DEAD & GONE

An absolutely addictive crime thriller with a huge twist

BILL KITSON

DI MIKE NASH BOOK 8

Revised edition 2020
Joffe Books, London

© Bill Kitson
First published in Great Britain 2015

**Please join our mailing list for free Kindle crime
thriller, detective,
mystery books and new releases.**

ISBN 978-1-78931-409-0

DEDICATION

For Val

Wife, lover, best friend, critic, editor and so much more

FOREWORD

2010

'I thought I was doing right.' The old man was plainly distressed. 'They were a good local company, so I thought. I even knew one of the directors, Linda Wilson; the one who has gone missing – known her family for years. It looked like a great chance to provide for the boy.' His gaze shifted to the photographs on the battered dresser.

The reporter didn't smile at the description of the farmer's son, for although now over forty years old, to the farmer, his son would always remain a boy. Indeed, where his mental capacity was concerned, he would stay a child until he died.

'My wife isn't well, and both of us are getting older. Our son can be a handful to manage, even for someone younger and fitter than us. What concerns us is what will happen when we're gone. So when they offered us this share deal it seemed too good to miss. If we could earn a tidy sum from the investments like they promised, we'd be able to set it aside to help with the cost of the upkeep when we're not around. That, plus the value of the farm, would be plenty, we reckoned. Instead of which it looks as if we'll have to sell up just to clear our debts; the money we'd invested in those shares has gone.'

The *Netherdale Gazette* reporter looked sympathetic. 'Can you tell me what happened, Mr Shaw? With the shares, I mean?'

'They did all right to begin with. I kept getting reports about the companies I'd invested in, and the share prices seemed to be moving the right way. The profit forecasts were good, so I was happy with the advice I'd been given by Bishopton Investments. The only thing was they hadn't sent us any share certificates. That should have made me suspicious, but it didn't. Not until it was too late.'

'How long was it before things started to go wrong?'

'A few months – six or seven maybe. The bloke we'd been dealing with said he'd been conducting a review of our portfolio and thought he could make one or two improvements. He suggested three companies that would offer better prospects.'

'And that didn't make you suspicious?'

'Why would it?' Shaw's tone was defensive. 'It seemed like they were looking after our interests, so I was happy to go along with it. The only drawback was the minimum investment they needed for the new shares was higher than the original amount we'd put in. Even that didn't make me suspect anything, so I borrowed money from the bank to top up our original outlay. It stretched me to the limit, but I was confident the risk would be worthwhile.'

He looked round at his familiar surroundings, and the reporter noticed a tear in the corner of Shaw's eyes, heard the tremble of emotion in his voice. 'Now, it looks as if we're going to lose the lot unless this court case produces a miracle. Five generations my family's farmed this land. I always knew I'd be the last. Our elder son and his wife were killed in a car smash, and my granddaughter's not one for farming. Our youngest isn't up to it, as you know, but despite that I hoped we'd end our days here. Looks like that isn't going to happen, though.'

The reporter was to remember those words later, but for the time being merely made a sympathetic noise, halfway

between clearing his throat and coughing. He'd heard similar stories several times already and his investigation was far from over. The others hadn't been as poignant, but the dreadful losses were beginning to mount up to huge sums. 'Do the police think they'll be able to recover any of your money?'

The farmer shook his head. 'They have to catch the bastards first. Even that won't be easy, they reckon. Apparently, when they went to the firm's premises, the buggers had cleared off and taken all the records with them. There was the bloke selling the shares, but the ringleader was Linda Wilson. She's the one behind it, and now she's gone abroad, or so the police say.'

'They don't seem too optimistic about your money by the sound of it?'

Shaw frowned. 'No, and the detective didn't say as much, but he implied it was as much my fault as theirs.'

The scandal rocked the community. North Yorkshire had never experienced anything quite like it. Most of the residents within the dale heard the news first on Helm Radio or read it in the leader of the *Netherdale Gazette*. The editor had some difficulty getting his paper's legal advisors to agree the headline, let alone the content of the article.

BIG FRAUD SUSPECTED AS B.I.G. GOES BUST

Bishopton Investment Group, whose advertising slogan 'Thinking investments? Think B.I.G' attracted many small investors to the local financial services company, was today placed in the hands of receivers. The *Gazette* understands that the insolvency practitioners appointed to handle the receivership called in police immediately after examining the books, fuelling rumours of widespread malpractice already circulating.

Nobody was available to comment, either at the receivers' offices, Bishopton Investments, or the local police station. However, a reliable source informed our reporters that the sums involved could run into millions. We understand that concerns about what was happening at the company were first raised by one of the senior financial executives at Wilson Macaulay Industries.

Bishopton Investments was formed in 1984 by local businessmen Stephen Wilson and Duncan Macaulay, co-founders of Wilson Macaulay Industries. The investment company remained independent of the rest of the group. Linda Wilson, company secretary and granddaughter of Stephen Wilson, along with Peter Macaulay, grandson of Duncan Macaulay, were still involved with the company at the time of the collapse. Mr Macaulay refused to comment on the appointment of the administrators, or the rumours regarding financial irregularities. All our attempts to contact Ms Wilson have been unsuccessful, and we understand that the police and the receivers are anxious to locate and interview her.

In a statement, local police highlighted the extent of the fraud. 'Our investigation has revealed that large sums of money have been systematically diverted from the company's funds to offshore accounts. We believe this was made possible by a corruption in the company's computer system which allowed one individual to make the necessary alterations. All the changes were authorized by the company secretary, Linda Wilson. However, efforts to locate Ms Wilson have proved unsuccessful. In addition to the theft from within the company, we are also attempting to locate another executive of Bishopton Investments, Mark Tankard, with regard to worthless shares that were sold to investors over the past few months.'

Despite the best efforts of the police, and international arrest warrants being issued for Linda Wilson and Mark Tankard, no trace of them was found, apart from a sighting of Linda Wilson boarding a cross-channel ferry in Hull, and confirmation from hotels in Amsterdam and Paris that the fleeing executive had stayed there. Later, after funds diverted

from Bishopton Investment Group and those from the sale of worthless shares were traced to a bank in the Cayman Islands, police there confirmed that Linda Wilson had stayed in a hotel several months earlier. Enquiries confirmed that the bank account in question had been closed following the withdrawal of the money, but there the trail went cold.

By the time the hearing to wind up the affairs of Bishopton Investment Group took place, no arrests had been made. The detective leading the inquiry admitted that all attempts to trace Linda Wilson and the missing share-pusher had failed.

On the day of the hearing, when it became apparent that no recompense would be forthcoming, the old farmer left Netherdale County Court and drove home. The foreclosure on the farm would be enforced within a week. Later that afternoon, he picked up the phone and dialled a local number.

'North Yorkshire Police,' the constable intoned.

'My name is Arthur Shaw, of Manygates Farm. I have just suffocated my wife and son. Will you please send someone as soon as possible?' He replaced the receiver, and as the young police officer was still wondering whether the call was a hoax, Shaw placed the twin barrels of his 12-bore under his chin and squeezed the trigger.

CHAPTER ONE

2013

In the dim light of the club, Naomi's feeling of unease deepened with every minute. She wished she hadn't come, wished her friends would turn up. She'd tried to phone them, to send them a text, but indoors the poor signal defeated her. Added to that, every time she looked up she had the feeling of being watched. After the third time, her unease deepened into apprehension approaching fear.

There was nothing new in the sensation of someone watching her. She was used to it, and sometimes even flattered. This, however, was something different. From her position seated near the bar, Naomi identified the source of her disquiet. It was a trio of men sitting at a table alongside the entrance. Admiring glances she could cope with, but there was something sinister in the way they looked her up and down; something dirty, dirty and threatening.

She glanced at her watch. Ten minutes more, enough time to finish her drink then she would leave, whether her friends had arrived or not.

One of the men had left the table. Naomi scanned the room but couldn't see him amongst the crowd of drinkers. She was still looking towards the far reaches of the room when the man brushed against her, seemingly on his way to the toilet. She didn't notice his hand move swiftly over her glass, depositing a fine trail of powder on the surface of the liquid.

Enough was enough. Totally unnerved by this encounter, she finished her drink in a couple of swift gulps, stood up, tucked her handbag securely under her arm and headed for the door. She felt strangely light-headed; not dizzy, more as if she was watching everything that was happening on TV.

She'd almost reached the entrance when the men began to move, standing up one by one, their decision to leave apparently unconnected with her departure. Had Naomi glanced back as the door closed behind her she would have seen this movement, appreciated the menace.

The followers slipped out of the club. They in turn failed to notice someone else on the point of leaving. From a table in the deepest shadow of the room, a man moved easily, gracefully, through the crowd of gyrating bodies on the dance floor, reaching the door before it swung to.

Outside, the cold night air made Naomi reel slightly. This was absurd. She had only had a half of lager, nowhere near enough to make her tipsy, let alone drunk. She looked for a taxi on the rank opposite. To her dismay, the space was empty. Normally, there would be a queue of vehicles waiting to transport revellers home, but not tonight. She would have to walk to the high street if she was to get a cab. And she would have to get one. Walking was not an option. She certainly couldn't walk from Helmsdale to Bishop's Cross. Not in the dark, and not in high heels. Even in daylight wearing trainers, she would have serious misgivings about attempting such a hike.

Getting to the high street involved walking down one of the narrow, badly lit alleyways or ginnels that criss-crossed the town centre. Naomi looked back. The street around the club was deserted. She decided to take the chance. The alternative route was much longer. Seconds after she entered the ginnel, the men emerged from the shadow of the doorway and headed towards the spot where she'd been standing.

The alley was dark, unlit, and smelt of urine and stale food, the latter from the wheelie bins along one wall. Naomi's heels clattered loudly on the cobbles. More than once she felt her ankle almost go over. Ahead, the lights from the high street were getting closer, but not fast enough for her liking.

She was halfway along the alley, at its darkest point, when she felt a hand grasp her arm below the shoulder. Naomi attempted to scream, but instantly something rough was forced into her mouth, making her gag and almost choke. As the fabric was pushed deeper, hands forced her backwards. She stumbled, her fall accelerated by more hands that pushed her knees forward.

Forced to the ground, Naomi writhed and squirmed, helpless as one of her assailants knelt on her shoulder, whilst another tore at her blouse and the button on her jeans. She felt the man's hand on her skin before he began tugging at her jeans and panties in an attempt to get them down to her knees, then to her ankles.

As he forced his knee between her legs, Naomi felt something brush against her cheek. Something warm. Something soft. Skin. Nausea threatened to engulf her as she choked against the gag. Dimly, as if from far away, she heard a confused medley of sounds.

The attack ceased abruptly. The pressure on her shoulders and legs eased. She freed herself, reaching up to rid herself of the gag. She heard a thump, a loud groan then a scream accompanied by a sharp crack as of a twig being broken. The crack was repeated; the scream intensified before tailing off to a whimper.

Naomi struggled to sit up, but recoiled at the touch of an arm round her shoulders, then realized someone was helping her, not imprisoning her. 'Pull your pants up and let's get out of here before they recover.'

The voice was young, male, but not threatening. Naomi reached down to comply, but blackness overcame her. Shock, relief and the effects of the drugged drink combined, and she collapsed, unconscious.

Their departure from the club had been watched with more than casual interest by one of the bouncers. He recognized the last person to leave and was curious enough to follow him into the street. From there, he saw the final part of the encounter in the alleyway, although given the lack of light, not clearly. He might have gone closer, but was called back via his headset to deal with a drunk. As he supervised the ejection of the troublemaker, his mind was still on what he had seen. He had no love for the girl's rescuer; in fact, he detested him.

The bouncer was proud of his reputation as a hard man. It had always been so; even at school. That was at the root of his dislike of the man; that was where he had been humiliated by his adversary. Admittedly, the bouncer had been the one who instigated the playground fight, but he had been confident in his ability to take on anyone of his own age, which made the shame even deeper. He wondered if there was some way the incident he'd just witnessed might be used to give him belated revenge.

Bright light, that was the next thing Naomi recalled. Bright, almost blinding sunlight. She forced her heavy-lidded eyes open. Where was she? This wasn't her room at home, or at the university. It was a bedroom, but not one she recognized, any more than the bed on which she had been placed or the duvet that covered her.

Memory came back with sickening clarity. She remembered the attack, remembered the release before…. She tried to concentrate. Someone had come to her aid, but what had happened after that? She sat up, feeling the discomfort from bruises on her shins, her shoulders, even her ribcage.

Naomi pushed the duvet back and realized she was wearing the clothes from the previous night: noticed a dark stain on the white fabric of her blouse. Blood? But whose blood? Not hers; of that she was sure. From the window, all she could see was the roofs of other buildings. She swung her legs off the bed, wincing slightly as the movement provoked more discomfort.

9

Her shoes had been placed neatly against the bedside cabinet. She struggled to put her feet in them, her brain registering with annoyance that her tights were torn. She gave herself a mental shake. If the laddered tights were the only casualty, she'd escaped lightly. But escaped to where? And who had aided that escape?

As if in answer the bedroom door swung open. A tall figure stood in the doorway. Was this her rescuer?

'Oh, good, you're awake.' The man walked across to the bed and helped her up. His voice sounded familiar. 'Come on, I'll make you a drink. Coffee? Tea?'

'Coffee,' she answered automatically. Her tongue felt swollen, painful, her jaw felt bruised. Naomi remembered the gag. She began to tremble.

'Steady on. No need to be frightened. You're safe now.'

As he helped her towards the door, Naomi felt a pounding sensation in her head and moaned slightly.

'Are you all right?'

'I've got a lousy headache.' Her voice sounded hoarse, little better than a croak.

'That'll be the after-effect of the drug.'

'What drug?' Naomi stopped dead, staring at him.

'One of them emptied a sachet of powder into your drink as he walked past. You were looking the other way.'

The stranger ushered her into a pleasantly furnished living room with a dining alcove at one end.

'Where am I? Whose place is this? What happened to those men? Who are you?' The questions tumbled out, matching the chaos of her thoughts.

'Hang on, one question at a time. First off, you're in a flat in Helmsdale; my flat, to be precise. As to what happened, those three scrotes were about to rape you until I discouraged them.'

'Discouraged them?' she echoed. 'How did you do that?'

He shrugged. 'I have my methods. Sit down, and I'll put the kettle on.'

Naomi chose an easy chair and sat pondering what he'd said; which was very little. What did he mean by 'I have my methods'? And she still didn't know his name. She wondered about him. The flat was well furnished. The curtains matched the suite, perhaps decorated with a woman's touch. Was he married? Not that it mattered. Naomi knew she owed him, if not her life then certainly a huge debt of gratitude. She shivered as she recalled her narrow escape.

'I put sugar in. It's supposed to be good for shock.'

She hadn't heard him enter the room. He seemed to have the ability to move swiftly and silently, despite being neither small, nor slim. She accepted the coffee and sipped it. 'Tell me what you meant when you said you discouraged them.'

He looked slightly uncomfortable. After a moment, he said, 'If you mention this to anyone, I'll deny it happened, deny I ever met you. I'm not supposed to get into fights, or trouble of any kind.'

'I won't say a word. Why would I?'

'Some people would disapprove of what I did.'

'You think I'd object? After you saved me from goodness knows what? Look, Mr Whoever-you-are, I owe you so much. I'm certainly not going to cause trouble for you. Unless you slit their throats of course?' Her eyes widened at the thought. 'You didn't, did you?' He smiled slightly and shook his head. 'Good,' she added with relief. 'If you want it to remain secret, I'm quite happy to go along with that.' She leaned forward and rested her hand briefly on his knee. 'But don't ask me to forget meeting you. That I can't do.'

He smiled again, and Naomi realized that he was quite good-looking.

'The thing is, I'm a serving soldier. If my CO got to learn of what happened I might be on a disciplinary, even a court martial. Taking it to the extreme, I could even be booted out.'

'Then I won't tell anyone what you did.' Naomi grinned. 'That's not difficult, because I don't actually know what you did. You can tell me because I won't be able to confirm or deny it.'

'I knocked out the one who was standing guard. That was easy. We're trained to do that sort of thing. The one who was about to force you to have oral sex – I stabbed with a biro.'

'Stabbed him? Where?'

'Where do you think? You've heard the expression "lead in his pencil"? He's probably got ink in his. He staggered off down the ginnel howling like a timber wolf. As to the third one, I broke a couple of his fingers then roughed him up a bit. Once they'd scarpered I brought you here. Carried, actually, but it isn't far. Just as well, because you were unconscious. Luckily, you're not a heavy girl.'

Reaction took over and Naomi began to weep. He was across the room instantly, placing a consoling arm about her shoulders. 'Don't cry, Naomi.' Her distress caused his anger to resurface. 'It's OK, you're safe now.'

She blinked away her tears and smiled slightly. 'How do you know my name?'

He pointed towards the table, on which was her handbag. He'd even rescued that.

'I don't know how I'll ever thank you and I don't even know your name.'

'Dean.' He smiled and added, 'And maybe one day you'll think of something.'

An hour later, when she was well enough to manage the journey, he escorted her to the bus station. At the depot, she asked casually, 'Will I see you again?'

'Are you sure the sight of me won't bring back bad memories?'

'I don't think so. Tell me, though, are you married?'

He stared at her, caught out by her question. 'No, whatever made you think that?'

'Then who was responsible for the decor of the flat? Not you, I guess.'

'My ... er ... my sister.' His answer was curt, rude almost; nevertheless, she noticed the hesitation.

'You didn't answer my other question,' she reminded him.

'About seeing you again? I'd like to, but I don't want to make any promises. I'm going overseas in a few days. But I'll call you when I get back, if you don't mind.'

'That'll be nice. I'd better give you my number.'

'No need, I already made a note of it. I had to go through your bag to see if there was anyone I could call. I phoned myself from your mobile so I could keep the number. In the army, we call that strategy.'

'Well, Dean, just make sure you do phone me.'

The bus pulled up alongside them and Naomi reached forward and kissed him lightly on the cheek. 'Take care, Dean, and come back safe. I'll be waiting for your call.'

He watched her board the bus and returned her wave as it drew away. It would be something to look forward to during his overseas tour of duty. He pulled his mobile out of his pocket and looked at the picture on screen; stared at Naomi's red-haired beauty. She really was a lovely-looking girl. He'd taken the photo surreptitiously when she was sitting in his lounge. He would treasure it. And he would certainly call her.

Naomi stared out of the slightly grimy window of the small Dales single-decker bus. She felt a warm glow of satisfaction, relief and pleasure, mingled. Her one doubt was that momentary hesitation when he'd answered her question as to who had decorated the flat. Was he really single? Or had she escaped from the frying pan of attempted rapists into the fire of an adulterer?

She dismissed the idea. Apart from the furnishings, there was nothing to indicate a woman's presence. The bathroom told her that. There were none of the usual ladies' toiletries in there. No waxing or depilatory creams, no shampoo or conditioner, merely shower gel and wet shaving gear. And aftershave. Of course, he could be married to the bearded lady, but somehow Naomi didn't think so.

CHAPTER TWO

A discussion between the victims of Dean's assault and the bouncer resulted in the wounded trio visiting Helmsdale police station. There, they gave the version of events the nightclub employee had coached them to produce. It varied significantly from the actual facts. No mention was made of Naomi Macaulay. They alleged that they had left the nightclub to return home, but being caught short, two of them had decided to use the passageway as a urinal. Whilst acknowledging that this was wrong, they claimed that the attack was both unprovoked and unwarranted. When asked for independent verification of their account, they suddenly remembered that the nightclub bouncer had been outside the club at the time, and that he might have seen something.

After they had left, DS Clara Mironova and DC Viv Pearce headed back to their office to compare notes. As they crossed reception the uniformed sergeant, Jack Binns, called to Clara, 'How did the weekend go, did you dissuade your father?'

'I'm not sure, but we tried,' she replied.

'Is he still intent on going back to Belarus?' Viv asked as they headed for the stairs.

'He might be, but until the regime over there changes, it wouldn't be wise. I think, after all these years, he's feeling his age and missing his brother.'

The tall West Indian took the stairs two at a time ahead of Clara. 'Well if my father wanted to return to Antigua, he'd be welcome to it. But I wouldn't go, only for a holiday. I'm a Yorkshireman and proud of it.'

The office door swung shut behind them. 'Anyway, what do you reckon to those two alleged victims?' Pearce asked.

Mironova frowned. 'The expression that springs to mind is one Jack uses. "I wouldn't trust them with the office cat."'

'Yes, whatever they were doing in that alley, I'll bet they didn't go there for a pee. Buying or using drugs would be my guess. Maybe this bouncer they all seemed so keen for us to talk to might shed some light on the reason for the attack. Do you want me to talk to him tonight?'

'Would you, Viv? But in view of the fact that they all suggested him, I'd take what he has to say with a pinch of salt. If there is anything worth following up, we'll talk to Mike about it.'

The following day, DI Mike Nash listened to his detectives relating the story of the assault. They presented it without comment, the factual account giving no clue as to their scepticism. 'The bouncer saw the tail end of the assault,' Pearce concluded. 'He recognized the attacker as someone he was at school with, a man he describes as "a vicious thug, even in those days". His words, not mine. He gave the man's name as Dean Wilson. I checked and found only one Wilson who matched the age criteria. He's a serving soldier who flew out to Afghanistan this morning.'

'In that case, we'd better put it on the back burner until we have chance to interview him. How long is his tour of duty, did you find out?'

'Six months, or so they said at the barracks.'

'OK, diarize it for after his return and we'll interview him then. Oh, and see if you can get a piece in the local paper. Someone else might have seen something.'

The article in the *Netherdale Gazette* wasn't exactly rich in detail. Under the headline MEN ASSAULTED OUTSIDE

CLUB, the piece merely stated that police were appealing for witnesses after an attack in Helmsdale town centre. Their injuries were not thought to be serious. Fortunately for their peace of mind, neither Dean nor Naomi had seen the item in the paper.

Naomi hadn't told her parents about the incident, or about her saviour. For one thing, she wanted to keep Dean to herself until she got to know him. More to the point, Naomi knew her parents wouldn't understand and certainly wouldn't approve. They would be shocked that she had visited a nightclub anyway. It didn't fit with their narrow, puritanical ways. These, Naomi knew, her father had inherited from his father. Her grandfather had terrified her as a child, but now, although she respected his beliefs, she was under no illusions about either him or her own parents. Her mother was careful, prim and easily shocked.

Naomi was painfully aware of the problems her father and grandfather had endured in business. They had lost money some years ago when Bishopton Investment Group collapsed. However, their wealth was too great for this to be other than an annoying inconvenience, unlike many of the other victims of the huge fraud. Listening to the seemingly endless debates on the subject, Naomi soon learned to revile the name of Linda Wilson, and to detest the wicked and heartless deception the woman had carried out.

The lurid speculation about the missing woman and her possible motives, which seemed to be centred about her rumoured infatuation with a fellow employee who had also vanished, did little to lessen Naomi's revulsion with the whole topic. As a less involved observer, she noticed that the topic caused her father much more distress than either her mother or grandfather, who seemed almost to salivate over each titbit of salacious gossip.

Dean couldn't remember ever having looked forward to returning to England before. When their overseas tour of duty was announced, most of his colleagues had been dismayed or at best non-committal at the prospect. Few of them were as happy to be leaving the country as Dean was, although right at the last moment, when he was all but ready to go, his meeting with Naomi had changed his view somewhat. It was refreshing to have something to look forward to when he returned home after six long months.

As he travelled from York to Helmsdale, Dean examined the photo of the girl on his phone, reminding himself, as he had often done during his spell abroad, of how attractive Naomi was.

His first act on reaching the flat would be to call her. He resisted the temptation to do it from the train, where others could listen in. Dean had little experience with girls and was desperately keen not to get it wrong.

Having stowed his kit in the flat, Dean was indecisive, unsure of the reception he would get. He opted to visit Good Buys supermarket first and stock up on supplies. By the time he returned and put the shopping away it was teatime, and he thought it would be unwise to risk disturbing Naomi when she might be dining. Instead he made something to eat, and by the time he'd finished his dinner, felt it was too late to call her that evening. He would phone the following day.

It was late morning before Dean plucked up enough courage to make the call. Naomi sounded happy enough to hear from him, but said she would be returning to university in a couple of days so it wouldn't be possible to go out with him before then.

He was beginning to wonder if this was a polite brush-off, until she added, 'I have to come into Helmsdale tomorrow to do some shopping. I could call round at your flat at lunchtime if you're about, and then we might be able to sort out something for when I'm at uni. As long as you don't mind travelling to York to visit me, that is?'

'I'd go much further than York for the chance of seeing you.' Dean was aghast at his own temerity, but Naomi seemed cheered by the statement.

'Oh good; until tomorrow, then.'

When Dean opened the door to let her into the flat, his first thought was to take his phone back to the shop and complain about the camera. The photo he had been admiring for so long completely failed to do justice to Naomi's looks. He reached forward to shake hands, but Naomi ignored the gesture, choosing instead to kiss him, lightly. Dean returned the kiss, surprised and delighted, before ushering her into the lounge.

She went automatically to the armchair she had used on her previous visit, and sat waiting as Dean went to make coffee. As she looked round the room, remembering the familiar objects, she heard the letterbox click and looked down the hallway. There were two envelopes on the mat. 'Postman's been,' she called through, 'shall I get it for you?'

'Yes, please.'

She walked over and picked up the mail. Without thinking, she glanced at the envelope, realizing that she didn't even known Dean's surname. She stood, rooted to the spot as she read the details. It couldn't be. Surely not. He couldn't be a relative, could he? Not of that person. It had to be an unpleasant coincidence.

Naomi walked back into the lounge just as Dean entered with the mugs. She held out the envelopes, her hands shaking. Two red spots of anger stained her cheeks, matching the flame in her hair. 'Lance Corporal Wilson? Is that you?'

'Yes, that's me.'

'Tell me you're not related to that woman. Tell me it's only the name that's the same.'

'Sorry, what do you mean?' He knew exactly to what she was referring, but was playing for time. Here it was again, a past he had no control over, rising up to spoil something he hoped was going to be good. At first, he couldn't understand why Naomi was so angry. Then he remembered her surname, and felt a rising swell of nausea.

'Tell ... me ... you're ... not ... related ... to ... Linda ... Wilson.' Naomi spat the words out as if each one was poison.

'I'm afraid I can't do that. I had no control over which bed I was born in. Yes, Linda Wilson is my sister. But I have had absolutely no contact with her since she ran away. And I had nothing to do with what happened before then.'

'Since she ran away? You mean ran away with the millions of pounds she stole from her employers and all the poor, gullible people who invested in the company, believing she was honest?'

'That was none of my doing, so why are you angry with me?'

'My name is Macaulay, as in Wilson Macaulay Industries.'

She looked at the coffee mugs Dean was still holding. 'You can keep those, Lance Corporal Wilson. A drink from you would stick in my throat.'

She flung the envelopes at him, spun on her heel and stormed down the hallway. The door didn't splinter behind her as she slammed it, but then it was a very sturdy piece of timber.

Dean's first week of leave had been miserable. During the months he'd been abroad, the prospect of seeing Naomi had been increasingly alluring. The disastrous outcome of that encounter had a shattering effect on the young soldier. For the rest of the week he remained inside the flat, nursing his self-pity until his mood of gloomy introspection bordered on depression. He had drunk more than was good for him, and the hangovers merely worsened his despair. His life seemed to stagger from one misfortune to a worse one.

On the Wednesday morning, he had just finished a belated breakfast when the doorbell rang. He wasn't expecting callers, nor was he expecting a postal delivery. Could it be Naomi? The wild idea buoyed up his hopes, if only slightly.

He opened the door to find a man and woman standing there. Dean blinked, still taking in this unexpected sight when the woman spoke.

'Dean Wilson?'

He nodded.

'I'm Detective Sergeant Mironova and this is DC Pearce. May we come in?'

Dean held the door wide. 'What's this about?'

'We want to talk to you about an assault outside a night-club before you were posted abroad.' She glanced down at the paper in her hand and quoted the date. 'We need you to go along with us to the police station, where we will conduct a formal interview.'

A short time later, Dean found himself in an interview room at Helmsdale. When asked to comment under caution, he felt trapped. He could see his army career ending ingloriously with a dishonourable discharge. His nature would not allow him to deny responsibility, nor would his moral code tolerate lies. At the same time, his sense of honour would not allow him to drag Naomi into the sordid affair, even as part of his defence.

Left helpless by the secret he would not reveal, and the lies he could not tell, Dean had no option. 'Yes,' he muttered, in answer to the repeated question. 'I stabbed him.'

Despite a barrage of questions, pressing him for a motive or anything by way of explanation, more than that he refused to say.

Later, Clara told Nash, 'There's something really odd about this business. Apart from the bizarre nature of the attack, I mean. Wilson's obviously hiding something, but what it is, I've no idea. He simply says he did it then shuts up. Not a word in his own defence, no explanation, no justification, extenuating circumstances, nothing whatsoever. At the same time, I don't believe much of what the so-called victim or the eyewitness has to say either. To be honest, if I'd to choose between them, I'd pick out Wilson as the good guy and the others as villains.'

'Did you ensure Wilson understood the possible consequences of his action on his career?'

'Yes, but it didn't seem to make the slightest difference.'

After the first week at university, Naomi was returning home for the weekend. It had been a hectic few days, settling back into the routine, but in spite of everything going on around her, she thought occasionally of Dean with much regret and a small degree of guilt. She knew how much she owed him, knew it was unfair to saddle him with his sister's wrongdoing. The realization of who he was had shocked her and in that moment her quick temper had flared, ignoring the injustice and hurt she was inflicting.

The sprinter train to Helmsdale was quiet for a Friday evening, and as she sat down, Naomi noticed a copy of the *Netherdale Gazette* on the seat near her. She picked it up, thumbing idly through the pages, until an item near the bottom of page seven caught her attention.

'SOLDIER CHARGED WITH ASSAULT' the headline ran. 'A soldier has been arrested and charged with assault following an attack last year in an alleyway in Helmsdale. The victim was treated in Netherdale General for his injuries. The alleged assailant, Lance Corporal Dean Wilson, was bailed to appear before magistrates on Monday.'

Naomi read the article several times. There couldn't have been two such incidents, surely? Dean wasn't the type to get into fights, of that she was certain. But if the incident referred to was the result of the attempted attack on her, why hadn't Dean spoken up, said something to defend himself? Surely, if the police had learned that he was defending her against three men, they wouldn't have proceeded with the charge. Had he kept silent to protect her? Was he unwilling to let her name be brought into it simply on the off-chance that the case might go public? If that was so, after the way she'd treated him that was incredibly noble. The more she thought about it, the more convinced Naomi was that such was the case. If so, the injustice would have to be put right. Naomi's jaw tightened with determination. She would have to be the one to put it right, whatever the consequences.

CHAPTER THREE

The rest of the team had left for the day, but Nash was still in his office when the phone rang. 'Yes, Jack,' he answered the sergeant.

'I've a young woman in reception, desperate to have a word with someone about that biro assault. She's seen the news of the arrest in today's paper and wants to tell her side of the story. Will you come down and talk to her?'

'Of course, just give me a couple of minutes to finish off here.' Moments later he headed down to reception.

'DI Mike Nash, how can I help you, Miss…?'

'I'm Naomi Macaulay.'

Nash listened to her story with growing interest. 'So you're saying there were three men, not one, and that they were trying to force you to have sex with them when Wilson intervened, beat them up and took you out of harm's way, is that it?'

Naomi nodded in agreement.

'I have to ask this,' Nash continued. 'What possessed you to go down that ginnel alone and in the dark?'

'I was desperate to get away from that club and there were no taxis on the rank. I didn't know they'd followed me out of the place until it was too late.'

'Lucky for you Wilson happened along at the right time.'

'It wasn't luck. He told me he was watching them inside the club; knew they were up to no good. He even saw one of them drop some sort of powder in my drink.'

'Probably rohypnol or GHB,' Nash remarked. 'But of course it's far too late to do anything about that now.' He finished taking her statement and added, 'The strange thing is, my sergeant who conducted the interview with Wilson was convinced he was concealing something: seems as if she was right. Thank you for coming forward, Miss Macaulay. In the light of what you've told me, we'll be talking to the alleged victim and the eyewitness again. They won't enjoy those interviews, I can assure you.'

'What about Dean? I mean, Lance Corporal Wilson, what will happen to him? He was very brave, putting himself in danger for someone he'd never met, and I don't want him to suffer for what he did. I'm grateful to him.'

'I think in the circumstances the charge for the assault will be dropped. In fact I'd go so far as to say that if I tell the men who were supposedly attacked that you're prepared to give evidence about the attempted rape, they might even forget that the incident ever took place.'

He saw the look of alarm in her face and hastened to reassure her. 'I shall only say it to them. That doesn't mean you'll have to testify, but they won't know that.'

Naomi lifted her head and looked Nash in the eye. She shuddered. 'If it came to it, even though I wouldn't relish the prospect, I'd be prepared to give evidence, as long as it meant that Dean didn't suffer a miscarriage of justice. He has suffered enough already, and what I put him through certainly didn't help.'

Nash looked at her enquiringly, but Naomi refused to elaborate, merely asking, 'Can I tell Dean that the charges are going to be dropped?'

Nash smiled. 'I think it will be in order for you to say that.'

Sergeant Jack Binns was more than a little surprised when Nash, after watching Naomi Macaulay walk out of the station, instructed him to contact the Crown Prosecution Service and ask them to cancel the court appearance.

'Is there a problem?' Binns asked. 'She's not some fancy solicitor he's hired, surely? No, she can't be' – he realized his error – 'she's far too young.'

'It seems that Clara's opinion of both the victim and the eyewitness was correct. She said she trusted Dean Wilson far more than those two. They also have selective memories. They conveniently forgot to mention that the guy with the mutilated member and his cronies were attempting to rape that young woman when Wilson intervened.'

'I suppose that's the sort of thing that can easily slip your mind when you're worried about your mangled manhood,' Binns agreed.

'Possibly so, and I think that it's our duty to remind them, don't you? I'll get Clara on it when she comes in on Monday.'

'I'm sure she'll get the bit between her teeth, if you'll pardon the expression,' Binns said, straight-faced. His expression changed suddenly. 'Of course, that's who she is.' He saw Nash's puzzled expression. 'The girl who's just left. Haven't you made the connection? His name's Wilson, hers is Macaulay. I'm surprised she didn't stab Wilson.'

'I don't get you. I know her name and address, that's all. Why, should I know more?'

'Didn't her name ring a bell? Didn't you realize the significance? For her to give evidence on behalf of someone called Wilson is remarkable, to put it mildly.'

'Sorry, Jack, you've lost me completely.'

'I forgot you weren't dealing with Bishopton area then, but surely you remember the scandal? Unless I'm mistaken, that girl is one of the Macaulay family, principal shareholders in Wilson Macaulay Industries. They were the biggest losers when Bishopton Investment Group went bust. In fact, now that I think about it, young Naomi looks a lot like another one of the family I knew slightly years back. She'd be Naomi's aunt, I guess. She went to live in America.'

'Of course, and the woman who legged it with the loot was called Linda Wilson, wasn't she?'

'Yes, and I'll bet all your money Dean Wilson is her brother.'

Dean was seated by the window in his lounge, from where the view was of the corner of the market square. He saw nothing of the vehicles or pedestrians that passed under his window, though, being immersed in his own woes. Would his life ever turn around? Would he ever be able to shake off the chains of the past, or free himself from the spiral of misfortune that had dogged his whole existence?

He had returned home following his release on bail and had started drinking within minutes of letting himself into the apartment. Today, in topping up the previous night's alcohol, he ignored the fact that he hadn't eaten since the slice of toast that had formed his breakfast.

During the time he was seated there, he had already downed a tumbler of whisky, and as his thoughts darkened, he poured another large glassful. He had gone to the girl's assistance, prevented her being assaulted, and what thanks had he got for his effort? None, apart from a mouthful of abuse from her, and an assault charge that seemed likely to end his army career. 'Well, yippee-doo,' he muttered savagely.

He lifted the glass to take another drink, and was mildly surprised to find it empty. He looked round suspiciously. Had someone sneaked in and drunk his whisky? Then he remembered he'd locked the door. 'Must be evaporating,' he muttered, 'better drink faster.' He refilled the glass and took another large gulp.

The doorbell rang, breaking into his melancholy. He frowned. He wasn't expecting visitors. He didn't want visitors. Visitors only mean trouble. 'Fuck off, fuck off, whoever you are,' he chanted.

The doorbell rang a second time. Either they were hard of hearing or insensitive. 'Which part of "fuck off" didn't you understand?' he shouted.

The caller was persistent, he'd give them that. When the bell rang a third time, Dean knew he would have to deal with it. He'd get no peace until he answered. He got out of the chair and lurched towards the hall and almost fell over the coffee table. He steadied himself against the arm of the sofa and glared down at the table. 'Somebody's moved it,' he growled, 'probably the same bugger that's been nicking my whisky.'

The doorbell rang again. 'All right, all right, I'm coming. Don't be so bloody impatient.' Dean squinted at the hall door, which appeared to be slightly out of focus. He reached it and fumbled with the catch, muttering under his breath all the time; nothing worth saying out loud, most of it unrepeatable. After several failures, he managed to unlock the door, and flung it back. The handle collided with the wall, dislodging a piece of plaster. Dean stared down at the grey lump on the hall carpet. 'Oops!' He looked up, peering myopically into the dimly lit landing. After a moment, he recognized Naomi, who seemed to have brought her twin sister along. 'What do you two want?' he demanded.

Naomi glanced round. 'Two?'

'You and her.' Dean pointed towards Naomi's left shoulder, but as he did so, his focus returned. 'Oh!' He glanced round. 'Where's she gone? She was here a second ago.'

'There's nobody here but me, Dean. Have you been drinking by any chance?'

'Bloody silly question. Course I've been drinking. Except some bugger keeps nicking my drink. If I catch the sod, I'll kill him. Amount they've nicked, there could be more than one. Thieving bastards, all of them.'

'All of who?'

'Them.' Dean swung round to indicate the empty flat. The move was disastrous. He staggered and would have fallen, but for Naomi's hand bracing the small of his back.

'Come on, you're not safe to be wandering around, the state you're in. Let's get you into bed where you can sleep it off without risking harming yourself.'

'Into bed?' Dean leered at her. 'You want me in bed? Are you propos ... propos...? Am I on a promise?'

'Not in the condition you're in,' she told him firmly. 'Not that you'd be much use to me even if I'd said yes.'

She guided him to his bedroom and tugged and pulled him until he was standing with his back to the edge of the bed. She removed the duvet before giving him a firm push and as he staggered back his knees caught the top of the mattress, leaving him spreadeagled on the sheet. She lifted one leg after the other and deftly unlaced and removed his trainers.

As she straightened the duvet over him, Dean squinted up at her. 'What are you doing here? Are you with them? Are you a shoe thief?'

'No, but you can't go to sleep with your trainers on. If you want to undress, the rest is up to you. I came to deliver some good news, but that will have to wait until you're in a fit condition to hear it.'

Naomi stopped there. She might have said more, but a loud snore from the bed told her that she hadn't got Dean's complete attention.

Waking up was a painful experience. Dean couldn't remember going to bed, couldn't remember much after coming back from the police station days earlier, but as he glanced around, moving his eyes cautiously to prevent the pounding in his head worsening, he realized he must have managed somehow, even if he hadn't been able to undress. That scarcely mattered. At least he'd had the sense to take his trainers off. The thought of his footwear stirred a vague memory, but he was unable to recall it.

He gave up on the futile effort; it wasn't worth the struggle. Besides which, he'd more important things on his mind. First of all, he needed the loo. When he emerged from the bathroom and walked into the lounge, Dean was surprised at how neat and tidy the room appeared. He frowned. He couldn't remember tidying up last night. Had he really done that before staggering off to bed? Something else that had slipped his mind?

Then, he heard a sound. It was a rustle, as of someone moving. It seemed to have come from the kitchen. Someone was in his flat! He crept to the archway leading into the kitchen and peered round the opening.

'Oh, hello, you've surfaced at last, have you? About time!'

Dean blinked in amazement. His mouth opened and closed a couple of times, but no sound came out.

'Coffee?'

'Er ... yes, please. I don't understand. What are you doing here? And how did you get in?'

'You let me in. Don't you remember?'

Dean shook his head. Not a good idea.

'You were a bit drunk.'

'I was more than a bit drunk. I was pissed, deluxe.'

'So drunk that I was unable to give you the news I came here to tell you.'

Dean was struck with a sudden, dreadful thought. 'What day is it today?'

'Saturday, why? Do you have to be somewhere?'

'No, but I got this awful feeling that it might be Monday, and I'm due in court on Monday.' The words slipped out before Dean could stop them.

'No, you're not. That was the news I came here to give you.' She passed him a mug. 'Will you be able to manage that, or do you want me to carry it through to the lounge for you?'

'I'll be fine. What did you mean about me not being in court?'

'It's cancelled. The charge is being dropped.'

Dean stared at her, mouth agape. 'How do you know?' he asked, eventually.

'Because when I read about your arrest in the paper I went to the police station and told the inspector what really happened that night.'

'You did that? You did that for me? But I thought....'

'Of course I did. You don't think for a minute I'd let you suffer and take the blame after what you did for me, do you? And by the way, it was sweet of you to try and keep my name out of it. However, I told Inspector Nash that if necessary I'm quite prepared to stand up in court and tell my story. Happily, he said he didn't think it would be needed.'

'You did? And did you tidy up in here? Did you put me to bed last night?

'Yes, yes and yes.'

'Did you stay the night?'

Naomi nodded.

'Where did you sleep?'

She pointed to the spare room. 'In there, despite your kind invitation.'

Dean groaned. She was teasing him. He'd obviously made a fool of himself. 'What invitation – or shouldn't I ask?'

Naomi grinned. 'Probably better not to. Now, would you like me to make you something to eat? I still don't think you're in a state to operate a gas cooker.'

Dean suddenly realized how hungry he was. 'Yes, please, I'm famished.'

'When did you last eat?'

'I'd some toast yesterday morning, I think. I'm not really sure.'

'No wonder you were in such a bad way, drinking whisky on an empty stomach. Was that a full bottle when you started?'

'I think so,' he admitted.

'There's only an inch left in the bottom now. I hope you don't make a habit of drinking so much.'

'No, certainly not. I was upset.' Dean looked at her. 'Partly because of the court thing, but mainly because of what you said.'

'I'll make breakfast. After you've eaten, I suggest you shower and clean your teeth.'

Dean demolished the substantial breakfast then meekly followed her instructions by going to the bathroom. When he emerged, he was surprised at how disappointed he was to find that she'd put her coat on.

'I have to go,' she explained. 'When I phoned my parents last night, I promised I'd be home for lunch. Will you walk with me to the bus station, like you did before?'

'Of course I will. You didn't tell them you were staying the night here, did you?'

'I'm not that daft. It wouldn't have gone down at all well, especially if I'd mentioned your name. As far as they know, I stayed over in York.'

As Dean reached to unlock the door, she stopped him, her hand on his. She stepped closer and kissed him, gently at first, then with increasing fervour, her tongue exploring his mouth, entwining with his. 'Now you know why I wanted you to clean your teeth.' She smiled at him, a trifle shakily. 'I'm not that keen on whisky.'

'If it's a trade-off, I'll never touch the stuff again,' he promised.

When they reached the street, it seemed quite natural for Naomi to take his hand, and to continue to hold it all the way to the bus station. As they waited for the bus to arrive, Naomi kissed him again. 'That's to say sorry for being so nasty to you. I thought about what you said and realized I was being completely unfair. If you got the flak from what your sister did, you must have suffered along with everyone else.'

She kissed him once more. 'And that's to say thank you for not telling the police about what happened that night.' Instead of letting go, she put her hand on the back of his neck, the flames of desire kindling between them, like the flickering forks of lightning before a storm. 'And that's from me to you, until we have that date. That is, if you still want to?'

He released her several minutes later as the bus pulled up alongside. 'I'll take that as a yes, then,' Naomi gasped. She walked towards the steps of the bus. 'I'll phone you and let you know when I'm coming home again,' she promised.

Dean wasn't certain if he walked or floated back home. He noticed one or two people looking oddly at him, which he found slightly puzzling. That was because he could not see what they could, which was the idiotic grin on his face that had one or two of them worried about his sanity. His first act on reaching the flat was to pour the rest of the whisky down the kitchen sink. He placed the bottle for recycling and, as he turned to walk back into the lounge, caught sight of himself in the mirror. There was a large scarlet stain on his face, from Naomi's lipstick. It looked as if she'd branded him. Which in a sense perhaps she had. He went to wipe it off – then changed his mind.

CHAPTER FOUR

Philip Lacey and his wife had booked a holiday. Nowadays they could more or less go when they wanted, and this was the trip they had promised themselves for years. 'Do you remember when we used to look at travel brochures and the adverts on TV that started on Boxing Day?' Philip asked her.

His wife smiled. 'You mean in the days when all we could afford was to look at them? When we had to save up for the TV licence?'

'That's right, and the holiday we fancied above all others was that cruise around the Norwegian fjords. Well, you'd better get packing, because I've booked one.'

'Philip, that's wonderful. When do we go?'

'Ten days from now.'

'What about the business?'

'Andrea can cope. She's well into the way of things now, and it isn't exactly rocket science. Besides, she's a bright lass.'

Andrea Lacey, their only child, was secretly delighted. Not only was she pleased for her parents, but she would be glad of the opportunity to show she could look after the family business.

Many years ago, whilst working as a salesman for an agricultural equipment dealer, Philip had spotted a niche in the market. Although the area had several farm supply companies, there was none dedicated to the specific needs of the equestrian community. This was surprising, bearing in mind that the region sported a greater proportion of horse riders than almost anywhere else in the country. In addition to those who rode purely for pleasure, there were the needs of the horse racing fraternity to be catered for.

After much heart-searching, and with the aid of his meagre savings added to a second mortgage on their house, Philip set up Lacey's Equestrian Supplies. In the early days, his wife had run the business whilst Philip continued his work selling agricultural machinery. The business had struggled for some years, and on more than one occasion, they had considered closing it down, but eventually, as word of mouth spread, their reputation for reliability, quality, customer service and value for money brought them an ever-increasing flow of new and repeat business. Eventually, Philip had been able to hand in his notice, and they had moved from the small, semi-detached house on the outskirts of Netherdale, where the garage served as a showroom and warehouse combined. They had bought an old farmhouse close to Bishop's Cross, where the former stable block and barns would serve their needs admirably.

On the Monday following her parents' departure, Andrea Lacey was in the office early. Getting there presented no problems, for it was no more than a fifty-yard walk from the house to the stables. On reaching her desk, Andrea's first task was to switch on the computer and check for incoming emails.

Philip Lacey had reached the point where most of the business was from previous customers, the majority of whom Philip knew by their first name. Andrea had persuaded her father that in order to extend both the area and turnover of the business, they should build a website and take online orders. Although Philip readily agreed, Andrea regarded it as her pet project, and was always keen to demonstrate its value in additional sales or enquiries.

She was gratified to see at least three emails enquiring about items in their online catalogue, plus a couple of confirmed orders. That would be a good start to the week, she thought, especially as one of the orders was for an item that ranked as almost the most expensive in their range. In addition to these, there was an email from a source Andrea didn't recognize, the subject being saddles. She opened it, but was disappointed to find that the message was from someone interested in supplying bicycle saddles.

Andrea framed a short, polite response and sent it, before deleting the email, and within minutes, when the sister of one of the nearby National Hunt trainers arrived to collect an order, she had forgotten all about it.

The week passed swiftly for Andrea. For the first time, she was aware of how much work was involved in running the business, especially single-handed. It was Friday morning before an email arrived that caused Andrea a few minutes' anxiety. The message subject was shown as computer fraud, and was from the local police force. Andrea read the body of the email with a sinking sensation in her stomach.

Have you received an email recently purporting to come from a person or persons interested in selling cycling accessories? If so, this email was an attempt at phishing which is a device to access information stored on your computer hard drive. If you received such a message, please indicate by ticking the relevant boxes below which of the following actions you took. If, on the other hand, you haven't received such a message, please tick the 'No receipt' box.

a) Deleted unread
b) Read and deleted
c) Replied to and deleted
d) Still in mailbox
e) No receipt

Please indicate also if you have noticed any unusual activity on your computer since receipt of the phishing email, by posting your remarks in the

*comments box. Please send your reply to Detective Sergeant Mironova at
the email address listed below. Thank you for your cooperation.*

Andrea followed the instructions and sent the response, glad
that she had no unusual activity to report. Once that was done,
she turned her attention to paying bills. It was the month
end, and her father was scrupulous in ensuring that suppliers
received their money on time. It was part of the reputation
that the business had become noted for. Nowadays, online
banking ensured that most of their suppliers could be paid
without resorting to cheques, but once Andrea had dealt with
those, she took the chequebook from the safe and started
dealing with the rest.

DS Mironova was studying the files her boss, DI Mike Nash,
had left on her desk, when the phone rang. It was Sergeant
Binns. 'I've a young woman in reception asking for you. She
seems to be in a bit of a state.'

'Asking for me? By name? Who is she? Any idea what it's
about?'

'Something to do with her computer and a load of money
that's gone missing.' Binns paused, then added, 'She says she's
had an email from you about it.'

Clara blinked in surprise. 'I'll be right down.'

She left the office and headed downstairs to reception,
introduced herself and listened to the young woman with
mounting astonishment. 'You say you had an email from me?
But I haven't sent any emails out. Certainly not in the last
few weeks, and definitely nothing to do with computer fraud;
I wouldn't know where to start, to be honest.'

'It is true,' Andrea insisted. 'Early last week I got one
from someone supposedly selling bicycle saddles. No use to
us, we deal in equestrian supplies.'

'No, I don't suppose it would be.' Clara had a fleeting
image of someone mounted on a chestnut gelding with only
a skimpy racing-bike saddle for support. She dismissed it and
concentrated on Andrea's tale of woe.

'Then on Friday, I got another email, this time from you, asking if I'd had the first one, and what action I'd taken. I had boxes to tick. I followed your instructions and didn't think any more about it until I got a call from the bank this morning, warning me we were close to going overdrawn.' Andrea paused and swallowed, and Clara could see the girl was near to tears. 'Someone's accessed our online banking and taken over £25,000 out of the account. My mother and father are away on holiday. Dad will kill me when he gets back.'

The tears she had been holding back spilled over. Clara looked round for support, and was relieved to see Nash entering the building. 'Mike,' she called, 'I think you'd better hear this.'

Nash looked from the distraught girl to his sergeant, noting Clara's grave expression as she introduced him. 'This is Detective Inspector Nash. I'd like you to tell him what you've just told me. Mike, this is Andrea Lacey.'

He listened to the story, and when she finished, asked, 'Did you print off a copy of the email that you thought came from Sergeant Mironova?'

Andrea produced a sheet of paper from her pocket. Nash scanned it. 'Very convincing,' he agreed, 'as it was intended to be. Unfortunately, that isn't one of our email addresses, and certainly not one of DS Mironova's. As for computers, Clara has to get the instruction book out to switch ours on. Which, I'm afraid, means you appear to have been the victim of a very clever fraud. Tell me something, the first email you got, is that still in your recycle bin, or have you emptied that?'

'No, I think it will still be there. The computer is programmed to delete them, but only once a month, and that isn't due for another week at least.'

'In that case, I'd like to send one of my officers round to see you. One that does know something about computers.' Nash smiled. 'He will retrieve that and with luck we'll get the sender's IP address. In the meantime you'll need an incident number. If I was you, I'd check with your bank. As your online banking account was hacked, and as you didn't release the password, I think you might be lucky. They might well reimburse you for the money that's been stolen.'

Had Clara been at all paranoid, by the end of the day she would have been stressed beyond belief. Following Andrea Lacey's visit, she received four more complaints about computer fraud, all of them from people citing her name and demanding to know what was going on.

Nash called on Pearce's expertise to help tackle the problem. 'How exactly do you think they did it?'

'It sounds like something called phishing. I'd say the first email can almost certainly be ignored. The part where the trap was placed would most likely be in the second email, where it requested a response from the recipient, asking them to tick certain boxes, or to leave comments. In doing that, they probably triggered a tracking cookie.'

'What on earth's one of those?'

'Tracking cookies are used by online marketers to identify shopping habits and websites that users visit. Then they target people with products or services tailored to their specific interests. In this case I'd say these were highly sophisticated tracking cookies designed to target the victims' online banking, and to identify the passwords used to access the accounts. Once they had those, all they needed to do was input the relevant information and withdraw sums of money that they could send to accounts they had already set up.'

'That's bloody cunning. I noticed that in all the cases, they left sufficient in the account to prevent it tipping into overdraft, which might have set alarm bells ringing earlier. How they did that, I wasn't sure, but if your theory is correct, and I believe it is, they would know exactly how much the victim had in their account. The next questions are, how do we stop them, and how do we identify them?'

'That's a lot harder to answer. The software program the scammers installed within the victims' computers would have to be designed specifically for the purpose. Finding it is way beyond my sphere of knowledge. Nor will we get much joy out of tracing the accounts where the money ended up.' Pearce shook his head. 'Because I'd be willing to bet the money didn't stay there longer than the time needed to clear the funds, and by the time we got to hear about it the money could have gone around the world and back several times. To be honest, when I said it was more than I could cope with, I'm not even sure whether our computer specialists would be able to solve this one. I could ask them, if you want?'

'I don't think we've any choice. Please do that, Viv, and make it a priority. We don't know if that's the end of it, or how many more people might have been targeted. Some may be in the process of being hacked even as we speak. I think we should issue a public warning as well' – Nash smiled wryly – 'but not by email. I'll ring Superintendent Fleming and tell her the bad news.'

Following his explanations, Jackie Fleming was exasperated. 'Damn it, Mike, that's the last thing we need. Do you reckon we'll have to get the specialists in?'

'I do, but more to the point, Viv does. And he knows far more about these things than I do. At the moment he's gone to visit all the known victims to examine their computers. However, if his theory about how the scam was set up is right, Viv thinks the fraud is so sophisticated, even our computer experts might struggle to get anywhere. For now I'd like you to sanction the release of a public warning. As things stand, all we can do is to try and limit the damage, because every day that passes gives them opportunity to access more bank accounts. I think the warning ought to be on every media outlet we can think of, even over the Internet. Poor Clara's getting so twitchy, she hardly dare pick the phone up because she's been made the focal point for one or two people's anger.'

'Leave it with me. I'll handle the media and hopefully we'll get something out today. Fax me a copy of the offending email and I'll get it distributed to the press and shown on TV.'

CHAPTER FIVE

The guest in room 21 at the Golden Bear Hotel in Netherdale paced his room, glancing at his watch frequently. She was late. That was unlike her. It only served to increase his excitement. He heard a discreet knock at the door. Just like her, always cautious. Soon, she would be in his arms, in his bed, all discretion gone.

He opened the door, and blinked with surprise – and dismay.

It wasn't her. It was someone else. It was the last person he expected to see – or wanted to see. Surprise turned to shock as he glanced down, then shock became pain, sharp, searing pain as the visitor lunged forward, again and again. The first blow penetrated his chest, as did the second and third. He reeled back into the room, turning in desperation to escape the wickedly sharp knife blows.

His assailant grabbed the guest's hair, jerking his head back, exposing his neck for the final cut. The knife slid across the victim's throat. He died instantly.

The attacker watched impassively as blood splattered the walls, the ceiling, the floor. He stared at the body, no trace of pity or remorse in his eyes.

Entering the bathroom, he dropped the weapon in the basin and washed his hands and face.

In the wardrobe he found a suitable jacket to cover his bloodstained shirt. He walked to the door and hung a 'Do not disturb' sign on the outer knob, before closing it and heading for the back stairs. Better not to scare the other guests. It might put them off their dinner.

He left the car park and half an hour later negotiated the series of hairpin bends towards the summit of Stark Ghyll. It was dark, his attention wholly on the road and its precarious route up the mountainside. Now in the early dawning of the day, he barely noticed the view. Although magnificent at any time, the prospect from his location was breathtaking. Despite its splendour, despite there being no traffic to distract him, he stared in complete oblivion. The road was little more than an ancient drovers' track that had been covered in tarmac. Unclassified, and all but unused except by the locals, many were unaware of its existence. On reaching the top, where the road straightened out as if to reward the driver for having overcome some hidden challenge, he pulled in to the wide grass verge at the side of the road and stopped the engine.

His eyes were unfocused, his thoughts elsewhere. A suspicious police officer might have assumed the glazed look in his eyes to be the result of the amount of drink he had taken, but that would have been less than wholly accurate. With the window open, the air was fresh and crisp. The driver shivered, but not from the cold. He shivered at the thought of his children. He conjured up mental images of them, each of the three in turn. Like a gate crasher at a private party, the image of the woman intruded and he could not dismiss it, no matter how hard he tried to evict her from his mind. Eventually, he succeeded in part, refusing to dwell on that topic too long. The memory was too recent, too raw, too sickening.

Betrayal was a word he had come to hate, and yet, in his mind it summed up everything that had happened to him. He didn't stop to consider how much he had contributed by his own actions to his misery and despair. There was a bitter irony to him finishing up here, so close to where all his troubles had started. Bishopton: the very name sent a chill through him. Bishopton – the home of Big Investments – a lot of good it had done him. Onto a winner; a sure thing, they'd said. He'd lost everything.

Betrayed then by his employer, a man he had mistakenly trusted to stand by him when things got tough. Even when the signs of trouble ahead were unmistakably clear, he hadn't thought for one moment that the man he called his friend would sacrifice him on the altar of expediency. How wrong could he be?

Then there had been the betrayal of those he thought of as his close friends. They had vanished like flies in December, at a time when he needed their support.

Worst of all, the betrayal had been that of the woman he loved; the woman he thought loved him. Discovering her affair with a man he loathed had been bad enough. Facing her with this knowledge had made bad far worse. Hearing her admit to her infidelity and recognizing a total lack of guilt, shame or embarrassment had been dreadful. And when she told him how much she enjoyed her liaison and stated her intention to continue it; that had been the last straw.

Desperate to free himself from a situation that had become intolerable, he had taken a reckless gamble with money he could ill afford to lose. Ignoring the gambler's maxim of only staking what you won't miss, he had plunged deeper and deeper into the mire of debt, ever hopeful of one slice of luck to reverse his fortunes. That didn't happen; all his foolhardiness achieved was to advance the unstoppable march of the inevitable.

Now, sitting on the summit of Stark Ghyll, he stared at the dale set out below. Over to the east, early morning mist gave the promise of a beautiful day to come. It hung over the land bordering the River Helm, all but obscuring the towns of Netherdale and Helmsdale. It was a strange sensation to be above the mist, almost like flying at an altitude above cloud level. Elsewhere, to the west and south, the fields and woods provided a widely contrasting pattern of colours and shapes, like a badly designed patchwork quilt thrown over an enormous bed.

He reached for his sole companion. The whisky bottle was already half empty; he had downed most of it since reaching his destination from the hotel. Prior to that, it had been the rented cottage. He laughed and shook his head. A week's break 'for the sake of the kids' had taken the last of his meagre hoard of cash. His wife was unaware of quite how desperate their plight had become. Unaware – or uncaring? He wasn't sure which, and it no longer mattered. That way, he had been able to pretend that things were somewhere near normal.

Normal? The word made him laugh aloud again. He took another deep swig from the bottle, then a second, then a third. After that he lost count. His mind went further back, to all that he had lost. 'Downsizing' they called it, and 'the inevitable and regrettable outcome of the recession and the nation's severe economic woes'. Glib phrases that concealed the misery that was to follow. With no job, no income and no prospects, events had followed with unstoppable force, like an express train out of control.

At some point in the next few hours, bailiffs would enforce the repossession order on their family home. 'Take it,' he muttered to himself, 'take the bloody lot. Why not, I've lost everything else. Except the car,' he added, almost as an afterthought, 'you can't have that. I need it.'

As if spurred into action by the thought, he started the engine and engaged reverse gear. He manoeuvred slowly and carefully until the car was at right angles to the single-track road. Inching the vehicle back, he was conscious of the drainage ditch behind him. He must take care not to let the rear wheels slide into that. It would be the anticlimax of all time.

He shifted the gear lever into neutral and examined the land beyond the road. There was a broad verge of sparse moorland grass. He remembered the previous time he had come up here. Sheep had been grazing on that verge. Luckily they had moved on since then. Beyond the verge was a rotting post-and-rail fence. Beyond that; nothing.

He engaged first gear, revved the engine, let the clutch out and pressed the accelerator. The high-powered saloon surged forward, gaining momentum rapidly as it raced across the tarmac, the broad swathe of grass, and demolished the wooden fence. For a brief second the huge machine soared forward through the clear morning air, until gravity dragged it down, sending it tumbling end-over-end as it fell. It struck the rocky limestone slope once, twice, three times before coming to rest, its roof crushed against an outcrop of rock close to the base of the sheer cliff.

The noise of the collisions echoed through the early morning silence like a series of gigantic gunshots. After the engine died, the only sound was the alarm call of a pair of grouse, their slumbers rudely interrupted.

The farmer gave his wife a cheery wave as he pulled the Land Rover out of the yard and set off along the winding country road. He turned the volume up on the Land Rover's radio. He wasn't a particular fan of the music being played, but it served to mask the constant rattling and banging from the empty livestock trailer he was towing. He hummed along to the tune. He was looking forward to the next couple of days. Spring lambs had been fetching a record price at auction recently. A trailer-load should fetch him somewhere in the region of £4,000. Better to get those that were ready to market now before supply became more plentiful and the price dropped accordingly. He would start with the flock he grazed on Stark Ghyll. He had checked them over the previous day and knew they were in good condition.

It took him a quarter of an hour to reach the summit. As he swung the Land Rover round the final bend, with the trailer protesting loudly, the farmer automatically glanced to his left, to where the flock had been grazing. He wasn't surprised to see that they weren't there. Experience prepared him for the fact that sheep wander. His glance didn't at first register that there was anything amiss, but when he took a second, closer look, he noticed the broken fence.

He stopped the vehicle and stared at the splintered railings with the huge, yawning gap in the middle, his face registering both alarm and dismay. His first thought was that something had panicked his sheep and they had crashed through the fence to a certain death below. The area was popular with the RAF as a place to train pilots in the art of low flying. He muttered something extremely impolite about the aerial branch of the armed forces and got out of his vehicle to investigate. If he'd lost this flock, or even part of it, it would be disastrous. He hurried towards the cliff edge.

He was halfway across the grass verge when he saw the tyre tracks. Once again, his thoughts went immediately to his flock. There had been increasing numbers of livestock theft cases reported recently in the farming press. Then he saw the direction of the tracks and a sick realization hit him. He reached the edge of the precipitous slope and peered cautiously over. Two raw, jagged scars across the rocks gave him his first clue, and then he saw the car, or what remained of it. Upturned like some giant dead insect, wheels twisted at impossible angles; the bodywork so battered it was impossible to discern the make or model. He felt certain whoever had been inside the car could not have survived such a fall. He reached into his pocket and took out his mobile.

The signal was poor, but he managed to get through to the emergency operator, and with some difficulty passed his message.

'What service do you require?' he was asked.

'That's a good question. Ambulance, I reckon, although a hearse might be more appropriate. Maybe fire brigade as well; and mountain rescue. There's a car gone over the edge on the summit of Stark Ghyll. It's fallen a few hundred feet, and it's in a lousy spot to get to.'

The farmer gave his name and agreed to wait at the scene for the emergency services to arrive. He ended the call and walked slowly back to his vehicle, staring morosely at his trailer. There was no need to hurry. One thing for sure, he couldn't guarantee to be taking any lambs to mart this day, and that meant they wouldn't be accepted for the following day's auction. Then he thought about what he'd just seen and his gloom vanished. He was a hell of a sight better off than the poor soul inside the car. He tried his mobile again and rang home. His wife answered and he could hear the kids bickering in the background; all reassuringly normal. He told her what had happened, and, uncharacteristically, ended the call by telling her he loved her. He wasn't sure why, but for some reason it seemed the right thing to do.

Mike Nash was usually first to arrive in the CID suite at Helmsdale police station. He had been in his office a little over twenty minutes when Sergeant Mironova walked in, bearing two coffee mugs. Nash looked up from the report he was reading concerning a drink-fuelled fight outside one of the pubs in the town the previous weekend. 'Morning, Clara,' he greeted her. 'All quiet last night?'

Mironova had been on call. 'Yes. At least I wasn't dragged from my bed in the early hours; in fact there's nothing to report. It was a lot quieter than it is at the moment downstairs. There's a real panic on. From what I can make out somebody's gone off the road at the top of Stark Ghyll.'

'I don't give much for their chances,' Nash commented sombrely. 'It's a heck of a drop. Is that all you know?'

'Except that Jack Binns is trying to organize an ambulance crew, emergency doctor, the fire brigade and mountain rescue, in between talking to traffic division and putting air-sea rescue on standby, together with the air ambulance.'

'If it's at the top, just reaching the vehicle is going to be a nightmare, let alone recovering anyone inside it. Still, it's not something we're going to be involved with, so we'll leave it to others to sort out.'

Nash was fond of warning his colleagues about the dangers of tempting fate, 'invoking Sod's Law' as he referred to it. This time, it seemed that he had ignored his own advice. Something that Mironova was to remind him of later.

The farmer had been waiting for what seemed like an age before a set of flashing lights signalled the imminent arrival of an emergency vehicle. It proved to be a Volvo estate car from the police traffic division. Any remaining faint hope the farmer might have entertained that he would somehow be able to load his lambs into the trailer and take them to market soon began to disappear after the officers surveyed the crash scene.

'This road will have to be closed to all but emergency vehicles,' one of the officers stated. He glanced around. 'That shouldn't cause too many problems, though. You'll be needed to give a statement as to what time you found the car, and what weather, road and traffic conditions were like at the time.' A faint smile flickered across the officer's face as he mentioned traffic conditions. This was obviously part of a well-rehearsed script. 'You're the nearest we've got to an eyewitness to the accident.'

The second officer, who had been talking on his radio, joined them at this point. 'Sergeant Binns has ordered paramedics and a mountain rescue team. They'll be here as soon as....' His voice tailed off as he stared at the verge near the farmer's vehicle. 'Would you mind driving fifty yards further up the road?' he asked.

'Look, officer,' the farmer replied, 'I came up here to gather some of my sheep. I've got to get them to mart today, otherwise I'll miss the sale and it could be costly for me – and my family,' he added by way of an afterthought to emphasize his situation. 'I only came across the accident, I didn't actually see anything. If I give you my name and address, can I come to the station in Helmsdale this evening and make a statement then? That way, I might still get my sheep in the sale.'

'I'm not sure. What do you think?' The officer turned to his colleague.

'I don't see why not. But you can't go to Helmsdale, the station will be closed. Let me check with my sergeant.' Reaching for his radio, he moved away.

While he waited, the farmer gave his details to the remaining officer and confirmed when he had driven up the hill; he was conscious of time slipping by and the fact that, as yet, he hadn't actually found his sheep.

'It's OK, but the sergeant says you'll have to go to Netherdale to give your statement.'

'Then I can go?' he asked hesitantly.

'I suppose so. But make it quick before we close the road. You'll have to go down the far side of the Ghyll.'

As the farmer hastily drove away, the officer signalled to his colleague. He pointed to the tyre tracks he had spotted on the verge, obscured by the farmer's Land Rover. 'What do you make of them?'

The second man stared at the tracks at the far side of the road, then turned to look at the ones close to where the vehicle had gone over the edge. 'The car was being driven across the road, not along it.'

'Yes, but it looks as though it was parked there and then manoeuvred before it went over: look at the ruts. Not even someone blind drunk would do that accidentally. It doesn't make sense, unless it was done deliberately, and that means....'

'It means that depending on the condition of the car's occupant we're looking at either suicide, murder or an attempt at one of the two. And that means we'll have to get CID involved. I'd better get back onto Jack Binns.'

CHAPTER SIX

The chambermaid at the Golden Bear Hotel in Netherdale enjoyed her work. She had lived in England for over two years, having been encouraged by her sister to move from Gdansk. She had been dubious at first, although she liked England and English people. She had heard some bad stories from other Polish migrants about people having to take menial jobs such as washing cars, but soon discovered that they were well rewarded for the work. Nevertheless, she preferred her job, especially when it rained or snowed, which she found it did a lot in England. She was halfway through her morning stint and was looking forward to sitting down with a mug of coffee. She reached the second floor and carefully steered her trolley out of the lift. She glanced at her worksheet: only one room to service on this floor then she could take her break.

Halfway along the corridor, she paused and stared at the door of one of the rooms. Something was wrong. Someone had splashed something on the door. It looked like paint. The 'Do not disturb' sign was hanging from the doorknob. It had been there since the previous evening. She remembered it distinctly, thinking that the man in that room must have gone to bed really early. Either that, she remembered with a giggle, or he was…. Well, as a chambermaid, you get to witness a lot of human behaviour that others don't see. She wondered if he'd gone out and forgotten the sign. Alternatively, he could be unwell. She didn't think so. She'd seen the man a couple of times, either entering or leaving his room, and he looked quite young and fit. Still, she ought to check. And at the same time ask about the paint.

She tapped lightly on the door. 'Room service,' she called out, but got no response. Perhaps he had gone out after all. She glanced at her watch. It was after 10 a.m. He couldn't still be asleep, surely? Unless he'd been, what was the English word? 'Bonking', that was it. Unless he'd been bonking all night. She giggled and knocked again, louder this time. Still nothing from inside the room.

Without conscious thought that she might be intruding on an intimate encounter, she took out her master key card. The room was in darkness, the curtains closed. 'Room service, Mr Jennings. Are you all right?'

There was no reply. She groped for the switch and turned the light on. At first, everything seemed to be in order, except that the bed didn't appear to have been slept in. She reached behind her and took the sign from the doorknob, intending to replace it on the small dressing table under the window. As she approached the table, she noticed a pair of feet protruding from alongside the foot of the bed. She stood still, and as her gaze travelled to the rest of the body she let out one long, shuddering breath. The pool of blood that covered the man's chest had flooded the carpet alongside him and splashed in liberal quantities across the wallpaper and curtains as well as the bedlinen. It was only when she regained her breath that she turned and ran from the room.

Sergeant Jack Binns strode into Nash's office without knocking. For him to do that meant trouble; the look on Binns' face merely confirmed it. In a few terse sentences, Binns explained what the traffic officers had found at Stark Ghyll.

'OK, Jack, we'll head on out there. Any word on who was in the car?'

'Not yet. Mountain rescue have arrived. They're rigging some form of block and tackle; reckon it's the only way to reach the vehicle. They're going to send one of their men down first – they're all first-aid trained – and then hopefully, if needed, lower a paramedic.'

'There's no chance this is someone disposing of an old banger, I suppose? And that the car was empty when it went over the edge?'

'No such luck. The traffic guys say that although it's now only fit for scrap, it appears to be a late model BMW. I suppose it could have been stolen and dumped. I'll check it out when I've got the details. But just to be on the safe side I've got an air-sea rescue Sea King and the air ambulance on standby, although the traffic officers reckon that's a wasted effort.'

Binns had just finished speaking when Nash's phone rang. He signalled to Binns to remain. 'Morning, Jackie,' he greeted the caller. The uniformed sergeant exchanged glances with Mironova. They saw Nash's expression change as he listened to Superintendent Fleming's opening words.

'More trouble,' Binns whispered to Mironova. 'They say troubles come in threes; I wonder what the third will be.'

They listened as Nash was speaking. 'Yes, we've a suspicious incident at Stark Ghyll. The first thought was that it was an accident, but the traffic officers reckon it was deliberate. However, in view of what you've told me, I'll send Clara and Viv Pearce out to deal with that. I'll head straight to Netherdale and meet you at the Golden Bear.'

He put the phone down. 'A chambermaid at the Golden Bear found one of the guests with his throat slashed from ear to ear. I'm off to meet Jackie and Lisa there. Clara, you know what to do. Take Viv and go to Stark Ghyll. See what you think.'

'The Golden Bear will be getting a bad reputation. That's not the first time something like that has happened there,' Clara remarked. 'And if Lisa is at the scene, it's sure to bring back unpleasant memories for her.'

Some years earlier, DC Lisa Andrews, based at Netherdale HQ, and Nash, had investigated a double murder at the Golden Bear. They cleared the main suspect, a man who later became Lisa's partner.

When Mironova and Pearce reached the scene, Stark Ghyll was bathed in warm sunshine, the magnificent views in total contrast to the grim nature of the task facing the emergency services. Where the winding ascent levelled out, the road was cluttered with all manner of vehicles. There were two Land Rovers, both bearing the logo of the mountain rescue team. Added to these were an ambulance and three police cars. The equipment from a fire engine was being offloaded.

One of the traffic officers who had been first on the scene hurried over to the detectives, bringing with him the team leader from the mountain rescue unit. 'We've rigged a line up, but the mountainside is so steep, anyone going down has to more or less abseil. One of our chaps is down there already. As far as he can tell there's only one occupant, and that's a male, trapped in the driving seat. However, the car's such a mess, he can't be one hundred per cent sure there's nobody else in there. Nor is he sure whether the driver is alive or dead; he thought he felt a pulse when he reached through the driver's window.'

The police officer continued. 'We needed someone down there as soon as possible and one of the paramedics has volunteered to be lowered.' The officer grinned. 'Actually, I think his boss volunteered him for the job. They've been instructed to smash the windscreen to access the driver better. Only after he reports will we know if we need to hurry or not.'

'I'm surprised you need to smash the screen,' Pearce commented. 'I'd have thought it would have smashed on the way down.'

'It must be one of those shatterproof glasses. The screen's broken right enough, but still intact, if you get my meaning.'

At that moment the radio held by the mountain rescuer crackled into life. 'I think I can see child seats in the back and there's another one further down the hill. I'm trying to see but it's just too much of a mess. Everything's crushed. God, I hope there's no little ones in there.'

The response was instant. 'You help the paramedic first and I'll send more help down to check it out with you.' He turned away and began firing instructions to others, similarly clad in climbing gear.

Pearce and Mironova walked to the edge of the cliff and looked over as a second man began the descent. They watched anxiously as he was lowered slowly down the steep mountain face, his progress made difficult by the rucksack strapped to his back. 'I reckon they're wasting their time,' Viv muttered. 'I don't see how anyone could survive a drop like that, especially when you see the state of the car.'

'I know what you mean. But we've seen plenty of instances where cars have ended up as crumpled wrecks and the drivers have walked away with barely a scratch.' She turned away.

'You OK, Clara?'

'Yes, it's just, well … if there are children….'

Viv Pearce smiled and placed a reassuring hand on her arm as she took a deep breath.

'Come on,' she said, 'we need to check with the traffic guys and see if they've taken any photos yet. Go talk to them. Ask them to take some of the vehicle from up here. If they use their telephoto lens they can try and pick up the registration from the number plate if the angle allows. But don't let them try if it's too risky; we don't want anyone else going over the edge. I'll go and talk to the mountain rescue people and the paramedics.'

'Morning, sir.' The officer stationed by the door to the corridor acknowledged Nash when he arrived at the Golden Bear. Nash accepted the bag containing protective clothing and continued past him to find Superintendent Fleming and DC Andrews waiting in the open doorway to the room. Standing in the corridor was a harassed-looking man who Jackie introduced as the hotel manager. 'The chambermaid identified the dead man as the room's resident. He's been staying here three days, registered as Paul Jennings, with an address in Leeds. Mexican Pete and a SOCO team are inside.'

Both women were clad in disposable suits and overshoes, which had already caused a number of curious glances from guests who had been asked to vacate their rooms temporarily.

'I take it you've been in?' Nash asked, glancing over their shoulders as he spoke.

'Yes, but luckily we didn't have to stay long, because SOCO arrived so we were able to make our escape. It's a bloodbath, I'm afraid.'

'I'd better take a look.'

'While you're doing that, we'll go downstairs. I think the manager is in need of a sit down.' Jackie began to remove her protective clothing, indicating that Lisa should do the same.

Nash ripped open the plastic bag and struggled into the paper suit, watched with interest by the young constable standing guard. As he stepped through the doorway, the pathologist, who was kneeling alongside the corpse, looked up. 'Ah, Mike, I felt sure it wouldn't be long before you arrived. Did you get a phone call, or were you aroused by the scent of blood?'

'No, I couldn't smell it. Unfortunately, the wind was in the wrong direction.' Nash stepped carefully round the stained carpet, looking around the room as he did so. 'What do you reckon was the cause of death? Poisoned?'

Professor Ramirez smiled slightly. 'Unlikely, nor do I think he cut himself shaving. Several stab wounds to the chest and his throat slashed. But I'll know more—'

'I know, after the post-mortem,' Nash finished for him. 'No sign of the weapon, I suppose.' Nash looked at the SOCO team leader, who was listening to the conversation.

'Yes,' the man answered. 'Found this in the bathroom.' He held up a plastic box, which contained a large kitchen knife.

Ramirez added, 'Which also rules out suicide. That, I guess, was going to be your next question. And as to the next-but-one question, I'd estimate time of death as yesterday evening sometime, say between six o'clock and midnight.'

'You seem to have answered all my questions without me asking them,' Nash said. 'Is there anything else I should know?'

'Only that I've got a meeting to attend tomorrow. So unless you find any other bodies for me I want to do the post-mortem today. I'll ring you with a time.'

The SOCO officer spoke again. 'There are a fair few fingerprints in here so it will take a while to eliminate the staff. I'll let you know if we find anything relevant. We've also recovered a mobile phone from the dressing table, which I assume belongs to the victim.'

'I'll need to take a look at that once you've finished with it,' Nash told him. 'Well, you seem to be playing nicely, so I'll leave you to it.'

The only reply was a grunt from the pathologist. It might have been 'goodbye', but Nash doubted it.

He placed the suit and overshoes in the bag provided before heading downstairs to find Jackie Fleming. Seeing three people clad like something from a science fiction film or an episode of *CSI* would have caused even more incredulous stares from guests.

The receptionist smiled at him and indicated a short passageway to the side of her desk. There, in the manager's office, he found the superintendent and DC Andrews. 'Like you said, a real bloodbath,' Nash told them. 'Has anyone asked if Jennings had any visitors? Apart from the one we know about,' he added with a grim smile.

'That's not as easy as it sounds,' Jackie told him. 'The receptionist on duty at the moment confirmed that she hadn't been asked for Jennings, or his room. But then, she only does the morning and early afternoon shift. Another receptionist takes over at three p.m. and works until just after midnight, and when she finishes, the night porter is in charge of reception.'

'That's rather late, isn't it?' Nash turned to the manager for explanation.

'We get a lot of coach parties staying here and some of them don't arrive until gone eleven, so by the time they've registered and been allocated their rooms it can be very late.'

Jackie continued. 'He has tried to ring the off-duty receptionist and the night porter, but got no response from either of them.' She smiled reassuringly at the man, seated behind his desk clutching a, by now, cold cup of tea and obviously struggling to come to terms with the morning's events.

'They probably switch their phones off in order to get some sleep,' Nash commented. 'I don't see that there's much more we can do here at the moment.'

The detectives thanked the manager and stepped into the reception area to continue their conversation. Across in the lounge, uniformed officers were taking statements from the guests on-site. The lift doors opened and Professor Ramirez stepped out. 'Ah, Nash, you're still here. Saves me a phone call. I'm going. My patient is leaving by the goods lift. I'll expect you at two, sharp, after I've had my lunch.'

Jackie Fleming smiled as she watched him leave. 'Talkative today, isn't he?' The others nodded in agreement as she turned to Nash and said, 'We need to look into the dead man's background.'

'SOCO found a mobile phone in the room. We're assuming it belongs to Jennings. I'd like to check that out as soon as they've finished with it. Who knows, it might provide us with a clue as to who killed him. What do you suggest we do in the meantime?'

'I think we should have a word with West Yorkshire and get them to send some officers to Jennings' house. He might have a wife and family. We also need to know why he's staying in Netherdale. It seems a little curious, when he only lives fifty miles or so away. Did he enter any car details when he registered?'

'Yes, he did,' Lisa answered. 'I looked in the car park at the back of the hotel, and it's there. I told SOCO about it.'

'Run up to the room and ask if they've found any car keys.' Fleming waited until Andrews was out of earshot. 'Will she be OK, Mike? She was involved in that double murder here a while ago, wasn't she?'

'Yes, leave it to me,' Nash said. 'I'll sort it.'

Lisa came back across the foyer. 'They have the keys. They were in the dressing table drawer along with his wallet. I suppose that rules out robbery?'

'You never know,' Nash replied. 'That's another job for forensics. His car will need to be checked over, but in the meantime we need to run Jennings through the PNC and see if he has form. Until we know more about him, we can't hope to make any headway.'

'I'm going back to HQ,' Fleming told them. 'I can ask Tom Pratt to do the PNC check. I'll also arrange for uniform to remain on-site. They'll be needed later.'

'That'll be a help.'

'Someone from CID also needs to interview members of staff and liaise with SOCO re fingerprints,' Fleming told them before leaving.

'I'll stay if Mike's going,' Lisa said.

'Are you sure you're all right being here? In view of what happened before?' Nash asked.

'It isn't easy,' she admitted, 'but I'll have to put up with it; there's nobody else available.'

Nash thought for a moment. 'No, you won't. I'll get Viv to come here and you can help out with the other job. I'm not leaving you here if it makes you uncomfortable. I'll ring Clara and get it organized. I need to know the state of play there anyway.'

Within minutes of arriving at the vehicle, the paramedic reported back via the mountain rescuer's radio that the man was alive and urgent medical attention was needed. The mountain rescue team lowered a portable generator and cutting equipment needed by the fire crew. Others began assisting the firemen and the second paramedic in their descent. In the midst of this, reports came back that all the child seats were empty, much to the relief of all those present.

Clara's mobile rang. She glanced at the screen. 'Hi, Mike, how are things in Netherdale?' She listened for a moment, then in response to his question told him, 'Miracle of miracles, the driver survived. From what we can see of the car, though, I didn't give much for his chances. However, he's unconscious and the paramedic isn't able to tell how badly injured he is. Added to that, he's trapped by his legs and the steering wheel. The only way to free him is by cutting him out of the car, which is going to take an age. That in itself won't improve his chances. It was first thought there could be children with him but thankfully, there weren't. Now we're waiting for the Sea King helicopter from RAF Leconfield. They were already on standby and have a doctor on-board. But it's going to be a very slow, laborious business, I'm afraid.'

'Any news as to who he is?'

Clara sighed, her frustration apparent. 'No, the front number plate is missing; probably ripped off. The rear number plate may be still attached, but it's jammed up against several tons of rock, so that's no help. I can't ask anyone to look for the plate either; they're all far too busy trying to save the driver.'

She listened for a moment. 'Anything else?'

She listened again. 'OK, I understand. I'll tell Viv.' She ended the call and turned to Pearce. 'Mike wants you to go to the Golden Bear and take over from Lisa. Take my car back to Helmsdale and pick yours up. Lisa's already on her way here.'

It was over fifteen minutes later that Clara phoned Nash back. 'Just wanted to let you know that the helicopter's arrived, and so has Lisa. We could be here for ages yet.'

'OK, thanks, Clara. As soon as Viv gets here, I'm going to the mortuary.'

It was nearly lunchtime before the firemen succeeded in freeing the driver. The doctor attending the scene told

Mironova, 'It's surprising he's survived this long given his injuries. If we hadn't got him out now I doubt whether he would have made it to hospital. As it is' – he shrugged – 'we won't know what his chances are until we've completed a scan. All I can say for definite is that both his legs and one of his arms are broken, as well as several ribs on both sides. He's also got head injuries, but how severe, I can't say. And those are just his external injuries. As to what's happened internally, I dread to think. The golden hour is well past,' he said as he shook his head, sadly.

Clara replied, raising her voice above the whine of the Sea King hovering over the crash site, waiting to winch the injured man on board. 'You had to cut his clothing off when you were treating his injuries. I suppose it's too much to hope that there was a wallet or some form of identification in them?'

'No, I believe not. I did give them to one of the officers to check, but I understand the pockets were empty. The hospital will need his name as well. Without recourse to his medical records we're limited as to the drugs we can give him. We don't want an adverse reaction with any current medication he's on.' The medic gave a weary smile. 'That's apart from the bottle of whisky he's ingested, which may well have saved his life.'

Clara looked puzzled.

'There's a smashed bottle in the car and the driver reeked of it. Chances are, he was not as tense as he may have been if completely sober when he went over the cliff – and therefore saved himself from death. Now I must go. I'm needed on board that helicopter.'

With the driver safely en route to hospital, the other emergency services began packing their kit and departing. Even the mountain rescue team seemed anxious to be away, although their leader did agree to leave one unit, along with a Land Rover and their equipment, to assist with retrieval of the wreck.

The senior traffic officer had now assumed command of police operations. As they waited for the recovery vehicle to arrive, he liaised with the men in charge of the hoist. 'They will need to assess the vehicle to see how we can recover it. I'd appreciate your help with securing the chains, if that's OK?' As they continued their discussion as to the best course of action, Mironova approached him. 'We still have to search the vehicle for some clue as to who the driver is. We could wait until the car's been hauled up the hill, of course, and see if the number plate's intact. But if it isn't, my boss won't want to wait until forensics retrieve the VIN number. And we're a bit short on time; there's a murder investigation back in town I need to help with,' she said, offering her most endearing smile. 'Any ideas?'

He stared at Clara for a moment as she waited for his reply, admiring her blonde hair and impish grin. 'OK, I'll go down,' he said, reluctantly. 'I'll borrow a helmet and harness from the Land Rover. I knew I'd find a use for my para-trooper training one day.'

He was kitted out from the equipment in the mountain rescue vehicle and headed for the cliff edge. 'Won't be long,' he called as he seemed to leap into the air and disappeared from view.

'Clara, why didn't you just flutter your eyelashes at him and have done with it?' Lisa asked.

'That would have been too obvious.'

When he'd been winched back up the cliff, the officer handed Clara an evidence bag containing a slip of paper. 'I found this wedged in what remains of the glove compartment. There may be other stuff in there, but I couldn't tell. The whole thing is so badly buckled the door won't open. I spotted one corner of this and managed to prise it out. Even then, as you can see, the paper caught on a jagged edge of metal and ripped as I was pulling it.'

She thanked him, donned gloves and opened up the folded sheet to examine it with Lisa peering over her shoulder. 'It's a rental agreement for Ivy Cottage, a holiday home in Gorton, let by an agency in Helmsdale. The person hiring the cottage is called Nigel Kirby with an address in Leeds.'

She paused and frowned. 'That's interesting. Mike said the man found dead at the Golden Bear this morning was also from Leeds. It may be pure coincidence, of course.'

'Do you think we should go to that holiday cottage and see what we can find out?' Lisa asked.

'We might as well. There's nothing more we can do here. Let's leave it to traffic to sort out. If we don't have any luck at the cottage, it might be worth trying the letting agents.' She looked at her watch, conscious that the day was passing them by. 'That's if they're still open by then,' she added.

CHAPTER SEVEN

Before Nash could enter the mortuary, his mobile rang. He glanced at the screen. 'Yes, Clara?'

'We've got an address for our car driver. It's Ivy Cottage in Gorton. The details were on a rental agreement in the car. Lisa and I are going round there. I'll let you know if we find anything.'

'OK. I'm at the mortuary so I'll ring you when I'm free again. Do you want me to pass on your regards to Mexican Pete?' He laughed as he ended the call, but his phone rang again immediately. This time it was the SOCO team leader from Netherdale. 'We've finished with that mobile from the hotel. The only prints on it belong to the dead man. It's all yours now. I think you'll find some of the recent text messages extremely interesting. Do you want me to read them out?'

'No, it's all right. I'm due at the post-mortem. If you leave it with reception at HQ I'll collect it from there.' He was about to open the door when his phone rang yet again. Nash muttered something vaguely impolite before answering. 'Viv, what news?'

'I've done all I can at the hotel, Mike. We've fingerprinted all the staff and taken their statements; there aren't very many.

Uniform are checking all the guests and I've got the details of those that checked out this morning. I've searched the room thoroughly, just in case SOCO missed anything. I even looked inside the Gideon Bible, but I couldn't find anything. SOCO left me the victim's car keys after they'd finished, but it's the same story there. Whatever Paul Jennings was doing in Netherdale is a complete mystery. There are very few personal items in the room, only a couple of clean shirts, socks and underwear in the wardrobe and the usual toiletries in the bathroom. I certainly don't think he was here on business. There were no suits, either in the wardrobe or the car, and no papers, no briefcase or laptop; nothing. That doesn't mean the killer didn't take them, of course.'

'Thanks, Viv. Make sure the room is sealed before you turn it over to uniform to guard, then you can leave. I'm due to attend the PM so will you nip round to HQ and find out if anything came from the PNC check on the victim? Whilst you're there, ask Superintendent Fleming if West Yorkshire had any success with Jennings' home address. And would she mind getting them to check out the address for a Nigel Kirby too; we think he's the man who tried to take the short cut off Stark Ghyll. Here's the address.' Nash repeated the details Clara had given him, before adding, 'SOCO have finished with the mobile from the hotel room and are leaving it at the front desk with the duty officer. Would you collect that for me whilst you're in the station? When you're done there, meet me round at Netherdale General, outside the mortuary.'

The post-mortem on Paul Jennings was routine, the only pertinent facts to emerge being confirmation of the cause of death, which had never been in doubt. The time that the victim had died, which Ramirez told Nash was exactly as he had forecast, was between 6 p.m. and midnight the previous night.

When Nash emerged, Pearce was waiting in the car park. He had his car window down and was devouring a sandwich. 'I didn't think you'd want anything to eat after you'd been in there' – he indicated the mortuary building as Nash slid into the front passenger seat beside him.

'Correct,' Nash replied. 'It doesn't matter how many times I enter that place, I'll never get used to it. So, got anything useful?'

'Tom couldn't find anything more sinister about Jennings on the PNC than a couple of expired speeding tickets,' he said, as he screwed the baker's bag into a ball and placed it in the car door. 'And when I left, Jackie hadn't heard back from West Yorkshire either, but she said she'll chase them up.'

'OK, let's have a look at this mobile. SOCO seemed to think we'd find the texts interesting. I think you'll be able to navigate round it far quicker than me.'

Pearce took the phone from the evidence bag and switched it on. He waited until the service provider's irritating jingle finished, and then began tapping the screen. He peered at the call log for several seconds. 'There appear to be a lot of calls to and from the same number. I'll try the messaging.'

He tapped the screen again. 'There's a lot of messages from the same number in here as well. I'll scroll back a bit.'

Nash waited.

'Well, I think Paul Jennings was having a fling with someone whose initials are K.M.'

'Oh, you do?'

Viv grinned. 'There are older messages here that imply that; times and places, that sort of thing. I don't think you'd sign a business arrangement with kisses on the end. And why would you send someone a two-word text saying only "Golden Bear"?'

'Go on, mastermind, tell me.'

Viv looked up, his face animated. 'Because, listen to this. "He's gone to York races. Back late. Mum got kids. Must CU 2nite." That's from the number Paul Jennings called most often. The message is signed K.M. and with a kiss. There's a reply. "Room 21. Can't wait. Luv U x, P".'

'When were those messages sent, can you tell?'

'Yesterday afternoon. The incoming one was at 2 p.m. The reply a few minutes later. Why do you ask?'

'Because I'd say that message was sent to trap Jennings. There was no racing at York yesterday, or this week at all.'

There was no sign of life at the holiday cottage. The detectives peered at the house. With no windows open, no car on the drive, the house looked as if the tenants had departed. 'I'll go and see if there's anyone in. You turn the car round. This might be a wild-goose chase,' Clara told Andrews.

There was no response when Mironova knocked at the door, even when she repeated the process. However, when Andrews joined her and tried the handle, the door opened easily. 'Hello, is there anyone in? Anybody at home?' Mironova's voice echoed down the hallway, but without eliciting a reply.

They inched their way cautiously into the house. Mironova pointed to a door to their left. Lisa nodded, and stood to one side before trying the handle. The dining room was empty, but there were unmistakeable signs of recent occupation. Clara pointed to the five place-settings. There were cereals, milk and butter on the table. Bowls and plates jostled for room on the small tabletop with glasses of juice. Two of the plates had crusts from toast on them. 'It looks as if everyone went out for the day and couldn't be bothered to clear up the breakfast things beforehand.'

'Without even locking the door? They must have left in quite a hurry,' Lisa added.

'Let's try the other rooms.'

The door opposite led to a lounge. Here, there was further evidence of the presence of children. A variety of toys were scattered over the carpet, the sofa and one chair. Mironova picked up a particularly handsome soft toy in the shape of a rabbit. 'I think one of the children is at the teething stage,' she remarked.

'How do you work that out?'

Clara pointed to the rabbit's ears. They bore the unmistakeable sign of having been sucked at great length. Lisa was about to congratulate Mironova on her powers of deduction when they were distracted by the sound of music. They looked at one another in surprise as a hit song from Take That filled the room.

Mironova spotted the source. 'There it is.' She picked up the mobile, which had been wedged between the cushions on the sofa, and stared at the screen.

'Are you going to answer it?' Lisa asked.

'I suppose I could. Then we'll know who it belongs to.' After a moment's hesitation, Clara tapped the screen. 'Hello,' she greeted the caller cautiously.

She listened for a moment and Lisa saw her expression change to one of shock. 'Mike, is that you? What are you doing ringing this phone?'

'Clara? Where are you? And whose phone is that?'

Mironova explained before asking, 'How did you get this number?'

'It's on Jennings' mobile; the man who was murdered at the Golden Bear. This number is the one he called most. Whoever it belongs to sent him text messages signed with the initials K.M. We think one of them was a trap to ensure Jennings would be in his room when the killer called. And that the person signing themselves K.M. is the killer.'

'K.M.,' Clara said. 'It could be K as in Kirby, I suppose.'

'No it isn't,' Andrews interrupted. 'Not exactly.' Lisa had been prowling around the lounge and found a woman's handbag. She held up a driving licence taken from the purse inside. 'K.M. stands for Kelly-Marie. Kelly-Marie Kirby, to give her full name.'

Clara relayed the information to Nash. 'We still have no idea where she is, or where the children are for that matter.'

'Children?' Nash's voice sharpened.

She explained about the toys.

'Better keep looking. I must go, I'm back at the station and my office phone's ringing.'

The caller was Superintendent Fleming, who had news from West Yorkshire. 'Leeds sent a couple of men to Paul Jennings' house. There was nobody at home, which isn't surprising. A neighbour they talked to told them Jennings lives alone; although they did say he had a woman visitor from time to time. Quite young and attractive, apparently. The neighbour thinks Jennings works for a printing firm somewhere in Leeds, but again he couldn't be sure.

'They also sent a man to the address Viv gave me that you think belongs to the man who went off the mountain. The officer interviewed one of the neighbours, who confirmed that Kirby lives there with his wife and three children. While they were talking, the bailiffs arrived with a van and began removing all the furniture prior to securing the property, which has been repossessed by the building society. According to what they told the constable, Kirby has been made bankrupt and they want to know where he is because the hire-purchase company intend to repossess his car.'

'I wish them joy with that,' Nash commented. 'It was only worth scrap value after the fall, and that was before the fire service began cutting lumps off it. But, I think that explains the suicide attempt.' Nash then told Fleming about the text messages he had read on Jennings' phone. 'It sounds to me as if Nigel Kirby was in danger of losing everything. I mean if, on top of losing the house, the furniture and the car, his wife was having an affair with Jennings, it would also provide him with a motive for Jennings' murder. Especially if she'd threatened to walk out on him and take the kids with her. We'll have to wait for the forensic reports and see if they came up with anything from the hotel room.'

'You may be right, but what about the kids? Where are they?' Fleming asked.

'We don't know,' Nash told her. 'We don't know where Mrs Kirby or the children are. Clara and Lisa are at the cottage now, but they tell me it's deserted. So we've no idea where they've got to. It all sounds wrong, though.'

'How do you mean?'

'Clara said they've found Mrs Kirby's handbag, complete with purse, at the house. Her mobile was there too. We know where the family car is. We just don't know about the family.'

'You check out the kitchen whilst I take a look upstairs,' Clara said.

Lisa walked back through the dining room. As she passed the table, she noticed the cereal in the small bowls was only partially eaten; the remaining milk had congealed. She prodded a piece of toast, which had dried out, in spite of the generous amount of butter smeared on it. Folded alongside was a morning paper, open at the sports page. She noted the date: yesterday. She called out to Mironova, 'The only thing I've spotted is yesterday's morning paper. I can't see one for today. Maybe they've walked to the village shop to buy one. I'll go and look around outside.'

All the rooms on the first floor showed similar signs of disruption or hasty departure to those downstairs. Beds were unmade; clothing was strewn around on chairs and on the carpets. The bathroom, which was the last room to be checked, had a heap of towels flung in a corner. Clara frowned; that wasn't the act of a wife and mother. She felt the towels. They were dry, as was the soap on the hand basin. Mironova was about to leave when she glanced at the bath. Her gaze focused on the area close to the plughole. Was it a trick of the light, or was there a pinkish stain around the chrome inset. She shook her head, dismissing her imagination looking for possibilities that may not exist.

She was halfway down the stairs when the front door swung open, thrust back with such violence that the handle struck the wall. DC Andrews stood in the doorway, her face devoid of colour, her expression one of absolute horror. She pointed to her left, towards the garage, her mouth working in an attempt to speak, but no words came forth.

'What is it, Lisa? What's wrong?'

Andrews swallowed once; then a second time, before managing to utter a few words, few in number, chilling in content. 'Garage …' she croaked. 'They're in the garage. All of them.' With that she burst into tears.

Nash had barely time to end his call with Fleming when his mobile began to ring. Although he knew it was Mironova from the name displayed on the screen, he was unable to make out what she was saying. 'Clara, slow down, take a long, deep breath and start again. And this time, speak slowly and clearly,' he said.

Pearce entered the room and could tell from Nash's expression that the call was not good news. He heard Nash say, 'OK, Clara, here's what I want you to do. Take Lisa and go sit in your car. Whatever you do, don't go back in there again. Stay in the car until we arrive. We'll attend to everything and be with you as fast as we possibly can. Got that?'

Even as Nash was speaking, he stood up and walked round his desk, removed his car keys from his pocket and handed them to Pearce, indicating the office door. They were already in the stairwell before he ended the call. 'Right, Viv, you're driving. We need to get to Gorton – fast! I'm going to be on the phone most of the way,' he told him as they almost ran past reception, to the bemusement of Jack Binns, and hurried across the car park to Nash's Range Rover. Pearce was turning the ignition key before he asked what had happened.

'Lisa and Clara have found four bodies in the garage of that holiday cottage where Kirby was staying. I have to assume they are those of Kirby's wife and children. You can imagine what sort of state Clara and Lisa are in, finding a family like that.'

As he drove, with scant regard for the speed limit, the removable blue light plugged into the dashboard and flashing, Pearce listened to Nash, who began by calling the pathologist. For once, it seemed that Mexican Pete had foregone the chance to comment on Nash's cadaver-finding instinct. Nash's comment that three of the victims were young children presumably scotched any ideas Ramirez might have had on that score. When he had finished with the pathologist,

Nash called Superintendent Fleming, then spoke to the head of the forensic section, who promised to have a SOCO team out there as fast as possible. His final official call was back to Helmsdale, where he spoke to Sergeant Binns to explain their hasty exit.

Pearce thought that might have been it, but once he'd got the official calls out of the way, Nash rang Mironova's home and spoke to David Sutton, her fiancé. He explained the situation briefly. 'Clara's going to need some moral support and a lot of TLC, David. Can you make it out to Gorton and take her home?'

'I'll be there as quick as I can. This sounds awful, Mike.'

Nash's last call met with no success. He had tried Lisa Andrews' home number, hoping to repeat the process with her partner, Alan Marshall, but there was no answer, the call going almost immediately to voicemail.

CHAPTER EIGHT

On their arrival at Gorton, Nash made no effort to inspect the crime scene. Instead, he and Pearce waited outside, talking to Lisa and Mironova. They elicited all the information they needed from the women, before Nash told them what he wanted. 'You're going home, both of you. I want you away from this place as soon as possible. I've already spoken to David,' he told Clara, 'and he's on his way.'

'There's no need, Mike. I'll be all right, it was just the shock,' she responded.

'I'm not listening to any arguments.' He turned to Andrews. 'I tried to get hold of Alan, but there was no reply.'

Lisa glanced at her watch. 'He went to a board meeting in Leeds. He's either sitting gossiping with Harry Rourke or on his way back.'

'Give me his mobile number and I'll call him. He can collect you from Clara's place, if that's OK with her.' He glanced at Clara, who nodded agreement.

Nash spoke with Marshall, who demanded to know if Lisa was all right before explaining his meeting had lasted longer than anticipated and he was about to set off for home.

Nash reassured him and explained the circumstances, before arranging for him to divert to Clara's house to collect

Lisa. After ending the call, Nash reinforced his earlier message that they were to go home and have a quiet night with their partners. He wasn't sure if their calm acquiescence meant that they had come to terms with what they had seen, or whether they were still in shock. Although every one of them had witnessed their fair share of the horrific after-effects of violent crime, some things were too terrible, even for the strongest stomachs. The murder of innocent children ranked high on that list.

Even when the pathologist and forensic team arrived, Nash refused to allow any of his colleagues to enter the crime scene. 'I'll go in with Mexican Pete,' he told Pearce. 'I want you to remain here with the girls until Sutton arrives. After they've gone, wait outside for Jackie.'

Having donned protective clothing for the second time that day, Nash joined the pathologist. Together, they viewed the distressing scene. The body of a woman, whom Nash assumed to be Kelly-Marie Kirby, was spreadeagled across a workbench in the centre of the room. In a far corner beneath a duvet were three further bodies; two young boys, the other, even younger, that of a tiny girl, barely a toddler. The children looked peaceful, almost as if they were asleep cuddled together.

'Madre de Dios, Mike, this is appalling,' Ramirez said, his voice little more than a shocked whisper. 'What on earth could have possessed a man to do such a terrible thing?' The use of Nash's Christian name, as much as the pathologist's words, conveyed the level of his distress.

'It seems to be the act of a man who has lost everything else in his life. When he knew his wife was about to leave him for another man and take the children, he decided to make an end to her, to his family, and to her lover – the man we found at the Golden Bear this morning. I'm going to leave you to it, Professor. I have two very distressed women outside to look after. Clara and Lisa Andrews,' he explained. 'They found the bodies.'

'They have my sympathy. Even after being warned, this was bad enough for us.'

When Nash emerged, he found that Pearce was alone. 'David's just left with the girls,' Viv told him. He looked past Nash at an approaching car. 'Jackie's here; and she's got the chief with her.'

They walked across the road to greet Superintendent Fleming and Chief Constable O'Donnell. Nash updated the new arrivals. 'By what Mexican Pete said, in between some fluent Spanish that I suspect was mostly obscene, he thinks the victims were killed between twenty-four to thirty-six hours ago. From that, it does seem to confirm what we suspected, that Kirby sent the text message arranging to meet Jennings in order to trap him.'

'How can you be sure? Perhaps she sent it and Kirby intercepted the message, or read it,' Jackie Fleming suggested.

'The timescale doesn't fit,' Nash explained. 'If Mexican Pete's estimate of the time of death is anything like accurate, Mrs Kirby was already dead before that message was sent. From the previous text messages between the two, which I believe *were* genuine, it seems she was on the point of scarpering and taking the kids with her. That must have been the last straw for Kirby. He'd lost everything else, and decided to kill himself after dealing with Jennings and his wife. The children had to go too, but they were secondary, I guess. Collateral damage. I think he disposed of them, sent Jennings that text, then went to the Golden Bear. After he killed Jennings, he drove out to Stark Ghyll, drank a full bottle of whisky and then this morning drove his car over the edge. The fact that he survived the fall is incidental, he obviously didn't intend to. Whether that's a good thing or not is open to question.'

'I know it's a bit early to ask this,' O'Donnell spoke slowly, choosing her words with care, 'but do you think there will be sufficient evidence to charge Kirby? And, will he be fit to plead? Given what he's done, I wouldn't be surprised if the psychiatrists decide he's not mentally capable.'

'I'm not at all sure it will come to that,' Nash told her. 'I haven't had chance to get an update on his condition from the hospital as yet, but there's no guarantee he'll survive. From what Clara told me, the doctor at the scene was none too hopeful.'

'I know this is going to sound terrible' – the chief constable glanced round as she spoke, presumably to check there was nobody else within earshot – 'but in one sense, perhaps it would be the best solution to the whole sorry business if he didn't.'

She could tell by Nash and Fleming's calm acceptance of her outrageous suggestion that they had both come to the same conclusion.

Nash was not surprised when both Andrews and Mironova reported to the CID suite in Helmsdale soon after his arrival the following morning. In truth, he was somewhat relieved, both for their sakes, and because with DC Pearce scheduled to give evidence in Netherdale Crown Court that day, their small team was in danger of being badly overstretched. Both women assured him they were fit for duty, whatever that entailed, although Nash thought he could detect a little nervousness that he might ask them to perform one particular task. He thought it better to clear the air on that matter immediately.

'OK, here's the situation. I'm going to be tied up all day. Mexican Pete has rescheduled a meeting in favour of the post-mortems. And with there being four, I can't see me being clear until very late this afternoon. As Viv's in court, that means the rest of the jobs plus anything new that might come in will be down to you two. There are a couple of specifics to deal with. We need someone to return to Ivy Cottage, I'm afraid, to be on hand until SOCO have finished. I also need someone to phone Netherdale General and check on Kirby's condition. They could do that whilst remaining here holding the fort.'

'Couldn't you check up on him whilst you're attending the post-mortems?' Mironova asked. 'After all you'll be almost in the same building.'

'In theory, yes,' Nash agreed. 'But the way I feel about Kirby at the moment, after what he's done, I'd not trust myself near him. And I don't think we want word of any of this getting out to the staff.'

'I'll go back to the cottage, Mike,' Lisa said.

Nash was surprised at her offer. He hadn't expected her to volunteer after the shock she'd suffered the previous day. 'Are you sure? Will you be all right with that? I know how distressed you were. I can get someone from Netherdale to go.'

'If I don't do it, I'm not sure I'd ever trust myself in a situation like that again.'

'A bit like getting back on a bike after you've fallen off, you mean?'

She nodded agreement.

'That leaves me here with only the hospital to phone,' Mironova said. 'A whole morning with next to nothing to do. A bit like your normal working day, Mike.'

She thought Nash had ignored her jibe, but his riposte was suitably cruel. 'I wouldn't say that exactly, Clara. You've still got that computer scam inquiry ongoing and there are reports to write up from the Stark Ghyll incident and the holiday cottage murders.' He gave her an evil smile. 'They call it the art of delegation, I believe.'

Despite her brave words to Nash, Lisa Andrews had serious reservations about entering the holiday cottage again, let alone the garage. After speaking to the officer outside the door, she made her presence known to the SOCO team in the house. She then plucked up courage to join the second set of forensic officers inside the garage and found that, with the corpses removed, it was just a garage again, despite the unmistakeable evidence of police activity. In fact, as she watched the SOCO team at work, she was able to look round the room for the first time and realized that it was far less of a garage and more of a workshop. Lisa found this rather surprising, as the building formed part of a property that was leased by people wanting to enjoy the beautiful countryside of the Yorkshire

Dales. She could not imagine someone taking their holidays and spending their time doing DIY. She could only assume that the workshop had been in situ before the property was acquired for its present purpose.

After a lunch of sandwiches from the village shop taken in the fresh air, the senior forensic officer told her their work in the garage was almost complete. They had documented the scene, found some fingerprints and had collected several tools from the rack for closer examination.

They returned to work and as Lisa moved to one side to allow working space, a random thought crossed her mind. If the owners had set this space aside as a workshop, why had they moved the workbench from its original position against the wall to the middle of the room? Perhaps Kirby moved it in preparation for killing his wife? But that didn't make sense: it would take more than one man to move the heavy object. From her vantage point, Lisa could clearly see the grimy mark along the opposite wall where the workbench had originally stood; cobwebs hung in its place. Moving it to the centre would give anyone wanting to work far less room. Besides which, the wall where it had been was the site of the only window. Even with the solitary strip light, the bench's new position would give the worker far less illumination.

She mentioned this fact to the technicians. Two of them seemed uninterested in her comment, but the third nodded his agreement. 'You're right. I thought that as soon as I came in. I've a workshop at home that's about the same size as this room, and my bench has to be against the wall otherwise I'd never get past it. And the light's all wrong too, just like you said.'

Encouraged by the man's support, Lisa prowled slowly round the bench. She had reached the far end when she noticed something, even in the shadow cast by the large wooden structure. She looked across at the forensic team leader. 'Lend me your torch for a moment, would you?'

She shone the beam down to illuminate the floor alongside the end of the bench farthest from the door. 'That's odd,' she muttered, 'very odd.'

'What's odd?' The SOCO member with a workshop joined her.

Lisa pointed to the area lit by the torch. 'Look there. See that crack? That's all newer concrete than the rest of the floor. Now why would anyone re-concrete just one section of the floor?'

She moved to the side of the bench, and on the far side was able to see where the join ended. 'It goes the full length of the bench. I think we should move the bench and see how wide the new section of concrete is.'

Lisa eventually managed to persuade them to shift the bench back to its original position. Now that it was no longer concealed, the officers could see that the newer section of concrete was approximately six feet long by three feet wide. The SOCO team leader gave voice to the thought that was in all their minds. 'That's just the right size for a grave. What do you want us to do? We could take a pickaxe to it and dig it up, only to find the pet dog buried underneath. It's your decision.'

'Thanks a bunch.' Lisa grimaced. 'Let me have a think about it.'

The decision wasn't an easy one. Digging up a large patch of concrete was likely to prove extremely unpopular with the owners of the property. On the other hand, Lisa could not think of an innocent explanation for the placement of the workbench in such a bizarre position. Certainly not something as innocuous as the burial of a pet. If it had not been done to conceal the concrete below, then why leave it in the middle of the floor? And just what was beneath? 'Do you think it could be drainage repairs?' she asked.

'No, if it were new pipework of some sort, the size and direction would be different. It would go through the building and continue on outside.'

What Lisa really needed was guidance from someone senior; Mike, for example. But she knew he was unavailable at the mortuary. She plucked out her mobile and pressed Clara's number. There was no response. She stared at her phone in dismay. She looked round at the technicians. 'Have any of you got a phone with a signal that works out here?'

A couple of the men shook their heads, the others checked their phones. They both had the same network. 'Is there a phone in the cottage?' one of them asked.

'No, we had to use DS Mironova's mobile to report in yesterday.'

'In that case, it looks as if it's down to you.'

'All right. Let's go for it. We'll make a start. I just hope we're not going to end up with hundreds of old copies of the *Beano* or something equally bizarre.'

It was nearly time for the shops to close before Nash emerged from the mortuary. He had planned a trip to the supermarket on his way home that evening, but food was the last thing on his mind. The post-mortems had been a harrowing experience, particularly those of the children. Even Ramirez had been subdued, and had kept what few remarks he had to make strictly business-like. Nash switched his mobile phone from silent and saw he had a text from Mironova asking him to call her. He pressed her speed dial number and waited.

'Mike, thanks for calling back. How did it go?'

'About as grim as you'd expect. Have you got news on Kirby?'

'I spoke to the hospital soon after you left. They told me Kirby had been taken down to theatre for an investigative procedure because of massive internal injuries. They couldn't tell me much more, but they said it would be a few hours before they'd know what exactly the problems were. I asked them to keep me informed. I got a call from the ward half an hour ago and they said he'd died on the operating table. Apparently the additional trauma of the procedure was too much. Either that or the injuries were too severe in the first place. They couldn't be sure, and with what he'd done, I wasn't really that interested, to be honest.'

'I was talking to Jackie and the chief about him last night,' Nash told her, 'and we all agreed that it would probably be for the best if he didn't pull through. I'll nip across to HQ and bring Jackie up to speed on things, and then I'll ring Lisa.'

'I could do that if you want me to,' Clara offered.

'What, and drag you away from your reports? I wouldn't dream of it.'

'To be honest, Mike, I've almost finished them and there's nothing else come in today that needs my attention. Uniform seems to be coping all right. The problem you have is you might not be able to raise Lisa. I needed to check something with her earlier and her phone seems to be dead. There are signal problems in the Gorton area.'

'I hope she's all right. As you're about clear with the paperwork, would you do me a favour? Nip out to Gorton and check she's OK. I know she reassured us this morning, but I don't want to take a chance.'

'No problem, Mike.'

CHAPTER NINE

The breakthrough came suddenly, with a blow from the sledgehammer that hardly differed from the countless previous ones. This time, however, the impact resulted in a large crack appearing, running from side to side. Levering with the pickaxe yielded no result, until a further hammer blow produced a second crack that ran at right angles to the first.

A short time later they had managed to remove almost all of the six-inch-deep concrete. 'No wonder it took so much bloody shifting,' one of them remarked. 'I hope this effort turns out to be worthwhile.'

'If nothing else it will help your fitness,' Lisa told him.

After loosening the hard-packed earth below with the blade of the pickaxe, they stretched a length of tarpaulin on the floor, brought a pair of shovels from their van and set to work removing the soil. Aware that at any point they might make a discovery of some sort, they slowed down and worked more carefully now. A further fifteen minutes had passed, and they had gone down over two feet, without anything untoward coming to light. Lisa surveyed the pile of earth removed from the hole. She was on the point of calling a halt when the SOCO leader shone his torch into the hole.

'There are a lot of worms in that soil,' he remarked. 'Makes you wonder what they find to feed on down there.'

Lisa was still pondering this statement when one of the diggers stopped work suddenly, straightened his back and stared down at where he'd been excavating. After a moment, he called to his superior. 'Shine your torch here, will you?'

As the beam illuminated the hole, the digger bent down and smoothed the soil back with his hand. 'I think you'd all better come and have a look at this.'

They moved forward to look. 'Well, now we know what the worms found so attractive here. It wasn't a false alarm after all,' the senior officer said.

Seconds later they all jumped at the sound of a voice. They had been so intent on their discovery that none of them had heard the arrival of a car. 'What are you doing in there?' Clara demanded.

Lisa hastily explained.

'Heavens! I dread to think what else this place is going to throw up. Does Mike know?'

'Not yet. My phone's playing up. We've only just made the discovery.'

'Here,' Clara said, offering her phone, 'try mine.'

Lisa pressed the speed dial and waited.

'Clara?' Mike answered.

'Sorry, Mike, it's Lisa here. My phone's on the blink. Clara's lent me hers. She's back here with me.'

'Yes, I asked her to check in. Has she told you that Kirby died a couple of hours ago? I think when we have the results back from forensics the evidence will show that he murdered his wife, their children and her lover, so perhaps it's the best outcome. Anyway, apart from tidying up loose ends and seeing to the paperwork, I guess that means it's probably all over.'

'No, Mike,' Lisa contradicted him, 'that's why I was trying to phone you. It isn't all over. Far from it.'

When Nash pulled up, he spotted DC Andrews, a slightly forlorn figure, walking to and fro on the parking space leading to the outbuilding. He immediately asked how she was feeling.

'Strangely enough it didn't affect me in the same way as yesterday.'

'That's a relief. Still not pleasant, though. Where are the boffins?'

'As soon as we found the body I ordered them to stop work. I thought it best not to disturb what I assume to be another crime scene to avoid possible contamination. Clara's in the garage with the SOCO lads, waiting for your instructions. They were muttering about the amount they had to do, until I reminded them they would be on overtime. They cheered up immensely after that. They sent me out for a breath of fresh air.'

'That's good work, Lisa. The first thing I'd better do is tell Mexican Pete and ask him to come, if Clara hasn't done already.'

'No, she hasn't. She told me to contact you first.'

Nash took out his mobile. 'Here goes.'

'This should be a laugh a minute.'

Nash eyed Lisa. 'You've got a strange sense of humour,' he said as he waited for the call to be answered.

Ramirez was caustic in his response. 'Another body?'

Nash explained that he would be required back at the holiday cottage.

'You've really excelled yourself, haven't you? You've got me bouncing around the county like a demented yo-yo, going from crime scene to crime scene. Why don't you take a nice long holiday somewhere thousands of miles away? Six months would be ideal; then the rest of us could get some peace.'

'Come off it, Professor, you'd be bored stiff within weeks. You'd be sending me text messages begging me to return.'

The pathologist's reply was unrepeatable, even though it was in Spanish. Nash grinned. 'I thought that as a doctor you would realize that what you're suggesting is physically impossible.' Nash ended the call, cutting off the flow of Castilian invective that followed. He looked across at Lisa. 'I'd better take a quick look inside. Mexican Pete's going to be a while before he gets here.'

'He didn't sound awfully happy.'

'Don't let that fool you. He's never happier than when he's got chance to insult me, or liken me to Dracula. You stay outside. I guess you've seen more than enough horrors,' he said as he struggled into yet another paper suit. 'I might decide to wear one of these permanently; it would save me a lot of time.'

The interior of the workshop was much as Lisa had described it, but for the addition of the slabs of broken concrete stacked in uneven disorder at one end of the hole, and the pile of soil. Soil that would need sieving, Nash thought.

He stared down at the makeshift grave, his expression sombre. In a way, the cold-blooded nature of what he felt to be a premeditated crime affected him more deeply than the original murders he had been called to at the property. This was different; this was planned and executed in a ruthless, clinical way that lent it an extra degree of horror. Nash wondered about the motive and the identity of the victim. He had already discounted any connection to the other bodies. The difference was so much at odds with yesterday's savage handiwork. This crime might never have been uncovered but for DC Andrews. Her intuition and persistence had ensured that the victim had been found, and might even be given the justice he or she deserved.

Two days later, Nash came from his office, a broad smile on his face, and briefed Mironova and Pearce. 'I've just taken a call from the forensic lab. Case, or should I say cases, closed.'

'You've got some results?' Clara asked. 'Is it the Kirby case?'

'That and the Golden Bear. The fingerprints in the hotel room belong to Nigel Kirby, as do several fibres found at the scene; those same fibres were found on the bodies of Mrs

Kirby and the children. The shirt removed from Kirby at Stark Ghyll after the crash was covered in blood; some of it was his, the majority of it belonged to Paul Jennings. Once the tech boys got to work on his car, they recovered a knife from the glovebox, which tested positive for blood from his wife. In the cottage, they found a second shirt which he had obviously worn when he killed his family.'

'He wasn't very careful, was he?' commented Viv Pearce.

'Why should he be? He wasn't planning on hanging around to get caught,' Mironova reminded him.

'Perhaps it's as well he didn't survive the operation, then. They love child-killers in prison.'

'I still don't understand why he felt he had to kill his children,' Clara said, sadly.

'I can answer that,' Nash said. 'One more piece of information I got was that the two younger children weren't his; their DNA was a match to Paul Jennings. Perhaps Kirby's wife taunted him with it and on top of everything else it would have been the last straw. One thing the professor did say was that the children hadn't suffered; they had been drugged.'

'One man's actions affecting so many families,' Viv added.

'And I can't imagine there will be many mourning his death either,' Nash said. 'However, we still have the body in the workshop. The first thing we need to establish is how long that corpse has been there. For that, we're waiting on Mexican Pete. I'll be attending the post-mortem, later this morning – yes, I know what you're both thinking,' he said, in response to their expressions, 'another one. Still, it has to be done. At least I got yesterday off while he attended his meeting. Hopefully, he'll give us a clue as to the dates we should be looking at and also some idea of how the person in that grave died. I can't think it was accidental, or natural causes, unless someone wanted to continue claiming an allowance by pretending the person was still alive, and that seems highly unlikely.'

'It's been done before,' Mironova pointed out.

'Yes, but hardly for such a long time. The remains were almost skeletal, so I don't think we're looking at something that happened recently. That leads me to the next part, which is going to be the identification. What I suggest in the meantime is that we all concentrate on compiling reports as far as is possible and submitting them to Tom Pratt. Let's get ahead of the game, because I've an idea we might get rather busy in the next week or two.'

Nash arrived at Netherdale General Hospital for the third time that week and made his way to the mortuary. He greeted Professor Ramirez and the post-mortem examination began.

'I have good news for you,' Professor Ramirez told him.

'Please tell me. I'm not exactly overwhelmed with glad tidings at present. It has been quite a week.'

'The victim is a woman; I suggest she was between twenty and forty years old. Cause of death: garrotting. Unfortunately, this lady's teeth have been removed, which suggests the killer didn't want her to be identified, even if she was found. I believe the removal was conducted after death.'

'Can you estimate how long ago she was buried there?'

'I'd say no less than two years and no more than five, but at present that's all it is, a guess. I'll need time to conduct further tests and get the results back from samples I'll send off for analysis before I can be more definite, and even then I can't give much in the way of certainties.'

'Thank you, Professor; that is so comforting.'

'If that's comforted you, my other news should make you ecstatic. There is a possibility that we might be able to get DNA from the remains. It will take some time, and even longer to analyse it, and at this stage I can't make any promises.'

'You rarely do, Professor, and I'll forego my ecstasy until I know one way or another.'

When he returned to his office, Mironova and Pearce were in the CID suite. He told them what the pathologist had said. 'Given the time span we could be faced with a long list of potential victims and equally large number of suspects. First off, I want to know more about the owners of that cottage, and the letting agents involved in renting it out. Viv, start with the agents, will you; they must know who the owner is. At the same time, find out how long they've had the property on their books. If it's more than eighteen months, they'll have to provide us with the names and addresses of all the tenants they let it to from before. If we're really lucky, they might have had the property in their portfolio for the whole of the period we're interested in, which would save us more work.'

'I doubt we'd be that lucky,' Pearce commented gloomily.

'Probably not, but we can always hope. I know it sounds like a mammoth task. You'll need help with all the information from the agents. I think you should ask Tom Pratt to collate the details as they come in, and then we can spot any that might be missing, or periods when the cottage was vacant. Of course,' he added with a rueful smile, 'the body could well have been interred during the winter, which would mean all that work would have been for nothing. However, it's the sort of job that Tom will enjoy.'

Pearce looked slightly more cheerful, from which Mironova guessed that the bulk of the work would fall on their civilian support officer, former Superintendent, Tom Pratt. Boredom had prompted Tom's return to work following early retirement caused by a heart attack some years earlier. His knowledge of the area and expertise were of great help to the team. 'Tom's going to be kept busy,' she remarked with a wicked smile in Pearce's direction.

Their attempt to obtain any information from the lettings agency was going to be delayed, as Pearce reported to Nash later the same afternoon. 'The firm is a husband-and-wife affair. I spoke to the receptionist, who is a bit on the dim side, to put it mildly. She told me her boss and his wife run the business and they're both on holiday until next week.'

'Couldn't the receptionist give you any information?'

'Couldn't or wouldn't, take your pick. I tried several different approaches, but all I got was "You'll have to speak to Mr or Mrs Baines when they get back from holiday."'

'Did you think about doing a Land Registry search on the property?'

'I did, but it would have cost us, and it might take even longer before we get the results.'

'OK, I suppose we'll have to wait, but it's frustrating, to put it mildly. However, if that poor woman has been buried as long as Mexican Pete thinks, I guess another week isn't going to make a lot of difference.'

Much as Nash had predicted, there was a lull as the team waited for the forensic evidence to be sifted and analysed. Nash was at last able to brief Superintendent Fleming and the chief constable on the closure of the Jennings and Kirby deaths.

Gloria O'Donnell was relieved. 'I suppose it will look good on the stats, although I can't say it's the sort of crime anyone wants on their patch. Well done, Mike.'

'Actually, ma'am, we didn't do much. The evidence was all there, it was SOCO who deserve any praise. They did all the work.'

'What about the remains Lisa recovered from the workshop?' Fleming asked.

'The body is that of a woman aged between twenty and forty. That's all we know at present. SOCO sifted the soil from the grave but that gave us nothing. There were no scraps of material, or fibres even, so we believe she was naked when she was put into that hole.'

'How long will it be before you know more?'

'I asked Mexican Pete that. He said it would be a week or two longer, but not to worry, she wasn't planning on going anywhere.'

'I imagine not,' O'Donnell commented dryly. 'By the way, that was excellent work by DC Andrews. But for her persistence, that poor woman's body might have lain there undiscovered forever. I think a mention on her file is merited.'

'I agree.' Fleming looked over at Nash. 'Do you want to tell her, Mike, or shall I?'

'I think she'd appreciate it more if it came from you, as the senior officer.'

'We'll have to wait for that report before we can consider how to progress the case,' O'Donnell commented. 'In the meantime, what about the other stuff we've got outstanding?'

Nash shrugged. 'I'm concerned about these computer scams. Fortunately, no more incidents have been reported in the last few weeks, but that's not to say we won't suddenly get another rash of them. So far, Viv's made no headway trying to get help from our experts, other than a few phone calls. He's tried liaising with them, and from the scraps of conversation I've heard, they could be talking Mandarin, for all I know. Mironova is coordinating both inquiries, which will leave me free to head up the "workshop woman" investigation.'

'Is that what they're calling it?' O'Donnell gathered up the paperwork Nash had supplied and placed it in her out-tray, signalling the end of the meeting. 'We'll meet again in a fortnight, unless there are any urgent developments in the meantime.'

CHAPTER TEN

Neil Ormondroyd was always first to arrive at the solicitors' office in Bishopton. He glanced at the brass plate by the front door. Ormondroyd & Partners was a little deceptive as titles go, although there had once been a partner and a clerk. That had been in the days when Neil's father had been the Ormondroyd, before Neil had qualified ten years ago; before everything had changed.

He really would have to get round to having a new plate made. But that would involve ordering new stationery and having the bank mandate changed. Then there would be all the official bodies to notify. The size of the task had deterred him, caused him to put it off time and again. But he would have to tackle it. The longer he deferred it, the more painful the reminder was. The reminder of things Neil would much rather forget.

All the legal work undertaken by Ormondroyd and the middle-aged woman who acted as secretary and receptionist was confined to civil matters, with Ormondroyd steering clear of criminal work. The most exciting aspect of his caseload was likely to be the titillating evidence from a divorce case.

As he opened the morning's mail, Ormondroyd's attention was not totally on the task. Part of his mind was still occupied with the memories his train of thought had stirred up. He worked his way through the pile, which contained no surprises until he came to an envelope near the bottom. Although the address was printed rather than handwritten, there was no company logo or franking mark. It was only when he removed the contents and unfolded the letter and sheet of paper within that his attention was fully caught. He read it through, then returned to the beginning and read it again. Not that there could be any mistaking the meaning or the disappointment the content brought him.

Later, after his secretary had left for the day, Neil sat for a while at his desk staring at the letter and the enclosed invoice. The demand was for services rendered, but they hadn't been. Not in the way Neil had hoped. Nevertheless, he took the chequebook for his private account from the desk and wrote out the sum, wincing slightly at the cost. It was money he could ill afford, certainly when the accompanying letter reported total failure. He addressed an envelope and enclosed the cheque.

He walked over to the filing cabinet, opened a drawer and lifted out a file and flicked through the first sheets containing information and computer prints from his research. He shook his head before replacing the folder, sighing heavily as he did so. He closed the cabinet, returned to his desk, pulled open the bottom drawer and took out a bottle of whisky and a small tumbler. He half-filled the glass and walked across the corridor to the other partner's office. He unlocked the door and stood, leaning on the frame, sipping the spirit as he stared at the interior of the room.

This had been his office when he joined his father's practice after leaving university. Following his father's retirement, Neil had moved to the larger room; his old room remained vacant. Ormondroyd sighed, sadness in every line of his face. How different things might have been, if it hadn't been for…. He shook his head as memory stirred.

The practice had grown to such an extent that the premises had become a little cramped, especially as the workload demanded two clerks. Much of the additional work was generated by the parallel expansion of their largest client, the Bishopton Investment Group.

B.I.G. had been the buzzword at the time. And then, back in 2010, it had all gone sour. As the group's solicitor, Ormondroyd's name had been on all the documentation. Although the Law Society investigation had cleared him of all wrongdoing, and the police inquiry into the fraud also stated that he wasn't implicated, the damage had been done. Word got about. Work began to drop off and clients left, one by one, never to return. The cruellest blow had been the loss of the money earned from the Bishopton account.

The B.I.G. receivership had happened shortly after Neil's love life had hit a low ebb. The cause was the same in both cases: Linda Wilson. The rumour was that the directors had been waiting to confront Linda with evidence of her misdemeanours. However, before they could, she had fled the country. Had it not been for that, the woman would have been arrested, the money recovered, and life would have been so different for Ormondroyd and many others.

Instead, she was probably sunning herself in some tropical paradise, whilst he struggled to keep his business going. And to what purpose? Sometimes the effort seemed futile, for he had never married, had nobody to succeed him. He had hoped to marry, but his hopes had been dashed. Ormondroyd's face twisted with pain and he drained the whisky in one swift gulp. The sharp liquid matched the bitterness of his loss and the memory of the woman who had betrayed him.

Neil closed and locked the door and wandered back to his own office. Before sitting down at the large, flat-topped desk, he took the letter to the shredder. Almost without thinking, he refilled his glass. He sat down and opened one of the desk drawers. As he had done many times before, he took out an envelope containing an old photo. It was of a young girl, a teenager, dressed in school uniform. Ormondroyd traced the outline of her beautiful features on the paper. This too he had done a hundred, a thousand times before, and, as always, with tears streaming down his cheeks.

Elsewhere, a young man stared at his computer screen and turned to his associate. 'We have a problem.'

'We don't deal in problems; we deal in solutions.'

'This is serious, not a matter for hackneyed 1980s selling clichés.'

'Sorry, couldn't resist it. What's the problem? Is it the bank transfers?'

'No. Someone's been snooping around.'

'That's not a problem. I told you before; there's no paperwork and without a paper trail we've nothing to worry about. Let them keep looking, they won't find anything.'

'You're missing the point. I don't mean someone's been looking through files. At least not that sort of file.' He tapped his screen. 'I mean someone has been using a computer to do their search. I'd say that represented a problem, wouldn't you?'

'Ah, yes, I see what you mean. Do you want me to take a look?'

'There's no need for that; the triggers you put in place have already deflected our nosy parker. What concerns me is the identity of the snooper, so I want you to make sure it doesn't happen again.'

'Does it matter? If the triggers worked, let them try to their heart's content.'

'That's all very well, but if they decide to combine physical and online surveillance, it could prove very awkward, and I think that's exactly the sort of thing a solicitor would dream up, don't you?'

'So that's who it is. I suppose given the connection, it had to be him. And in view of that, it does put another complexion on the problem. What do you suggest?'

'I think it might be time to reactivate Ivan the Terrible.'

'Phew! That's a bit extreme. Are you certain? It would be very expensive – even if he's available, which I can't be sure about. Last I heard he was languishing in a gaol somewhere in central Africa.'

'I'm sure even if Ivan himself isn't free, he'll have friends who would be happy to stand in for him if the price is right. And one thing we're not short of is money.'

'OK, I'll get onto it right away.'

'There's one other thing. And it could be far more worrying even than the legal eagle. This is only a rumour at present, but I heard something that might mean we need to give Ivan further work. Something along the lines of the last job he did. It seems there are others who might be getting suspicious, and they're people we can't deal with the same way. If that's the case, we either stall them until we've time to plan our exit strategy, or risk losing everything. From what I hear, they're bringing in an investigator: a woman.'

'We have no proof that when this woman begins work she will find out anything. Others haven't, so why panic over this one?'

'She has a very good reputation. That's why they use her.'

'I still don't see why you're so worried.'

'I wouldn't be, except for the discovery at the holiday cottage. Suddenly there are a lot of people interested in the identity of the remains that were found there.'

'The police, you mean? I don't think for a minute they'll connect that to what happened three years ago. For one thing, there was nothing left to identify the body, and by now I reckon it'll be no more than a collection of bones.'

'I'm not as confident as you, then. They can identify people, even if they've been dead hundreds of years. Do you remember that article about Richard III? They were able to get a DNA sample from that skeleton found in Leicester and test it against a known descendant. And that skeleton is centuries old.'

'You've been watching too much television. And anyway, even if they did identify who was buried in the cottage, there's nothing to trace it back to us.'

'I still don't think we should take chances with this woman, which is why I suggest we get Ivan working again. We can't afford her finding out anything before we're ready to go. How is that progressing?'

'Another two weeks, three at the most and then everything will be ready. Then I can press the button and we can leave.'

'That settles it; we'll have to use Ivan. The chance of an impromptu audit is like a ticking time bomb. We're so close now we can't afford to take the risk. If we take this one final precaution, we can proceed without fear of discovery until we're out of harm's way: a long way out of reach of the authorities.'

'Good, I'm getting fed up with this country. I want sunshine, a beach and the luxury we've worked for.'

'What about the woman?'

'Talk to Ivan. See what he has to say. If needs be, get him to do what he did before. This time tell him to pick a place where she'll never be found.'

'We thought he had last time. It was pure bad luck that she was discovered. Where do you suggest?'

'Another empty cottage would do. I suppose it doesn't matter that much if they find the body as long as it's after we've cleared out.'

'What if they catch up with Ivan? What if he tells them who he's working for? Or what if they follow the money trail?'

'I'm rather counting on that happening. If they do that, it will implicate someone else. That will give us more time to take up our new life with our new identities. By the time they discover their mistake it will be far too late.'

'OK, when I find Ivan, I'll have a word and see if he can frighten the woman off. If not, I'll tell him to go to the next level, but not to finalize things just yet. No point in doing it until absolutely necessary.'

'Still a bit squeamish? I remember you felt that way before.'

'Not squeamish, simply careful.'

It seemed as if Nash's prayers were on their way to being answered. The first piece of positive news came in a phone call from the pathologist. 'We've managed to extract a DNA sample from the skeleton found in the workshop. I'm sorry it's taken so long, but the first two we extracted had been corrupted by the surrounding material. This is the only clean sample we've obtained thus far, and I'll need at least one more to be absolutely certain we've got the DNA string one hundred per cent accurate. Hopefully, within the next few days we should be able to send one for analysis.'

'Thank you, Professor, now all we have to do is find a missing person who matches the dead woman's description and....'

Nash's voice tailed off.

'Nash, are you there?'

'Sorry, I just had a stray thought.'

Ramirez sighed. 'Usually when you get stray thoughts like that, my mortuary cabinets start to fill up.'

'Let me know when you have a viable sample and it's ready for analysis, and thanks, Professor.'

Nash rang off and remained seated behind his desk, his eyes staring at the painting of York Minster, his mind occupied with the theory he was beginning to develop. It was almost twenty minutes before he walked into the outer office. 'Viv, isn't it today that the couple from the lettings agency are due back from holiday?'

'Oh yes, do you want me to phone them?'

'No, better to go round in person, and don't leave without all the information you can get. They're bound to be horrified by what went on at the cottage, but I'm more interested in the other victim in the workshop, so keep their minds concentrated on what we need to know.'

An hour later Pearce returned, frustration written across his face.

'Problem?' Nash asked.

'Would you believe the office was closed? Closed, due to unforeseen circumstances, according to the notice in the window.'

'Well, in that case, we'll just have to wait until they reopen.'

Neil Ormondroyd had spent much of the week thinking of the women he'd loved – and lost. The pain of each was still raw, but now he had another worry. He wished he was more adept with computers. If he had been, he might have found out who was behind the crime he'd uncovered. He glanced down at the drawer where the decanter was secreted. No, that was becoming too much of a habit. Besides, he still had one more client to see, a client who would only speak to him and had insisted on a late appointment, and whisky-laden breath was not a good advertisement.

As if on cue, there was a knock on the outer door. He opened it, to greet the caller. Ormondroyd shook the man's gloved hand, noting the Slavic cast of his features. As the client followed Ormondroyd up the stairs, he removed a coil of thin wire from his pocket. Once inside the office, the caller placed his briefcase on the floor as Ormondroyd went to sit behind his desk. 'How can I help you?'

One quick stride took the caller behind the solicitor. He dropped the wire over Ormondroyd's head and tightened it. The struggle was swift, brutal and one-sided. 'Nothing for me. You do nothing for me. I do to you.'

Ormondroyd convulsed, kicked, choked and then went limp. His assailant allowed the body to slump over the desk, blood from the deep gash already seeping onto the blotter. The killer walked to the filing cabinet and began searching the drawers. He took out a bulky folder and stuffed it in his briefcase along with Ormondroyd's laptop. At the door he turned and said, 'Thank you, Mr Ormondroyd.'

Ormondroyd didn't reply, but then Ivan hadn't expected him to.

CHAPTER ELEVEN

Nash had just entered Helmsdale police station when Sergeant Binns stopped him. 'Mike, hang on.' The sergeant put the phone down.

'Morning, Jack, what have you got for me?'

'I've just had a message from the control room. They got a call from Ormondroyd Solicitors in Bishopton. When Mr Ormondroyd's secretary arrived at work this morning, the building was unlocked. She found Ormondroyd in his office. It sounds as if he's been murdered.'

'Tell control that Clara and I will go, she's getting tired of paperwork. What's the woman's name?'

'Mrs Lane.'

When they arrived, Nash looked at the exterior of the building. If a TV company wanted a setting for a small-town solicitor's office, this would fit the bill perfectly. The walls were grey and green; limestone, clad with ancient ivy. The window of the general office was opaque. Etched into the smoky coloured glass was the name, Ormondroyd & Partners, Solicitors and Commissioners for Oaths. Nash wondered who the partners were, or had been.

They were greeted by a uniformed officer who ushered them into a small vestibule. The general office was to one side; access was via a second half-glass door. Directly in front of them, a flight of stairs led to the first floor.

Nash and Mironova stepped inside the general office. The woman seated behind the desk was slightly the wrong side of forty, Nash guessed. She looked distraught.

'Mrs Lane? I'm Detective Inspector Nash. You made the call, I believe.'

Mrs Lane sobbed and nodded. Nash asked gently, 'Is it just you and Mr Ormondroyd here? Only, the sign on the window says, Ormondroyd & Partners.'

'That sign was put there by old Mr Ormondroyd, Mr Neil's father, but that was a long time ago. These days there isn't enough work to justify another partner. Now, I don't know what will happen.' She began to cry again.

'What I suggest is that you wait down here with the officer whilst DS Mironova and I have a look round.'

They headed upstairs. 'Do you want us to suit up?' Clara asked.

'Not for the moment, we won't go in the room; not until we have to.'

From the doorway, Nash had no doubt that Ormondroyd had been murdered. He pointed to the dead man's neck. 'Garrotted, by the look of things.'

Clara nodded agreement.

The killer's weapon of choice had bitten deeply into the solicitor's neck, stifling the dying breath, cutting everything in its path, almost severing the vertebrae. As the man had pitched forward, the heart, pumping resolutely to the last, had caused the blood to spew enthusiastically from the fresh outlets so recently opened up.

The blotter had been hard pushed to live up to its name, eventually giving up the unequal struggle to contain the escaping blood.

Later, after Clara had taken Mrs Lane home and Nash had handed the crime scene over to Ramirez and the forensic officers, he phoned Superintendent Fleming. 'SOCO will be at least twenty-four hours here, so whilst they're busy we can't search the offices thoroughly. We should go and take a look round Ormondroyd's house. I took his house keys off the ring, so we'll be able to get in easily enough. I've asked Viv Pearce to join us. I think if we take a look round the man's home, we might get some idea of the motive or even the identity of the killer from his lifestyle.'

'What lifestyle?' Clara asked when Nash had ended the call. 'I chatted to his secretary, after I'd taken her statement, and according to her, Ormondroyd was pretty much a recluse. Mrs Lane said that as far as she was aware, he hadn't been out for a meal or a drink; hadn't visited the theatre or cinema for as long as she could remember.'

'Maybe he wasn't a social animal.'

Mironova shook her head. 'No, Mrs Lane said he wasn't always like that. She reckons she knew Ormondroyd better than anyone else; had watched him grow up and she admitted that he was obsessively secretive. But she did believe he had been involved with someone up to a couple of years back. She said he changed after that, became even more of a hermit, and even less communicative. I asked her if she knew who it was he'd been involved with, and why it ended, but she has no idea.'

'That's not exactly a lot of help. Did she say anything else that might have given us a clue?'

'Not really. I did ask her one other question. It was the way she kept mentioning his secrecy that prompted it.' Clara smiled. 'It shocked her rigid. I suggested the person he might have been involved with could have been another man. When she got over the shock she admitted that it could have been a possibility, but she thought it was highly unlikely.'

'The other explanation for the secrecy could be that he was seeing a married woman. In a small place like Bishopton, it wouldn't take much for rumours of an affair like that to spread like wildfire. Anyway, let's go look at his house and see if we can find any answers there.'

Pearce was waiting for them outside the semi-detached Victorian building. Everything looked as it should. Once inside, they did a brief tour of the premises and could find nothing untoward. Every room bore the hallmarks of a solitary man living a bachelor existence. 'It's just as Mrs Lane said,' Clara commented. 'Rather sad and pathetic really; a man without friends or family.'

They were standing in the large airy room to the rear of the ground floor, which had been furnished as a study. Two of the walls were lined with bookshelves. A third wall, alongside the French window leading to the back garden, had a glass-fronted china cabinet, on top of which was a framed photograph of a good-looking young woman. Nash and Mironova examined the photo.

'Her face looks vaguely familiar. I feel I ought to know her,' Clara remarked. 'Hang on.' She pointed to the features. 'Viv, take a look, who does she remind you of?'

Viv stared at the photo, but with no success. 'Sorry, you've got me beaten. Who do you think it is?'

Mironova placed her hand over the lower half of the photo, covering the woman's body. 'Now, imagine the hair as short and try again.'

'Yes, I see it now. She looks a bit like Dean Wilson.'

'A bit? More than a bit. A lot, I'd say. I may be wrong, but at a guess, I'd say this was a photo of Linda Wilson.'

'Linda Wilson? Isn't she the woman who—'

'Disappeared along with several millions at the time that Bishopton Investments went bust. If the likeness is correct, she must be Dean Wilson's sister.'

'I haven't met him, so I bow to your knowledge,' Nash said. 'What intrigues me is why this photo has pride of place in Ormondroyd's private sanctum. Unless Linda was the woman he was involved with. That would tie in with what Mrs Lane told you, Clara. If Linda Wilson let Ormondroyd down the same way as she did the investors, he would have gone into his shell. Maybe he's been carrying a torch for her all this time.'

'Do you think her disappearance could be connected to Ormondroyd's murder?' Clara wondered.

'I can't begin to see how. Anyway, let's have a good look round in here and see what else we can find.'

They made a start, with Pearce concentrating on the two-drawer filing cabinet whilst Clara read Ormondroyd's diaries. Nash went through the contents of the desk drawers one by one. They had been at work for almost half an hour when Nash located another photo. He stared at it for several moments before muttering, 'Hell's bells!'

Clara looked up and saw the stunned expression on Nash's face. 'What is it? What have you found?'

Nash didn't reply, so she peered over his shoulder. 'Good Lord! That's obscene.'

'Did you meet Naomi Macaulay?'

Clara shook her head.

Nash continued. 'The girl in this photo looks very much like Naomi. However, the hair colour is totally wrong. This girl's a blonde, a natural blonde at that, and Naomi's hair is bright red. Unless Naomi's hair is dyed.'

Pearce hadn't seen the photo. 'How do you know the girl in the photo doesn't have dyed hair?'

Nash turned the photo so Viv could see it. 'Oh, I didn't realize it was that sort of photo. I can see now.'

'If this isn't Naomi, who do you think it is?' Clara asked Nash. Failing to get a response, she glanced at him. He was staring at the photo, his mind obviously elsewhere.

'Mike,' she prompted, 'if you could tear yourself away from ogling the nude for a moment.'

'Sorry.' He grinned. 'Did you speak?'

'I asked who you thought the girl was. Do you think Ormondroyd was into child pornography? Might that have been the motive for his murder?'

Nash didn't answer her directly. 'I'd like to know when this photo was taken.' His voice was quiet, pensive. 'Think about this. Naomi Macaulay is, what, eighteen or nineteen years old. We know Ormondroyd was thirty-three. What does that suggest?'

Mironova and Pearce exchanged glances, and it was clear they had no idea what Nash was driving at. 'Think about hair colouring,' he prompted them. 'Here we have a highly suggestive nude photo of a young girl with blonde hair, who I think looks a lot like Naomi Macaulay, although Naomi has red hair. When this photo was taken, I reckon this girl' – he tapped the photo – 'would be no more than fifteen or sixteen years old. Now think about Ormondroyd, and apart from a few flecks of grey, his hair is as red as Naomi's. Red hair isn't that common, and in a small place like Bishopton there can't be many people with the same colouring unless they're related.'

'You think Ormondroyd is Naomi's father? But he wouldn't have been old enough,' Pearce objected.

'Not legally, perhaps,' Nash agreed. 'But physically, he would have been quite capable of fathering a child, even if he wasn't over the age of consent. If I'm right, that leaves one unanswered question. Is this Naomi's mother? If she had an affair with Ormondroyd, then perhaps we should be talking to Mr Macaulay about the solicitor's murder.'

Clara was examining the photo. The pose was overtly sexual, and from the way the young girl was looking at the camera, Clara had little doubt that the object of her desire was the photographer. 'If your theory's right then this photo would have been taken before digital photography was widely available. So I wonder if Ormondroyd was interested in photography. I doubt you'd have got anyone to develop these. I can't see a young lad marching into the chemist's shop in Bishopton high street and leaving that roll of film, can you?'

'Good point, Clara. Maybe we should look round the rest of the house. However, let's concentrate on this room first.'

It was Mironova who made the only other significant discovery. The first entry in the diary to catch her attention was in the 2009 book. 'We were right,' she exclaimed. 'Neil Ormondroyd was dating Linda Wilson. It's in here. All it says is "Linda" followed by a time and place. However, they went away for weekends together. In the Lake District, to London, Edinburgh, all over.'

She turned her attention to the next in the sequence. 'The last mention of Linda is here, in February of 2010.' She continued reading. 'This is interesting. There's an entry that reads, "Linda, Netherdale station, 7.30, London train." Next day there's another. "Linda didn't show. Can't raise her at home or on her mobile. Where is she? Worried." Then another a few days later. "Bad rumours about B.I.G. and Linda. Can't believe it. Linda wouldn't let people down that way."'

Clara read on, her face registering the emotion. 'This is awful. The poor guy was heartbroken. He was obviously deeply in love with Linda Wilson. Her disappearance hit him very hard. After a few more entries, there's no further mention of her. And at the same time the tone of the diaries changes. It's almost as if his personal life has ceased to exist; either that or he's afraid to commit his thoughts to paper.'

Clara skimmed through the more recent diaries, and put them aside one by one. When she picked up the one for the current year, an envelope dropped out onto the desk. 'Hello, what's this?' She was intrigued, but her expression changed to one of disappointment. 'Oh, sorry.' She saw her colleagues looking expectantly at her. 'I thought for a moment it might be something interesting, but it's only some credit card statements.'

'Have a look at what he spent his money on,' Nash suggested.

Clara glanced through a few of them. 'Paying bills, mostly. By the look of this, I wouldn't be surprised if the business was in trouble. There are even a lot of calculations here scribbled in pencil that I can't make head or tail of, which suggest he was trying to work out how to pay his creditors. Sad, but hardly a motive for murder.'

She put the envelope back inside the diary cover and set the volume down. 'That's it, I'm done.'

Pearce had finished on the filing cabinets, but as he was about to turn away, he noticed a small curl of electric cable sticking out from behind the side of the wooden frame. He reached down and pulled gently at it. The cable proved to be connected to a voltage adapter and was plugged into the mains. He stared at the end for a moment. 'Mike, when you went into Ormondroyd's office, did you see a laptop?'

'No, but that doesn't mean there wasn't one. Our attention was taken with the body, to be honest. If there was one there, SOCO will have documented it, and the scene-of-crime photos will show it.'

When they had finished in the study, they turned their attention to the rest of the house. The sitting room was their next target and immediately on entering, Nash stopped and glanced around. 'Clara' – he gestured at the surroundings – 'does this look familiar?'

Clara looked at the Adam-style fireplace with a hearthrug in front of it, one with a distinctive pattern. 'That nude photo of the girl,' she exclaimed. 'It was taken in here. She was lying on that rug.'

'Exactly what I thought.'

Their next discovery came about almost by accident. As they were preparing to search upstairs, they walked down the hall towards the staircase. Pearce opened the cupboard under the stairs. It was then that he realized that it wasn't a cupboard at all, but the entrance to a flight of stairs leading to a cellar. 'Mike, here.'

They descended the steps, treading carefully in the semi-gloom only partly alleviated by the glow of a low-wattage bulb at the bottom of the flight. On reaching the basement, they looked round. 'Well, here's the darkroom,' Nash said.

Clara had found a bank of switches. She flicked them in turn, and the whole of the basement was bathed in light. 'Bloody hell!' Pearce exclaimed.

Around the walls were dozens of photos, all nudes, all in suggestive poses. There were only two subjects, Nash realized after close examination; the young girl whose image he had found in the desk, and the woman who resembled Dean Wilson.

'The dirty bastard,' Clara muttered.

'I'm not so sure.' Nash pointed to the images. 'I'd say these were the two loves of his life. I'd agree if there were photos of dozens of girls, but there are only two who posed for him. And if I'm right' – he stared at the young girl's face again – 'I'd say Neil Ormondroyd had extremely good taste.'

'Yes, but taking porno photos like this, it's perverted,' Clara objected.

'I'd agree with that but for the expressions on their faces. They were obviously up for it, clearly madly in love with Ormondroyd. There's no way they could have been coerced into allowing these to be taken, or have it happen when they were drugged or drunk.'

'Mike,' Pearce called, 'look at this.' The photo was of the blonde, taken in Ormondroyd's study. As with the others, the pose was highly suggestive. 'Check out the wall behind her.'

Nash grinned. 'What wall?' He looked closer. 'Oh, well spotted, Viv.' Behind the girl, a calendar showed the date quite clearly. 'That settles it. This is definitely not Naomi. However, I'm still curious to find out who she is.'

'Do you think she might be involved in Ormondroyd's murder?' Clara asked.

'She could be, I suppose. But what I'm more interested in is Linda Wilson. If, as we suspect, these other photos are of her and she is involved in Ormondroyd's death, why would she choose to resurface now, after all this time?'

CHAPTER TWELVE

When Nash reached the CID suite next morning, Pearce handed the DI a sheet of paper. 'We were speculating about the younger girl in those photos. The one you thought looked like Naomi Macaulay. I did a bit of checking up. I think we can discount it being her mother.'

Nash glanced down at the paper. 'Where did you get this?'

'I did a search of the *Netherdale Gazette* online archive. I simply typed the surname Macaulay and a load of stuff came up. Most of it was business reports about Peter Macaulay, but I spotted this article among the rest.'

'Good work, Viv.' Nash started to read the feature, which described a charity gala held in Bishopton the previous summer, the proceeds of which were going to a famine relief project. The chair of the organizing committee was Mrs Muriel Macaulay.

Nash recalled something Jack Binns had said about the family. 'They spend all week making money, and all day Sunday negotiating with God how best to take it with them when they go.' Reading the article, it seemed that the desk sergeant's cynical opinion could well be justified. The smugness of Muriel Macaulay's expression seemed to back that up. One thing for certain, she bore no resemblance to the girl in the photo. To describe Muriel Macaulay as plain would have been tantamount to flattery.

'We need to establish the girl's identity if only to eliminate her from our enquiries. There is an obvious family likeness to the Macaulay family, so we need to check them out.'

'Might that rule out Peter Macaulay as Ormondroyd's killer?' Pearce asked.

'I never rule anyone out, Viv, but go and ask Jack about the Macaulay family. If anyone knows, he will. No, you can't. I've just remembered, Jack's on leave until Monday.'

'In that case, I'll give Tom Pratt a ring. He might give us some idea.' Viv returned a while later. 'OK, here's all Tom can remember about the Macaulay dynasty. The family were farmers originally, but after the Second World War, Duncan Macaulay diversified and opened an agricultural merchants business. He struggled for a long time, but then he merged that company with one owned by Stephen Wilson. Wilson was a building contractor, and the new enterprise, Wilson Macaulay Industries, went from strength to strength.'

'Strange combination,' Nash said.

'That's what I thought, but Tom said they built milking parlours and the like, all sorts of farm buildings. Anyhow, Duncan Macaulay became a real entrepreneur, a risk taker, and by all accounts not above doing some very shady deals in the pursuit of wealth. Tom's father once told him the reason Macaulay was a Methodist, not a Catholic, was he would have blocked the confessional for hours getting penance for his sins.' Pearce grinned. 'Duncan died young; suffered a heart attack, which surprised a lot of people, who weren't aware he possessed one. His son Christopher took over the business alongside Stephen Wilson. A few years later, Stephen Wilson died and Christopher was left in sole control.'

'Didn't Stephen Wilson have any family to join the business?'

'Tragically, his son died in an RTA and later his grandson had to leave the business to care for his children after their mother died.'

Nash nodded. 'I get it. So this Stephen Wilson was Linda and Dean Wilson's great-grandfather.'

'That's correct. Linda joined the business when she was old enough and was doing very well for herself. How well, nobody realized until she fled the country with a few million.'

'And Christopher Macaulay is still the boss?'

'According to Tom, he's officially semi-retired now and leaves the day-to-day running of the business to Peter, his son. However, Tom reckons when any big decisions have to be made, it'll be Christopher that makes them, not Peter. Rumour is that Peter is terrified of his father, who has a reputation for being arrogant and quick-tempered.'

'Does Christopher Macaulay have any other children?'

'Tom reckons there was a daughter. He believes she'd be about seven years or so younger than Peter. However, as far as Tom is aware, she went to study at an American university and he reckons she stayed there.'

'Does Tom know her name?'

Viv shook his head. 'I asked him, and he said if he'd heard it, he can't recall it. I can do some more digging if you like.'

'No, you've done fine. If we need any more, we can resort to the computer later.'

Nash turned to Clara. 'I wonder if that could be Peter Macaulay's sister in the photo, but if that's the case, and she's been in the States for nearly twenty years, I think we can safely rule her out of any involvement in Ormondroyd's murder. Which puts us firmly back to square one.'

Nash was eating the sandwich brought for him by Pearce when his phone rang. He nodded to the DC to answer it. Viv listened to the caller for a moment then thanked them. 'SOCO have finished at Ormondroyd's office. There's very little to report, no sign of forced entry, only the expected fingerprints. But they've taken away his blotter for testing. They seem to think there is some writing on it hidden under the blood, so they're going to try and decipher it. Apart from that, the office is clear for us.'

'Right, we'll collect Clara as soon as we've eaten and get across there.'

When they arrived at the solicitor's premises, Mrs Lane met them by the reception desk. She looked forlorn, and a little bewildered, Nash thought. The cause of this was explained when she spoke. 'There are people ringing up, asking questions about the work Mr Ormondroyd was doing for them; questions that I'm unable to answer. Some of them are getting quite impatient. One or two were even rude. I simply don't know what to do.'

'Isn't there anyone who could help? Someone qualified, I mean?' Nash asked.

'I don't know of anyone.'

'Have you thought of approaching the Law Society? They must have someone they appoint in cases such as this, a sort of locum. I can't believe the same thing hasn't happened before within small law practices.'

'That's a good idea, I never thought of that. I'll phone them and ask for advice.'

'Now, if you would give us the keys, we'll get on with what we have to do.'

She held the bunch out. 'Your forensic officer told me I hadn't to go into Mr Ormondroyd's office until after you were finished.' She shuddered. 'I don't think I'll ever be able to go in there again.'

The office looked much as Nash remembered it, with the notable absence of Ormondroyd's body and the blotter from the desk. The work of the forensic officers had not caused too much upheaval, which was far from the case at every crime scene. As a precaution, they all donned plastic overshoes. He instructed Mironova and Pearce to start searching the filing cabinets. 'I'll set to work on the contents of the desk.'

Clara went to the left-hand side of the bank of cabinets. She drew a blank with the top drawer, but when she opened the second one, she immediately noticed a large gap between the suspension files. 'It looks as if something has been removed from here,' she told the others. 'There's a file missing; possibly two, judging by the size of the gap.'

'Maybe it was one Ormondroyd was working on, or had given to Mrs Lane to type up a letter or a contract or something,' Pearce suggested.

'That's probably it. I'll go down and check with her.'

When she returned a few minutes later, Nash noticed Mironova's thoughtful expression. 'No luck with Mrs Lane?'

'No, she hasn't got the file, but she did tell me which one she thinks it was. As soon as I told her it was between one for someone called Berry, and the file after it was labelled with the name Bowden, she said it could only be one file, a big one, and she certainly doesn't have it. In fact she said she wasn't aware that it had been out of the cabinet in the last eighteen months. There was no reason to remove it.'

'Why's that?' Pearce asked.

'Because it was a dead file. One there was no possibility of further action on.'

Nash waited patiently, aware that Clara was enjoying the suspense, savouring the announcement she was about to make. 'The missing file is the one for Bishopton Investment Group. They were one of Ormondroyd's *biggest* clients before they went bust.'

Nash groaned at her attempt at humour.

Clara continued, 'What I can't work out is why it's gone missing. What relevance could a file concerning a company that went into liquidation three years ago have to do with Ormondroyd's murder?'

'Perhaps it isn't connected. If Ormondroyd was so upset by what happened, perhaps he destroyed the file,' Viv suggested.

'He couldn't do that, Viv. He wouldn't be allowed to. We've searched Ormondroyd's house, and the file certainly wasn't there. I can't see any sign of it in here, unless of course it's been filed in the wrong place. However, let's not jump to any hasty conclusions. Although it may be connected and may have been removed by the killer, we've no proof one way or another yet.'

'Another piece of information I gleaned from Mrs Lane that you might find interesting is who was also a client of Ormondroyd.' Clara was still enjoying herself.

'Go on then, surprise me.'

'Wilson Macaulay Industries!'

'Now that is interesting. So why not now?'

'It had cost them a lot of money to repay the people cheated when B.I.G. went bust, and for some reason they held Ormondroyd responsible. They took all their business, both commercial and personal, elsewhere.'

Nash returned to his search of the desk, and in the bottom left-hand drawer found a brown envelope with a photo inside it. 'This looks familiar.' He held it up for the others to see.

'That's the girl you said looked like Naomi Macaulay,' Clara said. 'Although this one is far less explicit than those at the house.'

The young girl was clad in a white blouse and pleated skirt. Although it looked as if her clothing formed part of a uniform, there was nothing that would identify her school. Her pose, smiling for the cameraman, bore only the slightest hint of familiarity. 'I wonder who she is and where she is now,' Nash mused, not realizing he'd voiced his thoughts aloud.

Mironova winked at Pearce. 'Is that because of her connection to Ormondroyd, or because you fancy her?'

'Certainly not, although I admit it would be interesting to see what she turned out like. I was thinking that the likeness to Naomi is even more pronounced in this photo. Maybe that's because she's not striking a pose.'

'And because she's fully clothed,' Clara pointed out, 'and therefore less likely to distract you.'

Nash stared at her coldly. 'Speculation is idle, until we discover who she is. And that's not what we're here for.'

He returned to his task, but there was little else of interest until he came across a folder which, when he opened it, proved to contain financial information regarding the business and Ormondroyd's private affairs. He began looking through the sizeable mound of paperwork. It consisted of bills, all neatly appended with the date of payments, invoices to clients, sundry petty cash receipts, mortgage and bank statements. 'It looks as if Ormondroyd took out a hefty mortgage soon after the Bishopton Investment trouble. I guess that was because the firm was facing big losses, from what I can judge by the accounts.'

He continued looking through the papers, but stopped suddenly. Clara, who had finished the first of the cabinets, glanced across as she moved to the next set of drawers. She stopped, seeing the puzzled expression on his face. 'Found something, Mike?'

'I'm not certain,' he replied, his voice thoughtful. 'I'd say Ormondroyd was an extremely neat and tidy person, wouldn't you? A bit like my mother's favourite expression, "a place for everything and everything in its place," she used to say.'

'I'd go further than that,' Clara agreed. 'I'd say it was almost an obsession with him. Why do you ask?'

'I find it curious that he has some of his credit card statements in this folder, and the others in his desk at home. You remember; the ones you were looking at?'

'I see what you mean. It does seem out of character.'

'Perhaps they were from different years,' Pearce suggested.

Clara walked across and glanced at the statements. 'No, that isn't it. Some of these are from around the same time as the ones in his study. So why separate them?'

She began turning the statements over, examining them one by one. As she was looking at them, Nash's mobile rang. He identified himself and listened to the caller, eventually saying, 'Thanks for that, will you email the exact details to me?'

He ended the call. 'That was forensics. They've got a result from the writing on the blotter. Apparently there was

111

one word, written several times, and below it a short phrase. The word was the name "Sam" and the phrase was, "Must find Sam", although who Sam is, and why Ormondroyd was trying to find him, I've no idea.'

'Perhaps this bloke Sam is the killer,' Viv suggested. 'Maybe he found Ormondroyd before Ormondroyd could find him.'

'Nip down and ask Mrs Lane if she knows who Sam is, or if the name means anything to her. She might have heard Ormondroyd talking about him.'

Pearce was away several minutes. 'She was on the phone to the Law Society,' he explained. 'They're going to appoint someone to supervise the winding-up of the business. She doesn't know of anyone called Sam, and certainly never heard Ormondroyd refer to him. She can think of no reason why he would have the name scrawled on his pad.'

Mironova returned to her study of the credit card statements. 'I don't know if this means anything,' she told Nash, 'but I have spotted one difference between these statements and the ones at his house.'

'What's that?'

'All these have had the whole balance paid off, whereas the ones at his house were obviously covering times when cash flow was at its worst, because he only paid off the minimum amount. I guess he wouldn't want to leave them here, in case Mrs Lane or a client caught sight of them, and jumped to the worst possible conclusion.'

'That sounds logical, and I suppose that means it's another dead end. Back to work, then.'

As Clara reached the final statement, the one covering the previous month's transactions, she noticed another sheet of paper. She turned it over, and found it was an invoice. 'I wonder what this is about?'

'What have you got?'

'It's an invoice from a company called In Confidence.'

'What's it for?'

'It doesn't specify. It just states "to services rendered". There's no indication of what those services were.'

'Give me their phone number and the invoice number and I'll ask them.'

'That's another odd thing. There is no phone number on the invoice. In fact there isn't even an address. I thought you had to put the address on invoices.'

'I think you do. Without that, where would you send payment? This all looks very strange.' Nash inspected the invoice. 'Whatever they did for Ormondroyd, it was quite expensive. £500 plus VAT can buy you an awful lot, even these days. And the other intriguing part is that the invoice is addressed to Ormondroyd personally, so this was a private transaction rather than a business one.'

'Do me a favour, Viv, get hold of Tom Pratt and ask him to try and locate this In Confidence firm. I want to know who they are, where they are, and what they did for Ormondroyd.'

The detectives could find nothing else remotely pertinent to their inquiry, but when Nash returned the keys to Mrs Lane, he warned her that they might want to conduct a further search, and that she should ensure that neither she nor the locum solicitor removed anything from the room.

It was much later, as Nash was preparing his evening meal, that he remembered something they had missed. He picked up his mobile and phoned Mironova to check his facts. 'Remember that electrical lead Viv found at Ormondroyd's house? I didn't spot a laptop in his office, did you? So, where is it? Mrs Lane says she couldn't face going into his office, so I don't think she took it for safe keeping, which leaves only one other possibility.'

'Won't SOCO have taken it?'

'There was nothing on the list they sent me.'

'So you think the killer might have removed it and the B.I.G. file after he murdered Ormondroyd?'

'I don't know. All we have at present is speculation. A few hard facts would be a real step forward.'

CHAPTER THIRTEEN

Pearce had left in his second attempt to discover the owner of Ivy Cottage. Nash turned to Mironova. 'Busy?' he asked.

'Not really, why?'

'Grab a couple of coffees and come into my office. I've had a wild idea, and I want you to tell me it's nonsense.'

As Nash finished expounding his theory, his phone rang. 'Yes, Professor?'

'Ormondroyd was garrotted, in the same way as the woman found in the workshop. In other words, such a level of violence was used that he was almost decapitated.'

'You think the same person killed them both?'

'I can't say that for certain, but it is possible. I should remind you that my work ends when I establish the cause of death. Identifying the killer is down to you. I believe that is what you're paid for.'

Immediately after Ramirez had ended the call, Nash's phone rang again. He listened for a few moments, and then said, 'Thanks, Viv. Collect all that information and take it through to Netherdale. Get Tom Pratt to help you collate it.' Nash put the phone down and turned his attention back to Clara, who had been thinking about his wild idea.

'I don't believe your theory's likely; all the evidence points the other way,' she said.

'I'd almost convinced myself of that until Viv's call just now. He's found out who owns the cottage at Gorton.' He explained and saw Clara's surprised expression.

'Where do we go from here?' she asked.

'There's only one way to get confirmation for my theory, and that depends on the DNA results from the skeleton. Once they're available, we'll have to pay one or two visits. The one to the Macaulay family in particular should be interesting, to put it mildly.'

'What shall we do whilst we're waiting? We can hardly sit around twiddling our thumbs.'

'I think we should return to Ormondroyd's office. There's another file which I hope hasn't been removed; one that I particularly want to look through.'

'Which one is that?'

'Wilson Macaulay Industries. I'd also like to take a look at Duncan Macaulay's will. If Ormondroyd and his father handled the Macaulays' legal affairs, I feel sure there will be a copy of it in the office. Failing that, it should be on public record. With the amount of wealth swilling about in that family, it would have to go for probate.'

'Why do you want to look at the will? Old man Macaulay must have been dead a fair while, going by what Tom told us. The will and its provisions will be ancient history by now, surely?'

'Think about it, Clara. Tom said he thought Peter Macaulay's sister went to America years ago, to study at university. She was the granddaughter of one of the richest men in the county. It seems inconceivable that he didn't leave her a sizeable chunk of his fortune, plus in all probability a block of shares in the family business.'

'Yes, I'll go along with that, but he may not have left her anything. I still don't see where you're heading with it.'

'So, where is she? Did she come back to claim her inheritance? Did she demand the money she was entitled to? If her return and that demand occurred shortly after the Bishopton Investments crash, her father, Christopher Macaulay, might not have been in a position to pay her.'

'You don't think he…? That's a wild theory, even for you, Mike.'

'Exactly what I thought – until Viv told me that Ivy Cottage has been owned by Macaulay Property Holdings for the past fifteen years. Who's to say that one or other of the Macaulay clan didn't kill her and bury her in the workshop, confident that as long as they owned the property her last resting place would remain undisturbed?'

'Put like that, it doesn't seem quite as wild, but what about your other candidate?'

'Linda Wilson? You've more or less ruled that out. According to what we know, Linda was spotted on CCTV boarding the cross-Channel ferry in Hull, and later booked into hotels in Amsterdam and Paris. To do that she would have had to produce her passport, and police at the time checked the passport number recorded by the hotels, and that was a match. Likewise with the Cayman Islands. She was there at the time the missing millions were withdrawn from the bank there. She could hardly have done that if she was under six inches of concrete in Gorton village.'

'Which of your two theories do you prefer?'

Nash sighed. 'Neither of them, I suppose. Far more likely that someone bumped off his wife or partner during their holiday, panicked and buried her in the workshop, covered her in concrete and pulled the workbench into the middle of the room. They've probably been sweating on the possibility of discovery for years, and the recent events will have sent their fear into hyperdrive.'

'The other possibilities still need checking out.'

'I agree, if only to discount them. By the way, Tom Pratt rang me yesterday afternoon. He's remembered the Macaulay girl's name. She's called Susan, he thinks. I did a Google search of the Ivy League universities and amongst all the others, I found a Susan Macaulay who was a student at Princeton around the right date, but for some reason, the entry had a tag on it that read "All biographical detail withheld" – whatever that means.'

'Maybe her family didn't want her traced back to the UK, or having her old college friends turning up here looking for her and asking awkward questions.'

'That might be the reason, but what I find far more suspicious is why nobody from the Macaulay organization has contacted us after the horrific events that took place in one of their properties. You'd have thought they'd show some level of concern, unless they have something to hide. Especially later when the other body was discovered. To be honest, it's only their failure to get in touch with us that keeps my wild theory alive.'

'Do you intend to confront them?'

'I certainly mean to ask them for DNA samples, purely for elimination purposes. And I want you along with me when I do, because I can't watch two people at once, and I'm particularly anxious to see the reaction of Peter Macaulay and his father when I make that request.'

Their second, more focused, search of Ormondroyd's office yielded little of value to begin with. The Wilson Macaulay folder in Neil Ormondroyd's office contained only a couple of letters, including a curt note from Christopher Macaulay, requesting that their files be transferred to Potter and Co. of Helmsdale. 'Macaulay was really putting the boot in by the look of it; obviously blamed Ormondroyd for the Bishopton Investment thing.'

'Maybe it was more personal than that. Perhaps your theory about Naomi's parentage is correct.'

Nash gestured to the folder. 'There must be more than this. Even though the legal work was transferred, Ormondroyd would have had to keep copies of anything the firm had done for Macaulay in the past. So, where is it? I hope that hasn't been removed as well.'

'I'll ask Mrs Lane.'

Clara returned and held up a key. 'She said they may be in old Mr Ormondroyd's office, the one across the landing. We only took a quick look inside the room, because it had obviously not been used for years.'

'I don't suppose by any chance the Bishopton Investment file is there as well.'

'No, when I asked Mrs Lane, she said that one was definitely in this room.'

There were several Macaulay family files. In the first of these, Clara found a document headed Deed of Trust. She scanned it briefly. You were right,' she told Nash. 'This is a codicil to Duncan Macaulay's will appointing trustees on behalf of the girl. And here is the will itself. In it there is a major bequest to his granddaughter, Susan Arabella. He did leave her a stack of money and shares. In fact' – Clara continued reading – 'although he left money and shares to her and Peter, he seems to have ignored his son, Christopher, altogether.'

'How much did he leave Susan?'

'There was a thirty per cent stake in Wilson Macaulay Industries, plus a cash sum of half a million. Peter got twenty per cent and £250,000.'

Nash whistled. 'Well worth killing for. I've known less compelling motives for murder.'

Clara continued examining the folder's contents. 'Hang on,' she said. 'I think this blows your theory out of the water. The trust was set up when the girl was nineteen years old. This document,' she held up another sheet of paper, 'revokes some of the terms of the first one.'

'What is it?'

'A deed of transfer of some sort.' Clara began to read. '"The trustees hereby transfer the shareholding of thirty per cent of the ordinary share capital of Wilson Macaulay Industries Ltd, a company registered in the United Kingdom", and then it gives the registration number and address of the registered office, "in equal parts, to Christopher James Macaulay and Peter Louis Macaulay. We hereby also relinquish the trust's interest in the sum of £500,000 being the amount bequeathed in the terms of the will of Duncan Macaulay, deceased, by the mutual consent of all parties." I think that might explain why she didn't return to claim her inheritance. It no longer existed.'

'It all sounds very dodgy to me. I don't think a court would look too kindly on the trustees making such big decisions on behalf of a young girl without some very convincing reason. I also think that if she felt aggrieved and thought she'd been swindled out of her inheritance, she might well have come back to England and threatened the family with exposure. A court case, their name being dragged through the mud, would be the sort of things the strait-laced Macaulay family would have hated. Silencing her because of the trouble she might have caused could be an even stronger motive for killing her than to avoid having to pay up.'

Nash signalled to Mironova that she should join him and told Pearce, 'Clara and I are going out. See if you can get hold of Dean Wilson. Check if he's going to be at home today. We'll call around lunchtime, if that's convenient.'

'Where will you be?'

'Visiting Wilson Macaulay Industries.'

'Have you made an appointment?' Clara asked as they walked across the car park.

'Certainly not. I don't want either Peter Macaulay or his father forewarned about our visit. I want to gauge their genuine reaction to our questions, not some blank poker face they've learned to put on.'

The receptionist in the foyer was about as unhelpful as she could be, leaving Clara to wonder if the act was part of her training. She admitted that Peter Macaulay was in. That was from necessity, as the Mercedes bearing his personalized registration number was parked directly outside the glass-fronted building. However, the woman told Nash, 'Both Mr Christopher and Mr Peter gave strict instructions that they were not to be disturbed at all today. I suggest you phone for an appointment sometime next week.'

Clara waited; her sympathies marginally on the side of the receptionist, who had clearly not had to deal with anyone like Nash before.

He smiled sweetly at the woman. 'That's a very great shame. We've travelled from Helmsdale specially to talk to them. Now, I'm going to have to go back and prepare arrest warrants. I shall need your full name and home address to put on one of them.'

As he spoke, Nash reached into his pocket and took out his Sheaffer pen and pocketbook. He waited, looking at the receptionist expectantly.

'My name and address? Why do you need them?' The receptionist looked alarmed.

'The warrant.' Nash's smile turned into a wolfish grin. 'For obstructing the police in the execution of their duty.'

The bluff worked, to the extent that the receptionist asked them to take a seat in the waiting area, saying, 'I'll see what I can do. I may be able to get a word with Mr Peter, if he's not too busy.'

'I do hope so, all this paperwork is such a nuisance.'

The receptionist disappeared upstairs at haste. As they waited for the woman to reappear, they were joined in the open-plan seating area by several visitors, some of whom were carrying sample cases. Clara guessed these to be salesmen hoping for orders from the prestigious group. She wondered if the buyers set aside specific days and times to see representatives. The receptionist returned. 'Diane Carlson, the finance director, is with Mr Peter at the moment. He will see you when they've finished if you'd care to wait.'

Some fifteen minutes later, a young woman appeared. 'Mr Nash?' she asked.

Nash's voice echoed round the glass walls. Clara noticed that he was speaking much louder than normal. 'Detective Inspector Nash, Helmsdale CID,' he corrected her.

'I'm Mr Peter's secretary. What is the reason for your visit?'

'We need to speak to both Christopher and Peter Macaulay about the bodies of a family found in one of your company's properties. And also about the human remains under the floor of the garage to that property – another murder victim.'

Clara saw that one or two of the visitors were staring at them, curiosity and alarm in their expressions. She turned abruptly and stared out into the car park, biting her lip to avoid laughing aloud.

Within minutes, the secretary ushered them into a well-appointed office on the first floor. 'Do you want me to stay and take notes, Mr Peter?' she asked.

Peter Macaulay, the sole occupant, rose from behind the large desk and shook hands as Nash introduced himself and Mironova. 'No, thank you, that will be all.'

Macaulay was still in the act of sitting down when Nash asked abruptly, 'Where is your sister?'

Macaulay sat down heavily. He glanced to his right, clearly alarmed by the question. Nash repeated it, taking a sheet of paper from his pocket as he spoke. He continued, 'We know she studied at Princeton University but we've been unable to find any trace of her since then.'

'I've no idea where Susan is.' Macaulay's reply was barely audible, in contrast to the strong statement which came from the connecting doorway to the adjoining room.

'Why do you want to know about my daughter?'

The detectives glanced to their left, from where the interruption had come. Standing in the doorway was an elderly, powerfully built man with steel-grey hair that curled slightly at the nape of his neck. He was leaning on a walking stick for support, and Clara noticed that the hand grasping the stick trembled from time to time. Parkinson's disease, she wondered.

The man looked like an older version of Peter Macaulay. Despite his age, his voice was strong, his tone the sort that defies contradiction.

Nash opted for shock tactics. 'What I'd really like to know is whether it was you, your son, or the pair of you acting together, who murdered your daughter and buried her beneath a slab of concrete at Ivy Cottage?'

Both father and son were clearly shocked and horrified by the allegation. Christopher recovered first, albeit marginally, and his voice was much less hectoring when he replied. 'We were obviously sad to learn of such dreadful things happening in one of our properties, but I fail to see how we can help. I was given to understand that the victims were killed by the father, who had become deranged. Is that not true?'

'The family certainly were,' Nash told them. 'However, we have not thus far identified the remains found buried under concrete in the garage. We believe the victim had been placed there several years ago, certainly during the time you've owned the property. I am curious as to why you failed to contact us in the light of events at one of the properties belonging to your company. That would have been the natural thing to do, especially given the horrific nature of what happened to the family. Or, could it have been that you were hoping that during our investigation the presence of another body would remain unnoticed?'

'Don't be ridiculous. It was nothing of the sort,' the old man snapped angrily. 'We were unaware that the property was one of ours until a few days ago, by which time it was far too late.'

'You didn't know that you owned Ivy Cottage? That's not exactly a very good way to run a business, is it?'

'The cottage is part of a portfolio of more than fifty such houses that are owned by one of our subsidiary companies, Macaulay Property Holdings. Neither of us has any involvement in the management of that company. Our finance director, Ms Carlson, oversees the portfolio, and the lettings agency we employ see to the day-to-day affairs of the houses, maintenance, that sort of thing. Ms Carlson was abroad when the bodies were found. As soon as she returned, she informed us, but as I said, things had all moved on by then, and we believed everything had been cleared up.'

'So you can't help us with the identity of the woman in the workshop,' Nash spoke softly, as if thinking aloud, 'which means that you can't either confirm or deny categorically whether the remains are those of your daughter,' he paused, 'or of Linda Wilson.'

For a moment, Clara thought that Christopher Macaulay was about to collapse. He swayed like a boxer who has taken a heavy punch, his hand reached for the wall to steady himself, but then recovered sufficiently to reply. His voice, however, had lost all its previous strength and bluster. 'As I said earlier, Inspector Nash, we can't help you. We have no idea who the woman is, but I very much doubt if it is either of those you have mentioned.'

'If you have no idea where either your daughter or Linda Wilson is, you can't confirm whether they're alive or dead, is that correct?'

'It is.'

'You don't seem very good at keeping track of the women around you, do you? As you can't help us eliminate either possibility, I'd like a DNA sample from both of you. If we fail to get a familial match, that will confirm that your daughter may still be alive, which I feel sure will please you immensely.'

Even Clara winced at the biting sarcasm in Nash's voice. She thought the demand would be impossible to refuse, but Christopher was made of sterner stuff.

'I'm sorry, Inspector Nash,' Macaulay said after a while, 'that isn't going to happen. You have to accept our assurance that the unfortunate woman is not my daughter.'

They were pulling out of the car park when Clara's mobile bleeped. She read the text from Pearce. 'Dean Wilson's at home until late this afternoon,' she reported.

'OK, we'll head there now.'

Driving towards Helmsdale, Nash asked Clara what she thought about the men they had just interviewed.

'Giving my opinion of Christopher Macaulay would involve use of language I'd prefer to avoid, and you wouldn't want to hear,' Clara said.

Nash laughed. 'I don't shock that easily, but he doesn't exactly go out of his way to charm people, does he? What about Peter Macaulay, apart from his obvious nervousness?'

'Difficult to say; he never uttered a word whilst his father was in the room.'

'I noticed that and it intrigued me. Maybe he's another that Christopher has cowed into submission.'

'He looked appalled by your suggestion that his sister might be the workshop woman; appalled or terrified. Apart from that, I thought he was a bit pathetic.'

'There was an expression on Christopher Macaulay's face that I can only describe as shifty when I mentioned his daughter, and Peter looked positively sick with fear or guilt, I'm not sure which. I don't know what went on in that family, but if I had to guess, it's all to do with Duncan Macaulay's will and the revoking of the trust. Christopher Macaulay must have been mortified at being completely ignored in his father's will. Whether there's something even more sinister than possibly cheating his daughter that we haven't discovered yet, only time will tell.'

CHAPTER FOURTEEN

After what Naomi had done for him, Dean Wilson began to entertain a wild idea that perhaps she would agree to a date, that she might even consider seeing him on a regular basis. As often as he thought of it, he dismissed the notion. Naomi had merely been kind, as he guessed was part of her nature. What use would a bright, intelligent and pretty young girl have for someone like him? A girl who was university-educated, from a wealthy family, consorting with a mere squaddie? And one whose family name was blackened by what his sister had done. There were more preposterous ideas around, but not many. Even if Naomi had wanted to get to know him better, the knowledge of what had happened in the past would always come between them.

When his phone rang, his heart skipped a beat. To say he was disappointed to find the police were intending to visit was a huge understatement.

If their visit to Wilson Macaulay Industries had been difficult, the meeting with Dean Wilson was equally trying; but for totally different reasons. Having to explain to the young soldier that they needed to collect his DNA because his sister could be a murder victim was a daunting task. Not for the first time, Clara was thankful that it fell to Nash rather than her to explain.

'This isn't about you, or at least not directly,' Nash began after Clara introduced him. 'I want to talk about your sister.'

Clara had an odd feeling of déjà vu as Nash asked virtually the same questions as he had when meeting Peter Macaulay. And for a second time, the questions had been greeted with a guarded, defensive expression.

Apparently, Nash had also noticed it for he hastened to reassure Wilson. 'I didn't intend to talk about the fraud, not in the first instance, but we might as well clear one thing up. You don't believe Linda stole that money, do you?'

'I have never thought she did' – Wilson's face reflected his anger – 'and I got into one or two scraps because of it. I'd joined my regiment by then, and although the army like their squaddies to fight, they prefer them not to fight each other, so I was lucky not to get kicked out.'

Wilson leaned forward, anxious to put his point across. 'I know about all the evidence, the paper trail, the fact that Linda was the only one with access; the only one with the right computer codes, and all the other stuff. The relationship with that bloke and her being seen on the continent and in the Cayman Islands; none of that tallies with my sister.

'She was nine when I was born, and my mother died when I was seven, by which time Linda was sixteen. I didn't realize it at the time, in fact it's only recently that I've thought about it, but how many sixteen-year-olds can you think of who can be bothered with a noisy, quarrelsome, energetic seven-year-old brat? Not many, I guess. Most would be off enjoying themselves and would leave the kid to his own devices. Not so Linda, she became more of a mother to me than a sister, and after father died, even more so. It seemed the most natural thing in the world for her to buy this flat for us from the money she got for the sale of our parents' house. That would have been the ideal chance for her to free herself of the responsibility of a spotty, petulant, moody teenager.'

Wilson paused, looking around him reflectively, sadness in his eyes as he checked out the familiar scene. 'Linda furnished this place, chose the wallpaper, the lampshades, everything. She gave up her social life for me. She was really good-looking, but more than that, she was a good businesswoman and a very caring person. That's who I remember. I don't recognize the money-grubbing fraudster and cheat portrayed in the press.'

If Nash had been hoping for a reaction from Wilson, Clara thought he'd got it and far more besides.

'Do you have a photo of Linda I could see?' Nash asked.

Wilson pointed to the picture frame on the windowsill. 'That one was taken of her with me when I joined up.'

Both detectives looked carefully at the photo. The young couple did look alike, and if Wilson was a handsome young man, his sister was an equally attractive woman. More to the point, however, their inspection of the image convinced them that Linda was the woman whose portrait was in Neil Ormondroyd's study, and who he had taken such intimate snaps of.

'Were you aware that she was in a relationship?' Nash asked.

Clara noticed that Nash had made the question appear like a statement, as if they were already aware of the fact.

'I suspected as much, and in a way that was the only explanation of Linda running away that made any sense to me. She would never have done it for the money alone; never have cheated so many people unless she was being influenced by someone else. I suppose she might just have done it because she was under the spell of some man or other – frightened of losing him. I assume you're talking about that bloke Mark Tankard. He vanished at the same time, didn't he?'

'You said you suspected as much; did Linda tell you anything about the man she was seeing?'

'No, not directly, but I knew there had to be someone. On my leave before she vanished, Linda was different. She was livelier, really light-hearted; happier than I'd seen her for years. On several occasions I heard her singing around the flat. That had never happened before.'

'If she didn't tell you the name of the man she was seeing, you've only those press reports and the coincidence of them both vanishing at the same time to believe that it was Tankard?'

'It must have been him, surely.' Wilson frowned. 'Who else could it have been? If it wasn't him, why did she run off with him?'

'If she did,' Nash said quietly.

There was a long silence as Wilson tried to puzzle out Nash's last remark. 'I don't understand,' he said, eventually. 'Are you suggesting she didn't run away with Tankard after all? Do you mean that she went with someone else? If that's the case, where's Tankard?'

'I've no idea where Tankard is. I've no real idea where Linda is, only a half-formed theory. What I do know beyond all doubt is that Linda was indeed seeing someone, and the man wasn't Tankard.'

'Who was it?'

'A Bishopton solicitor called Neil Ormondroyd. We were fairly sure, because he had a lot of photos of Linda. We thought it was her, because of her likeness to you, but that photo proved it.'

'Ormondroyd? Isn't that the man who was murdered a week or so ago?'

'Correct, and if my half-formed theory is correct, his murder might have been because of his relationship with Linda.' Nash paused, and when he spoke again his tone was gentle, as if he was trying to soften the impact of the unpalatable suggestion he was about to make. 'We're also seeking to establish the identity of another murder victim. A woman whose remains were found in a workshop in Gorton.'

Wilson stared at Nash, and from Nash to Mironova, and they could see the dawning horror on his face. 'You think that was Linda? That she was....'

'Hold on, Dean. The only reason I believe it could be her is that our pathologist says the body was put there sometime within the last five years or thereabouts. We're following up on anyone who went missing during that time frame. The reason we're here is to take a DNA sample in order to eliminate Linda from our enquiries. I haven't a shred of evidence to support my theory. For all I know, Linda could be sunning herself on a beach in South America, or living with a tribe in the Amazon rain forests, or with the Inuit people in the Arctic.'

Nash's absurd suggestions worked, and Wilson relaxed sufficiently to smile faintly. 'I think you can safely rule the last two out,' he told them. 'Linda disliked rain and positively detested snow.'

Once they had the DNA swab and left the flat, Clara asked, 'Where do we go from here?'

'Literally? Back to the office. With the enquiry stalled in other directions, I think you and I should request the Bishopton Investment Group file from the archives and study it in depth.'

Their study of the fraud at Bishopton Investments told them little that they did not already know, except for the mechanics of how the embezzlers had accessed funds and channelled them abroad. Nash read the pertinent paragraphs before passing the document to Mironova.

SUMMARY OF THE INVESTIGATION AT BISHOPTON INVESTMENT GROUP

The software at B.I.G. was corrupted by someone with a high level of technical skill and knowledge of the relevant computer access codes. We enlisted the help of Jonathan Farrell, chief technical and senior operations officer at Security Solutions (Helmsdale), who provide and install computer software security programs. After inspection and analysis of activity on each computer terminal, he identified the point in the LAN (Local Area Network) where the amendments that allowed the diversion of funds were input. The terminal was in finance director Linda Wilson's office, and the login ID and password were hers. He was also able to pinpoint the date and time the changes were made, and we checked the whereabouts of the only other people within the company able to access that part of the system. They were the managing director, Peter Macaulay, who was in Birmingham at a trade exhibition held at the NEC all that week, and Linda Wilson's assistant, Diane Carlson, who was on holiday in Spain. Our conclusion is that Linda Wilson alone had the means and opportunity to alter the software.

A copy of Farrell's report is attached, but to précis the contents, it appears the corruption enabled the diversion of amounts ranging from ten per cent to sixty-five per cent of the profit on genuine share transactions. It also enabled funds from the sale of worthless shares sold to gullible members of the public by the salesman, Mark Tankard, to be transferred direct to the fraudsters' accounts in the Cayman Islands. The money reached its ultimate destination via a number of different routes, passing through as many as seven different banks en route. We believe this was done to avoid arousing suspicion of money laundering activity.

With regard to the worthless shares, the companies recommended by Tankard to investors did exist. However, the share certificates were fakes, their certificate numbers relating to shares that have never been issued. B.I.G. never purchased shares in those companies, but when investors checked the share prices they were able to see the progress of their supposed investments. In line with the sophisticated nature of the rest of the fraud, dividends in respect of the phantom shareholdings were paid out from the general funds at B.I.G. to keep the investors happy whilst the capital was being transferred to the offshore account.

Farrell concluded his report by commenting that in his opinion the software at B.I.G. was open to the sort of abuse that happened, and he was surprised that a company handling such large amounts of money didn't have better protection in place.

The report concluded with the investigating team's efforts to locate Linda Wilson and Mark Tankard. It listed the CCTV footage showing Linda Wilson boarding a ferry in Hull, gave the dates, hotels and even the room numbers where she had stayed in Amsterdam and Paris, the flights she had taken to reach the Cayman Islands and confirmation that the number on the passport she had produced in each location tallied with the one issued to her by the Passport Office.

The final paragraph gave some indication of the frustration felt by the detectives investigating the case.

With regard to Mark Tankard we can find no trace of this man. All the references and identification he provided when applying for the post at Bishopton Investments were forgeries; even the National Insurance number referred to someone who had died some years previously. No photograph of him exists, and even the description provided by Peter Macaulay and Diane Carlson is less than comprehensive. Apparently, he worked from home, a rented flat in Bishopton, and was rarely seen at the company's offices. The flat was leased from Macaulay Property Holdings, and the person who signed that lease on behalf of the company was Linda Wilson.

'What do you make of all that?' Nash asked Mironova when she had finished reading the report.

'It's fairly damning for Linda Wilson. It also doesn't say much for the way Bishopton Investments was run. What puzzles me is how this Tankard character was able to operate with complete freedom, and even how he got to work there when all his credentials were so obviously false.'

'I agree, and we're still no wiser as to what happened, either to him or Linda Wilson.'

After giving the matter some thought, Nash phoned Dean Wilson. 'Tell me something, how good was your sister with a computer?'

'I'm no expert, but I'd say she was very good. I remember her sitting at the table here in the flat and watching her fingers flying over the keyboard of her laptop, and zooming from one website to another, or switching between different programs with a speed that made me dizzy.'

'What happened to her laptop after she disappeared? Have you still got it?'

'No, I thought she must have taken it with her. I never saw it after she … went away. It certainly wasn't in the flat. Is it important?'

'I don't know yet. It could be, but until we've some hard evidence we're simply guessing.' He put the phone down and said to Clara, 'Somewhere in that file there's an inventory of Linda Wilson's possessions that were seized by the team investigating the fraud. Have a look through it and see if there's any mention of a laptop.'

She scanned the form. 'No, there's nothing listed here. Neither a laptop nor a mobile, but then surely she'd have taken them with her, wouldn't she?'

'I'm not sure. It depends on whether she actually went away or if she ended up in that workshop. Either way, I have my doubts as to whether she'd take them with her, particularly the mobile. Don't they have GPS tracking devices built into them so that people's location can be pinpointed?'

'Most do now, I believe, but I'm not sure if they did then.'

'Let's suppose Linda didn't steal the money, didn't scarper, but was murdered and hidden away to make her into a convenient scapegoat. We already have one link to Ormondroyd's murder in the way both victims were killed. Now, there's another, with the two missing computers.' Nash shook his head in frustration. 'I'm off to Netherdale to update Jackie. Until we hear from Mexican Pete, I don't think there's much more we can do.'

Jackie Fleming greeted Nash with a wry smile. 'I bumped into Professor Ramirez this morning and he was complaining about the workload you've given him recently. He suggested I should transfer you to traffic division; then changed his mind because he reckoned there'd be an upsurge in road accident fatalities.'

'That's ingratitude for you. I keep him in a job.'

'You do seem to be collecting corpses. Tell me how things are going.'

'To say we've been busy would be the understatement of the year. First of all, we're waiting on identification of the remains found in the workshop. They could either be those of Susan Macaulay or Linda Wilson. Alternatively, they could be of someone completely different.'

'Who are these women?'

Nash explained about the teenager who had gone to America, adding, 'Susan Macaulay stood to inherit a fortune until the trust was revoked in what Clara and I deem to be suspicious circumstances. However, the body could equally well be that of Linda Wilson.'

Nash smiled at Jackie's puzzled expression. 'Do you remember the scandal over Bishopton Investments? The big financial firm that went belly up? She was their finance director. She supposedly vanished with the loot three years ago, but I'm not so sure. We believe she was having an affair with Ormondroyd, the solicitor who was murdered. Her involvement with him rather discounts the popular belief that she ran off with this shadowy figure, Mark Tankard. That's not the only connection if the body turns out to be Linda's.'

Nash explained about the garrotte, and the missing computers. 'There's another possible link as well. We believe Susan Macaulay might also have been involved with Ormondroyd back when they were both teenagers.'

'It all sounds very convoluted and highly theoretical.'

'That's about all we can do, speculate, because we've nothing concrete.' Nash smiled ruefully. 'Sorry, bad pun. I mean we've nothing we can build a case on.'

'What action have you in mind?'

'As soon as I know one way or the other about the victim's identity, I shall go back to talk to Peter Macaulay and his father. I feel sure they're hiding something, but whether it's to do with Susan or Linda, I couldn't say.'

'Very well, I'll await developments there. Now, what about this online scam that's cost people a lot of money recently? The one that quoted Clara's name?'

'I'm desperate to get our technical people involved in the case. That's why I left that message for you the other day. They're not answering my calls and Viv Pearce can't get any help from them.'

'No, I realize it must be frustrating, so when I got your message I rang the head of that section. He's very apologetic, but they've a couple of big cases they're working on with the Serious Fraud Office, ones that run into many millions. Until they've finished them they can't accept any other cases. I asked him how long that might be, and he said three to four months all being well. Apparently it isn't just us who are short of manpower. That doesn't help you, I know. You'll just have to manage without them.'

'I don't see there's much more we can do. Viv's exhausted the limit of his knowledge, which is by far the greatest locally. We could get outside help in, but there would be a cost.'

Jackie winced. 'Don't use nasty four-letter words such as "cost",' she complained. 'You know how tight the budgets are.'

As Nash was leaving Netherdale headquarters, Tom Pratt stopped him. 'Mike, you asked me to find out about that company In Confidence that billed Ormondroyd? It turns out they're a private detective agency. Ormondroyd hired them to trace Susan Macaulay, but apart from an old address in America and her time at Princeton University, they were unable to discover anything. They reported that, and apparently he was very upset at their failure.'

'Thanks, Tom.'

CHAPTER FIFTEEN

Chance plays a part in the detection of crime, more often than many police officers acknowledge. Chance was certainly involved in DS Mironova spotting Peter Macaulay's car parked in a quiet cul-de-sac near Helmsdale town centre. Clara had visited the street to interview a teenager suspected of supplying cannabis to pupils at Helmsdale Grammar School. Having delivered her cautionary talk to the boy and his parents, Mironova returned to her car to set off for home, her thoughts on the casserole simmering in her slow cooker.

Manoeuvring her car around a badly parked van, Clara's headlights picked out the personalized number plate on the Mercedes parked on the drive of a house on the opposite side of the road. What, Mironova wondered, was Peter Macaulay doing in Helmsdale at 9 p.m. on a weekday evening? Or any other evening for that matter? She knew he lived at Bishop's Cross, and with the company being based in Bishopton, Macaulay would have no need to drive to Helmsdale following a day's work. So why was he there?

Around the time that Mironova was puzzling over this, Nash reached home, having called in for a pint at the pub in Wintersett. His old friend Jonas Turner had recently moved into the village, having swapped his rickety bicycle for an equally ramshackle and similarly ancient Land Rover. Since losing his wife to cancer, Turner lived alone apart from Pip, the Jack Russell that was his constant companion. Nash liked the old man, and what sergeant Jack Binns didn't know about the inhabitants of the dale, Jonas could certainly tell him.

After the pleasantries and enquiries as to how Nash's son Daniel, was faring at boarding school and Nash's delight at regaling Jonas with his son's prowess on the cricket field, as was usual, the conversation centred on gardening and allotments. After a while, the old man mentioned the remains found in the workshop. 'Got any idea who it is yet?'

Nash shook his head. 'I've a couple of ideas, but I can't talk about it. You know how it is with our job.'

'Who does t' cottage belong to? Is it that Macaulay lot?'

'It is,' Nash admitted cautiously.

'They'll not be content till they own all t' dale, I reckon. Christopher Macaulay in particular.'

'Do you remember his daughter? Susan, I think her name was.'

'Aye, she might have been christened Susan, but she was allus known as Suzi. Went to America, didn't she? By gum she were a reet cracker, even as a kid. A bit of a wild one, though.'

'What do you mean by that?'

Turner chuckled. 'She were blonde, sexy, wi' a cracking figure, legs up to her armpits and liked to let the world know it. I reckon one or two lucky lads around here got their first taste of the pleasures of the flesh along with Suzi Macaulay.' Turner frowned as he thought for a moment. 'There were some trouble, as I heard. She and her father never got on, but I reckon it were more than that. She disappeared suddenly. They put it about that she'd gone to t' States ter study, but it didn't seem right, she vanished that quick.'

'Thanks, Jonas, you never know when anything might come in useful. I'd better get home.' With that, Nash downed the last of his pint and waved a cheerful goodbye to the landlord.

When he entered Smelt Mill Cottage, his first act was to scoop the post up from the doormat, hoping for a letter from Daniel. In the kitchen, as he waited for the oven to reach temperature for his pizza, he opened the envelopes. Most of it was junk mail, which would go straight for recycling. The contents of the last envelope caused him to frown with annoyance. Nash was usually meticulous in payment of his credit card balance, but they had been so busy following the events at Gorton that he had missed the deadline by a couple of days. He was about to thrust the credit card statement to one side, muttering about the amount of interest charged for a mere couple of days, when he stopped.

He stood for a minute, staring at the sheet of paper, their investigation suddenly in the forefront of his mind. Why had Ormondroyd kept some statements in his study at home and others in his office at work? Was there some significance in the fact that they were the ones with an outstanding balance? And what were the figures the solicitor had scrawled on them? He decided to collect the statements next day and inspect them.

It had been chance that Mironova saw Peter Macaulay's car that evening; chance that Nash had been charged interest on his credit card and chance that he had connected his oversight with Ormondroyd.

He was in the middle of his evening meal when the phone rang. He answered it, and was surprised to hear Christopher Macaulay's voice.

'How did you obtain my number?' Nash asked.

'I have my ways.' Nash could almost believe there was a hint of laughter in Macaulay's tone.

'Would you be able to come to my house tomorrow morning?' Macaulay continued, 'I want to explain about my refusal to give you a DNA sample, and assure you there is no sinister reason behind it.'

Nash was intrigued enough to agree. The following morning, he phoned Mironova and explained that he would be late in, and why.

'That reminds me,' she said, and explained about seeing Peter Macaulay's car the previous night.

'Maybe he's got a bit on the side,' Nash suggested. Whatever their theories, speculation was thrust aside for the time being, after the news delivered that morning at Christopher Macaulay's house.

On the outskirts of Bishopton, Nash parked at the end of the short drive. Macaulay let him in and indicated they should go through to the sitting room. 'I thought I should explain, to save you the time and trouble of applying for warrants and the expense of conducting futile DNA tests. It has taken a lot of heart-searching before I decided to let you in on a secret we have guarded closely for many years.'

He indicated Nash should take a seat and continued. 'My daughter Susan was spoiled; not only by my wife and me, but my father too. The result was she thought she could have anything she wanted. Her behaviour was wild and we couldn't control her. She would come home at all hours, sometimes drunk, sometimes drugged, occasionally with the unmistakeable signs that she'd been having sex.' Christopher's face reflected a father's anguish as he added, 'This started when she was only fourteen. We stood it for as long as we could, trying to reason with her and get her to sort her life out, but eventually, things got worse and we sent her to America to live with members of my wife's family and study at university there. We hoped that a change of scene and being separated from what we saw as the corrupting influences around here would straighten her out. But in fact things became worse. Her addiction to drugs and alcohol wrecked her sanity and we were forced to have her institutionalized. She was committed to a sanatorium in Kentucky after she was sent down from Princeton, and she has been there ever since. My wife and I visit her three times a year.' There was a world of sadness in Macaulay's expression as he added, 'Sometimes she recognizes us, at other times she asks who we are.'

'And does she ever ask about her daughter?' Nash's question was blunt, but the time for finesse was over.

Christopher's face twisted with pain. 'They told me you were a good detective.' He took a moment to compose himself, sighed heavily and continued. 'Yes, Naomi is Susan's daughter. Hers and Neil Ormondroyd's, but Naomi doesn't know that. Nor do I want her to find out. She doesn't need to know, does she?'

'I can't promise anything, but I'll try to keep it from her.'

'Peter knows all about what happened to his sister. He and his wife took Naomi from Susan when the baby was only a few days old. We were afraid that Susan might harm her, either by neglect, or in one of her manic episodes. It worked out well for them, as it transpires they were unable to have any children of their own. Peter's marriage has not been a conspicuous success, I'm afraid, and it has only been having Naomi to raise that has held it together. He knows that if anything happens to me, it will be his task to continue to support Susan and pay for her upkeep.'

'Is that why the trust was set up, and later amended?'

Macaulay smiled, but with little humour. 'Very astute. Yes, we had to do that to protect her.'

'Did you blame Neil for what happened? Is that why you moved your legal work away from his company? Or was it to do with the Bishopton Investments fraud?'

'Both, I suppose. I did blame him for what happened to Susan for a long time, but recently I've come to realize that it wasn't his fault. If it hadn't been him, it would have been someone else; someone far less suitable. What's the expression, Inspector? "There is none so blind as he who will not see"? I was blind to the flaws in my daughter's character simply because I didn't want to believe them, and therefore I put the blame on those around her. If I could have done so, I would have apologized to Ormondroyd for my decision to remove the group's legal work from him. It was a petty, spiteful action, and I'm not proud of it. However, it's too late now, sadly. Now I have the extra worry about what Susan might have passed on to Naomi from her wicked, sinful ways. Do you think those things can be genetic, Inspector?'

'I don't see that at all,' Nash contradicted him. 'As far as I can tell, the only thing Naomi has inherited from her mother is her looks. She has great determination and very strong principles.'

Macaulay stared at the detective in surprise. 'How do you know so much about Naomi?'

Nash explained, but didn't mention Dean Wilson by name. 'I think that demonstrates what I mean,' he ended.

'I'd like to meet that young man and thank him.'

'You'll have to talk to her about that,' Nash said in parting.

He was in the Helmsdale CID suite before 9.30. He had barely reached his office when the phone rang. Moments later, he emerged and signalled to Clara. 'That was Mexican Pete. He's identified the remains from the workshop. Now we have to deliver the news.'

True to her promise, Naomi phoned Dean.

All Dean's time had been spent on a ferry ride between hope and deep depression. Then, when any expectation of her actually calling him had all but evaporated, the phone rang.

The conversation was polite but stilted to begin with, but after a while, Naomi said, 'It's a short week at uni, and I'll be coming back from York on Thursday. I wonder if you fancy meeting up for a drink, if you're free?'

Dean spent the rest of the time between then and Thursday trying in vain to remember the rest of the conversation. All he was able to recall was the arrangement they had made to meet at 8 p.m. at the Horse and Jockey.

After four agonizingly slow days, Dean was in the pub twenty-five minutes before the time they'd agreed. Despite being so early, Naomi was there before him. 'I managed to get an earlier train,' she explained.

'I didn't want to risk being late,' he responded.

Both stories were factually correct, although the motives behind them were less than one hundred per cent honest. They had a couple of drinks in the pub, then, in response to Dean's question, Naomi admitted to being hungry and agreed they should go for a meal. Dean suggested a curry, but Naomi vetoed that in favour of an Italian.

As they dined, Dean told her about army life and his enjoyment of it shone through in every sentence, except the part when he mentioned the colleagues he had lost and the trauma of seeing them die.

'You love being a soldier, don't you?' Naomi suggested.

'Oh yes, it's fantastic. The last few months were a bit dodgy at times, but mostly, well, it's the closest thing to being part of a family I've ever known.' Dean stopped, aware of the touchy subject he was close to approaching.

Naomi reached across the table and placed her hand on his. 'Dean, you can't be held responsible for what your sister did.'

In the silence that followed, Naomi squeezed his hand. 'You have a brilliant career; you've already demonstrated your courage and self-sacrifice in helping me. Can't you see how terrific that is?'

Dean wasn't sure he agreed with Naomi's glowing tribute, not at all certain he recognized himself in her description, but he wasn't about to argue. After they paid the bill, which Naomi insisted they should share, Dean asked, 'What time is the last bus?'

Naomi didn't even glance at the clock. 'It'll have gone by now.'

'Do you want me to walk you to the taxi rank? I could ride out to your place with you if you like, to make sure you get home safely.'

'I don't think that will be necessary.' Naomi's reply was a little evasive.

They left the restaurant and walked hand-in-hand down the market place. Halfway down, they reached the taxi rank, where three drivers were standing talking, leaning on one of the cars. Dean stopped walking, but Naomi continued past the rank. He caught her up in a few strides. 'I thought you wanted a taxi home?'

'No, Dean. It was you that mentioned taxis.'

'But where will you stay?'

'I thought I'd stay at yours. If that's OK?'

'What about your parents?'

'I wasn't thinking of inviting them.'

'Of course it's OK, but won't they worry?'

'I don't think so. They're not expecting me home tonight anyway. So, is it OK?'

'Of course it is.'

'I have one condition.'

'What's that?'

'The bed in your spare room is very uncomfortable. I'd prefer to try yours.'

'All right, I'll sleep in the spare room.'

Naomi shook her head slightly and sighed gently. 'Dean, if you're going to talk nonsense, I'll go back and get a taxi.'

At last the message sank in. Dean stopped dead. 'Naomi,' his voice was gentle, a caressing whisper in the dark, 'are you certain about this? It isn't the wine talking?'

She patted her shoulder bag. 'I hadn't drunk any wine when I left York, which was when I put my toothbrush, a spare T-shirt and underwear in here. I don't normally wander around carrying those. I take it you do have some toothpaste?'

Naomi woke late next morning. The sun was streaming through the bedroom window. Alongside her, she could hear Dean's breathing, slow and deep, regular and comforting. She stretched lazily before turning her head to look at her lover. Last night had been wonderful, all she could have hoped for. Regrets there might be, but they would come later; if at all.

She glanced at his bedroom clock and wondered whether to get up or wait for him to wake. She was tempted to force the issue and was actually on the point of reaching out to caress his chest, wanting the feel of his body, when she heard the doorbell sound. Dean slept on, so Naomi shook him gently. 'Dean, someone's at the door.'

His only response was to roll over onto his back and begin to snore. She shook him again, slightly more vigorously. The snoring increased in volume. The doorbell sounded a second time. Naomi muttered something impolite. She flung the covers back. 'Lazy bugger,' she said as she reached for his dressing gown hanging on the back of the bedroom door.

The vinyl flooring of the hall was cold on her bare feet as she struggled with the unfamiliar lock. She opened the door to find a man and woman standing in front of it. The woman was a complete stranger, but after a second, she recognized the man. 'Inspector Nash!' Her blush was scarlet enough to put her flame-coloured hair to shame.

'Hello, Naomi,' Nash said easily. 'Is Dean about? This is Detective Sergeant Mironova, by the way.'

'He's still asleep.' Naomi's cheeks felt as if they were on fire.

'May we come in? Don't rush to disturb him, though.' As Clara closed the door, he told Naomi, 'I'm glad you're here. I take it you and Dean are what I believe is termed "an item" these days?'

'I ... er ... yes,' Naomi stammered. This was awful. Far worse than she could have dreamed; even in her worst nightmare.

'I hoped that might be the case. I'm afraid we've come on an errand that's not very pleasant. I think he might need as much love and support as he can get over the next few days and weeks.'

As Nash finished speaking, Dean emerged from the bedroom, wearing nothing but a pair of boxer shorts and a broad smile. 'Naomi, have you nicked my dressing gown?' As he finished the sentence, he saw the visitors eyeing him curiously. 'Oh, Lord!' He did a swift about-turn and vanished into the bedroom, to emerge minutes later wearing a pair of jeans and tugging a T-shirt over his head.

Clara noticed the soldier's expression; recognized it immediately from her own experience. Her fiancé David was a serving officer, and whenever he saw or heard of a fellow soldier being killed in Afghanistan, the combination of pain and anger was unmistakeable. Wilson's expression was just the same, and she knew that Nash didn't need to explain.

Dean already knew what they were there to tell him. Which wouldn't make it any the easier for him to accept.

Nash watched Wilson sit down on the settee alongside Naomi; saw the protective way she took his hand, gripping it tightly.

'I think you've guessed why we're here,' Nash said. 'I'm sorry to have to tell you that our pathologist has confirmed that the sample you gave us shows a close familial link to the DNA recovered from the remains found in the workshop, via both parental strands. There is no doubt that the body is that of your sister Linda. I'm most terribly sorry. We will do everything in our power to track down her killer and prosecute him – or her. I cannot promise results after all this time, but we will do our level best.'

'I think about the only consolation is that Naomi was there to comfort him,' Nash told Clara as they left the flat.

'Yes, but even so, I think we should keep our eye on him, and if we do get close to identifying whoever murdered Linda Wilson, we'd better make sure we arrest them before Dean gets within striking distance. Going by the look on his face when you confirmed the findings, if the killer had been in that room, we'd have Dean under arrest for murder by now.'

'I suppose that's understandable, but I think Naomi will be an enormous help keeping him on the straight and narrow.'

'Yes,' Clara agreed, 'by the sound of it she's completely different to her mother, who was ...' her voice trailed off.

'What is it? What have you thought of?'

'That message scrawled on Ormondroyd's blotter. The name was Sam, wasn't it?'

'That's correct.'

'Except that it isn't a name. It's a set of initials. SAM: Susan Arabella Macaulay. That was who Ormondroyd was thinking about. His long-lost flame, the mother of his child.'

'Brilliant, Clara, but I don't think it gets us any further forward with the investigation, except to prevent us looking for someone who doesn't exist.'

CHAPTER SIXTEEN

Next morning, Nash and Mironova went straight to the offices of Wilson Macaulay Industries. This time, they weren't made to wait. As the receptionist saw them enter the building, she picked up the phone, and within a couple of minutes an anxious-looking secretary ushered them into the boardroom.

There were three people seated at the oblong table. All three had folders open in front of them. Peter Macaulay invited them to sit down and his father introduced the other occupant of the room. 'This is Diane Carlson, our finance director.'

Clara guessed the woman was in her early thirties. She was wearing a pinstriped suit, her blonde hair drawn back tightly, and had glasses perched on the end of her nose. She acknowledged their presence with a polite nod, but seemed more preoccupied with the papers she was studying.

Nash wasted no time. 'We have identified the remains found at your holiday cottage. The dead woman is Linda Wilson, your co-director. From the decomposed state of the body, our pathologist estimates she has been there since around the time of her disappearance. Cause of death was by garrotte, and the force was so excessive that she was almost decapitated.' Nash paused before adding, 'The way she was killed is identical to the murder of Neil Ormondroyd. Putting all the facts at our disposal has raised some very interesting questions.'

Clara knew that her brief was to watch the men for their reaction to the news, but to begin with she was equally intrigued by Diane Carlson's demeanour. The finance director seemed so little concerned at the fate of her predecessor, or the link to the death of the company's erstwhile solicitor, that Mironova was at a loss as to whether Nash's announcement wasn't news to her; or whether she simply didn't care.

'What questions?' Christopher Macaulay demanded. 'Surely it must be patently obvious, Inspector. Linda Wilson and her fellow conspirator fell out over the money they stole. He killed her and disposed of her body so he could keep all of the ill-gotten gains. Greed: one of the deadly sins.'

'Yes, that remains a possibility,' Nash conceded. 'However, if that is so patently obvious to you, perhaps you can explain how the man Tankard managed to get access to that workshop? And also, as you're such a good detective, could you explain why he apparently murdered Ormondroyd? It seems contradictory that having vanished with the money he should then return and draw attention to himself.'

'That might not have been him. It could be pure coincidence,' Peter Macaulay ventured.

'Sorry, Mr Macaulay, but the wounds are such that it is virtually certain they were inflicted by the same killer. So, returning to my original statement, there are several distinct possibilities. One, I agree, is that Linda Wilson was complicit in the fraud and was murdered from greed. However, the far more likely theory is that she was merely a convenient scapegoat. Her disappearance gave the real thief chance to get away, cover his or her tracks, and hope that Linda's body would never be found. If that is the case, and the real fraudster is still at large, my guess is that Ormondroyd somehow stumbled on the truth and had to be silenced. If I'm right, the principal suspects are in this room.'

'That is a ridiculous statement.' Christopher Macaulay reacted angrily. 'Why would any of us steal from our own company? It doesn't make sense.'

'A lot of things don't make sense at present. However, stealing from one's own company is by no means uncommon, and there are plenty of reasons for that. It could be an addiction to drugs, or being blackmailed over an illicit relationship. Are any of you guilty of that?'

Peter Macaulay's suntanned face turned grey. Well, well, well, Clara thought, so that's why he visits Helmsdale. But does that in itself make him a thief and a murderer? Try as she might, she couldn't see Peter Macaulay in that role.

'This is leading nowhere.' Christopher Macaulay had regained his composure. 'Is there any other reason for your visit, Nash, apart from insulting us?'

'Yes, there is. I want to know where each of you were when Neil Ormondroyd was murdered.'

All three claimed to be at home during the period in question. Nash looked at them in turn. 'And I take it you have someone who can vouch for that?'

If Peter Macaulay had looked sick before, he looked positively ill now, Clara thought.

'This is only the beginning of the inquiry,' Nash warned them. 'Over the next few days and weeks we will be examining the business affairs of Bishopton Investments again, and also those of all the companies within the Wilson Macaulay Industries group, plus the personal lives of anyone with any possible connection to the missing money.'

On arriving back at Helmsdale, Clara asked, 'What did you make of all that? I thought Peter Macaulay was going to throw up when you mentioned blackmail and illicit affairs. I think that confirms my theory as to why he was parked in that cul-de-sac.'

'Yes, but that doesn't make him a killer. There could be far more unpleasant things come to light when we start looking under the rocks. First, we need to find out what exactly went wrong at Bishopton Investments.'

'How do you suggest we go about that? Everyone concerned seems to be either dead or gone.'

'We could do worse than talk to the man who compiled the report on the fraud. The man from that software security firm, whatever they're called.'

Clara searched the file until she found the relevant section. 'The company is called Software Solutions (Helmsdale) Ltd and the man who signed off the report is their CEO, Jonathan Farrell.'

'Get him on the phone and tell him what we want. Ask when it will be convenient for me to visit him. I think I'd better take Viv along. If he starts spouting technical jargon I'll need an interpreter. At least with Viv in the room, we've someone who knows the difference between a gigabyte and a download when they trip over one.'

If Nash and Pearce had any preconceived notions about Farrell, the computer specialist's appearance destroyed them. Nash guessed his age as being somewhere in his mid to late thirties. His sober suit and tie, neatly trimmed hair and clean-shaven face gave him more the appearance of a banker or accountant than a geek. 'I understand this is to do with Bishopton Investments?' Farrell asked, after Nash and Pearce identified themselves.

'Yes, I read the outline of a report compiled by you after they went into receivership. Can I ask who commissioned that report?'

'Officially, the police requested it, but it was Peter Macaulay who persuaded me to take it on. I'd only recently started this business and I was hoping to sell one of our security packages to Wilson Macaulay Industries. I'd just done a demonstration, only a couple of weeks earlier, which I suppose is why my name was top of Peter Macaulay's list. They needed someone independent, and luckily for me, they chose my company.'

'Why didn't the police use their own experts?' Pearce asked.

'I believe it was a combination of reasons, but mainly availability and cost. Macaulay knew he could get me to do the report without charging, in return for them promising to install my software on a trial basis. I believe the lead officer in the case jumped at the idea.'

'Seems as if nothing changes,' Nash observed wryly. 'I can see the benefit of getting an independent opinion, but the work involved must have been both costly and time-consuming, especially for such a young company.'

'Actually, it was neither as long a job or as expensive as I feared. The reason for that, sadly, is that Bishopton Investments' software was woefully inadequate. They had little more protection than you would find pre-installed on any PC or laptop you can buy on the high street.' Farrell paused, before continuing. 'As it turned out, agreeing to give my services for free was one of the smartest moves of my career. Peter Macaulay was very grateful and they installed the full package throughout their group. He talked to other company directors too, and word soon got about. Within a year of doing that favour, I'd been forced to employ extra staff because of all the new clients who were asking for our services. Some of them really big outfits, too. I'm talking about companies like Good Buys Supermarkets and Shires Financial Services, Dales Sports, Helm Construction and a lot more besides. I'm not sure any of those accounts would have come our way but for the work I did for nothing. It was a cheaper and far more effective form of advertising than any other I could have used.'

Farrell looked from one to the other of the detectives. 'I can understand the frustration you and your colleagues must feel in being unable to bring the case to court, but I'm curious as to why you're taking such an interest in the fraud again.'

'There have been one or two new developments,' Nash told him, without specifying details. 'You stated in your report that it was Linda Wilson who had stolen the money from Bishopton Investments. Are you one hundred per cent certain that she was the guilty party? Or, could someone else have used her computer to commit the fraud?'

Farrell frowned in an effort to recall the details. 'I seem to think that at the time I was fairly convinced it had to have been her. Bear in mind, I can only report on what I find; a bit like your job, I suppose.' He smiled. 'However, I don't think I'd be prepared to say it was a cast-iron certainty. The trouble with computer fraud is that it is impersonal. That's why identity theft is so easy. It is possible that someone else used her identity to log in and gain access to the parts of the system that allowed them to steal the money. As I told you at the beginning, Bishopton's software was pretty basic.'

Nash decided to confide in the computer expert. 'The reason we're reopening the inquiry is that we've identified human remains found at a cottage in Gorton as being those of Linda Wilson. Far from living a life of luxury in some tropical paradise, Linda was brutally murdered and buried under a slab of concrete only a few miles away from her home. What we can't yet decide is whether she was party to the fraud and suffered because her partner in crime got greedy, or whether she was innocent. That was the reason I asked if you were sure it was Linda who stole the money. Because if it wasn't her, who else could it have been? Who else could have accessed that information using Linda Wilson's login name and password?'

Farrell thought for some time before answering. 'It's possible that any number of people could have done it. Any of the other directors, certainly. Then there's Linda Wilson's assistant, Diane Carlson. Although she wasn't a director then, she would have been able to get into the system easily enough. And she's about the only person to have benefitted from the fraud. By that, I mean she was promoted to take Linda Wilson's place and is now finance director of the whole Wilson Macaulay group.'

'Not quite the only person to have done well out of it,' Nash pointed out. 'You did OK as a result of your report.'

'Agreed, but I certainly couldn't have predicted the outcome beforehand. Going back to your question, I suppose the likeliest candidate has to be the bloke who disappeared at the same time as Linda Wilson. Tankard, wasn't that his name? My guess is that if you find him, you'll find the money and find your murderer.'

'Do you have a copy of the full report? All we have on file is a summary. There's none of the technical detail, like login codes et cetera.'

'I thought you'd ask that, so I downloaded a copy.' Farrell passed Nash a CD.

Nash thanked him and they took their leave. Farrell stood by his office window watching them walk across the car park. He'd told them finding Tankard would probably give them the answers they needed. However, he reckoned that was probably far easier said than done.

When they were on their way back to the station, Viv asked, 'Do you think we should talk to the Carlson woman? Farrell made a good point about her being the one person who gained from the fraud.'

Nash thought for a moment. 'I think you're right. However, I'm going to take Clara with me when I talk to her. I want a woman's perspective on what makes Diane Carlson tick. In the meantime, Viv, I want you to look through that report Farrell's given us. Check every detail you can. There may be something significant in there that wasn't obvious at the time, because nobody knew that Linda Wilson had been murdered. Also, give Tom Pratt a call and ask him to find out who lives in that cul-de-sac where Peter Macaulay's car was parked. It may not help, but if we discover he's having an affair and who with, it might come in useful at some point.'

Nash gave Mironova the gist of their conversation with Farrell, and explained what he wanted from their planned interview with Diane Carlson. 'Get her address and we'll pay her a visit.'

They left Pearce and drove across the dale to Bishopton. Diane Carlson expressed her surprise at finding the detectives on her doorstep but invited them into her neat semi-detached on the outskirts of town. She revealed little that was either new or interesting. 'Yes, I had access to all Linda's codes, but so did others. After all this time I can't be sure exactly who did or didn't have them, but they were hardly kept secret. Back then, we were far more trusting. Perhaps too trusting; gullible, almost. Ever since the B.I.G. disaster, the board has insisted that every group company has adequate security software installed, and that passwords and login codes are both kept secret and changed on a regular basis.'

'Jonathan Farrell admitted he'd done very well as a result of the work he'd carried out on the Bishopton fraud,' Nash stated.

'Yes, I suppose he has. I can think of a few companies who have installed his programs since the fraud. In fact one or two of our clients asked us directly for our opinion of the software he supplied.'

'He's not the only one to have gained, though. Your career seems to have flourished.'

'I wasn't exactly doing badly before then. I'd already been earmarked for a seat on the board. Linda's departure merely accelerated that.'

'You knew you were going to be appointed to the board?' Clara asked.

'Not in so many words, but all the directors liked my work, and the way the business was expanding at the time, we needed more senior executives. The losses at Bishopton and the economic downturn reversed that fairly quickly, but the need for a competent finance director was, if anything, even more vital.'

'Do you believe Linda Wilson was involved in the fraud?'

Diane didn't pause, even momentarily, before answering Nash's question. 'I didn't believe it at the time, I'm even more certain now that she wasn't involved. Somehow, it came as no surprise when you told us she'd been murdered.

I could never equate the cold-blooded theft with the woman I'd worked with. I couldn't believe the theory that she went along with it because she was besotted with that man Tankard. In fact I thought she was involved in a relationship with someone else.'

'Neil Ormondroyd, perhaps?'

Diane looked surprised, the first sign of emotion Nash had detected in her. 'How did you find that out? Even I wasn't sure. And apart from her brother I was perhaps closer to Linda than anyone.'

'What did you make of Tankard?'

Her reply surprised them. 'Actually, I only met him once. He wasn't a direct employee of Bishopton Investments. He worked on a commission-only basis. As such, I believe he didn't report into their offices, except with sales. We rarely saw him.'

'We have next to no information about him. Can you describe him for us?'

'That's not as easy as it sounds. Like I said, I only met him once. He looked like a typical salesman, if you get my meaning? He was medium height, certainly not tall, average build, dressed well, a bit flashy. His hair was brown, little ponytail at the nape of the neck, goatee beard, but I can't tell you what colour his eyes were, because he wore sunglasses. About the only distinctive thing about him was his voice.'

'Distinctive? In what way?'

'It was a high, falsetto voice. It made him sound effeminate which was totally at odds with his appearance.'

Nash thanked her, and stood up to leave. 'One thing I ought to ask,' he said as they shook hands. 'Is it Mrs Carlson, or Ms?'

Diane shook her head. 'Definitely not Mrs,' she remarked, showing some feeling for the first time. 'I've never had time or inclination to become involved with anyone. My work is what interests me. Relationships are messy, more trouble than they're worth. You know where you stand with facts and figures.'

After they had returned to the CID suite, Clara asked Nash what he thought about their meeting and Ms Carlson.

'About the only thing of interest was her description of Tankard. That's the only one we have, and it's about as much use as a chocolate teapot. If you wanted to disguise yourself, I can't think of a better way than a beard, long hair and sunglasses. Added to that, her description of his voice made it sound as if he was trying to disguise that as well.'

'Why would he need to disguise his voice?'

'I've absolutely no idea. As for my opinion of Diane Carlson, I'd be interested to know what happened to make her fight shy of relationships.'

'You don't buy into the cold, hard accountant line?'

'Not for a minute. I think she's repressing her feelings, but that they're present, under the surface, a bit like a volcano waiting to explode.'

'It all sounds unnatural to me. She's still young and not exactly hideous. In fact if she lost the glasses and wore her hair loose, I'd say she was a very attractive woman.'

Nash smiled. 'If I'd said that you'd accuse me of fancying her.'

'You don't?'

'To be honest, I haven't given it any thought. Perhaps I'm getting old.' He seemed quite offended by Clara's laughter, which merely increased her amusement.

Viv entered the room and Nash changed the subject quickly. 'Did Tom have any success with the mystery of Peter Macaulay's car?'

'He was busy, so I checked out the electoral roll for the address where it was parked and then handed it over to Tom. Her name is Hope Morgan. But Tom's having problems. He can't find her on any other records.'

'That in itself doesn't mean a lot,' Clara pointed out. 'She might have been born overseas. Or recently married, or changed her name for other reasons.'

'I think we'll have to investigate the woman, if only for elimination purposes,' Nash told them. 'In the meantime, Clara, I think you'd better explain what's going on to Viv.'

The phone rang. Pearce picked it up and listened. 'OK, Jack, I'll tell him.'

He replaced the receiver. 'Dean Wilson is waiting downstairs to see you. He reckons he's found some information that might be important. He's got Naomi Macaulay with him.'

After greeting the visitors, Nash asked Wilson what he'd found. 'It wasn't me that found it,' Wilson said. 'It was nosy Naomi.'

'I wasn't being nosy. I was looking for somewhere to hang my clothes.' She blushed slightly. 'It seemed pointless carrying them to and from York all the time. I've moved out from home,' she explained. 'I told my father and mother I was seeing Dean, and they went ballistic. There was a terrible row. The pair of them went on and on at me for hours until I told them to stuff it. Told them to stuff their money and give it to the chapel. Dad even got my grandfather involved. I sometimes think the gypsies must have swapped the real Naomi for one of their own babies. I have nothing in common with the rest of my family. I even have red hair like a lot of gypsies.'

Nash hastened to change the subject. 'What was it you found?'

Wilson took up the story. 'A few months after Linda … disappeared, I was sorting things out at the flat, and in the spare room I found some cardboard boxes. They were tucked away at the bottom of the wardrobe. I looked inside and all that was in them was a load of computer printout sheets. They meant absolutely nothing to me; just ream upon ream of numbers. I'd forgotten all about them until Naomi mentioned them. Do you think they could have anything to do with why she was killed?'

'Impossible to say until we can get an expert to look at them. Have you brought them with you?'

'No, they're a bit heavy to bring on the bus.'

'In that case, I'll let you know when I've arranged something and either send the expert over to your place or collect the boxes and bring them here.'

CHAPTER SEVENTEEN

The hotel was part of a chain that provided comfortable low-cost accommodation. As such, it was ideal for both private and business users.

For Patricia Wain, who spent most of her working life as an auditor away from home, it suited her purpose ideally. Her room was comfortable, and once she had eaten her evening meal, she would be undisturbed, checking the results of her day's work on her laptop, sending an interim report to the client and preparing for the following day's tasks.

The location was unimportant. She could have been in any one of a dozen cities, the hotel would be the same and so would the work. At one time, location had been a problem, which was why she had left the security of her role within one of the major financial institutions to work independently. At least that gave her the chance to pick and choose her clients.

Sitting in the restaurant, Patricia remembered the events that had decided her move. It might have been something in the way the tables were set out, or possibly the waiter's Eastern European accent that made the memory come flooding back. She remembered the cafe in the small market square of the town in Kazakhstan where she had dined. Two days after returning home, she had seen footage on the television news of the same cafe; destroyed by a bomb attack. That had been the last straw. She had almost made her mind up to resign before then. As an internal auditor, Patricia's first task on entering a bank branch was to inspect the insurance policy, which should be kept in the manager's safe. In response to Patricia's request on meeting the manager of the bank branch in Kazakhstan, he had laughed and produced an efficient-looking machine pistol from under his desk.

'This is the only insurance I need,' he asserted confidently.

Although shaken, Patricia was proud of her response. 'And how will that protect you against fraud, or staff dishonesty?'

Despite this, Kazakhstan had been the end of the road for her. She knew there was no mention in her job description of either bombs or guns; nor did her salary contain an element of danger money.

Patricia's thoughts returned to the present. The decision to strike out on her own had proved successful, more so than she could have imagined. She silently thanked the politicians who had drafted the Financial Services Act. The provisions of that piece of legislation had toughened the banking sector's requirements, resulting in a huge volume of work for Patricia and others like her. Admittedly, the large institutions had their own internal audit teams in place, but that was neither a practical nor financially viable option for many smaller companies who were crying out for the services of independent auditors. That accounted for much of the work in Patricia's full diary. However, there was one case in particular where she knew other, less straightforward reasons might be behind the urgent demand for her services.

The head of the company concerned had voiced his unease, but had admitted that he had no solid evidence on which to base his suspicion of malpractice somewhere within his organization. Patricia's challenge was to find out if he was wrong, or, if his suspicions were correct, to identify where the problem was. So convinced was he that something was amiss, that he wasn't prepared to wait for a spot check to be carried out at some point in the future by quality assurance managers from the banking authorities. Patricia remembered his words, and recalled the note of near-panic in his voice. 'I need to have it sorted beforehand. The company must be seen to be proactive in this. We cannot afford to be otherwise. I am prepared to pay over the odds if you will promise me this can be your very next job.'

The lure of a substantial bonus, added to the lucrative rate for the work, had decided her. As soon as she finished the audit she was currently carrying out, she would head north. If she put in some overtime during the evening, that would shorten the time-scale even further.

She finished her meal and headed for her room, oblivious of another diner who left immediately after her. A diner who followed her, taking the stairs instead of the lift, and arrived on the same floor at the same time. She didn't see the man standing at the top of the stairwell, watching as she struggled with the key card. Once she'd closed and locked the door she was unable to see the man walk swiftly down the corridor, pause outside her door, noting the room number, before continuing to another room at the far end.

Patricia switched on her laptop, closed the curtains and began work. She was soon engrossed in the maze of figures onscreen and failed to notice the passage of time. It was over an hour later before something disturbed her concentration. She looked up, mildly annoyed because she had been making such good progress. It had been a sound, faint but definite. She looked round in time to see the door handle moving slowly back to horizontal. Patricia knew the door to be locked. But someone had definitely tried it.

Although she dismissed the incident and returned to work, her nerves were on edge. Eventually, as time passed, she forgot about the attempted intrusion. She had almost reached the end of the work she had to do, when she heard the sound once more; saw the door handle move again. She leapt to her feet, intending to fling the door open and challenge whoever was out there, and had actually taken a couple of angry strides towards the door when common sense prevailed. She was alone, and unlike the manager in Kazakhstan, unarmed. The lack of such an insurance policy decided her next move. She rang reception.

The duty receptionist promised to look into the matter and again at 1.15 a.m. when Patricia's sleep was disturbed, at which point she abandoned all hope of getting any rest. She took breakfast early, and told the duty manager that if the incident was repeated during the final night of her stay she would insist on the involvement of the police.

Although she expressed her views calmly and forcefully, Patricia was unsure whether the manager viewed them as anything more than the imagination of a mildly hysterical female. She was also unconvinced that he had taken her threat of police involvement seriously.

When the following evening passed without any repetition of the disturbing incidents, Patricia had all but forgotten the attempts to enter her room by the time she closed her laptop and went to bed. She had finished her report, and all that remained to do was present her findings the following day.

Exhaustion caused her to drop off within minutes of snuggling down under the covers. Before sleep overtook her, Patricia thought drowsily that it would need something in the order of a small nuclear detonation to wake her.

She was uncertain how long she'd been asleep when something roused her. Still only half-conscious, she listened for a few moments.

She sat bolt upright, her hand groping for the switch to turn on the bedside lamp, blinking in the sudden brightness. She waited, watching and listening. Eventually, so softly as to be barely audible, she was able to make out the sound of breathing: heavy breathing, laden with tones of sexual intent. Someone was standing outside her door. Someone with one goal in mind. The threat was unmistakeable.

The silence was so absolute that Patricia was able to hear the stealthy sound of footsteps retreating along the corridor.

With hands that were trembling violently, she reached for the phone.

She explained the problem, her tone abrupt; the threat of police involvement explicit. When she had finished, Patricia sat trembling. This had not been a hotel guest mistaking the room or one who had taken too much to drink. This was something way more menacing.

'Where are you?'

'I am at railway station. Woman is waiting for train.'

'Where is she going? Which train is she catching?'

'She bought ticket to York. After, I do not know.'

'So you can't be sure if the frightening worked or not?'

'She was scared. Scared and angry. She spoke to hotel manager and he called police.'

'OK, here's what I want you to do. Take the same train and try to scare her a bit more on the journey. Use your continental charm. When she gets off at York, find out which connection she takes. If she boards the train for Skipton, leave her be, because that means she's going home and you've done the trick. On the other hand, if she takes the train for Netherdale, I want you to stay with her. It'll be easy once she reaches the place she's staying.'

'What do you want me to do?'

'The same as you did three years ago.'

'Exactly same?'

'Yes, exactly the same.'

'Is all ready?'

'It is. There will be a car waiting in the station car park. The keys will be on top of the rear wheel. I'll send you a text with the registration number once you're on the way.'

'Where do I take woman?'

'I'll send you the address in the same text.'

'Is place lonely, deserted?'

'Very lonely, but you should know. You've been before. Why do you ask?'

'Is better when I don't have to use gag. I like hearing screams. It excites me.'

Ivan's caller shuddered. There are some things it is better not to know.

It was nearly lunchtime when Patricia reached the station. As she waited to board the train, she was conscious that she ought to spend the journey planning for the meeting she was due to attend early next morning. Her client had sent her some information which was now stored on her laptop, and she knew she should use it to prepare her work schedule. However, the disturbed nights had left her too weary, and she had virtually decided to postpone her efforts. If she could get a decent night's rest, she could set her alarm for early next morning and still have time to do the work ahead of the visit to her client.

In the event, the decision was taken out of her hands. The train was crowded, almost every compartment being packed solid with football supporters heading for York and a connecting train to an away match that evening. Patricia knew that she would not have been able to concentrate above the din they were making, even if she had been fortunate enough to obtain a seat at one of the tables. She was lucky to get a seat at all. She sank into a window seat at the very rear of the train and sighed with relief. Almost at once, alongside her, the last remaining vacant seat was taken by a man of about thirty-five to forty years of age, Patricia guessed. He was of strong build, the sort of muscular physique that would quickly run to fat if neglected, and his features had a vaguely Slavic appearance.

As yet more passengers boarded the train with little sign of them being denied access, Patricia wondered if the operating company was exceeding its maximum load limit, or indeed, if such a limit existed. She glanced round at the other occupants of the compartment. Apart from the football supporters, who were talking loudly in a language that

161

bore a slight resemblance to English, the other passengers seemed oblivious to their surroundings, and unaware of the existence of each other. Some were sending text messages in a seemingly endless stream. Were they all to the same recipients or did they really have so many friends, Patricia wondered. Several were listening to music on iPods, their lips moving in sync with unheard lyrics. Would a lip-reader be able to tell the title of the track? Yet more passengers were staring fixedly at the screen of their tablet PC, iPad or smartphone. Only a few were reading. Momentarily curious, Patricia recognized the covers of a vampire story, the adventures of a boy wizard, the latest Ian Rankin thriller, and, despite the efforts of the young woman to disguise it, an erotic romance.

The journey seemed interminable. It was one of those services that stopped at every station en route, and rarely got up to anything approaching express speed. The compartment had been over-warm when she entered it. As the train continued its snail-like progress it got even hotter, even stuffier. The warmth, her exhaustion and the lack of something to occupy her mind soon combined; Patricia dozed off.

She began to dream. Instead of being on the train, her dream-scape transported her to home, to the comfort of her sitting room and her favourite armchair. She snuggled deep into the soft cushions, smiling at her partner Julian. He was seated on the floor alongside her, as often happened when they were in a romantic frame of mind. He was caressing her leg, his hands gently sliding over the smooth skin of her knee. As if in response to the implicit invitation in her smile, his hand moved upward, the caress became more vigorous, matching the heat of his growing arousal.

She awoke with a start as the train jolted to a halt. At first she thought that no one had noticed that she had fallen asleep. But one man all too obviously had. The man seated next to her had seized the opportunity to pay far too much attention to her. She slapped his hand, pushing it off her knee. He smiled, and Patricia felt vaguely nauseous.

Undeterred by the rebuff, he spoke quietly. 'Beautiful lady, I would like to know you better. To know you as a man should know a woman.' He accompanied the words with a gesture as obscene as his smile. The accent was Eastern European, confirming her guess.

Patricia was well used to admiring glances; used to men staring at her long legs, her trim figure, sometimes even seeing the desire in their eyes. That, she could tolerate, conscious of her beauty without flaunting it, but this was altogether different. This was skin-crawlingly loathsome. 'Well, you're not going to,' she snarled angrily.

'That would be shame, for so much loveliness should be to share, not to keep hidden away. It should be like work of art in exhibition: free for many peoples to enjoy.'

'Listen to me, buster. I share it with who I want, when I want and that certainly doesn't include the likes of you. So keep your filthy comments, your greasy smile and your oily, sweaty hands to yourself or I'll pull the communication cord and have you thrown off this train and arrested for molesting me. Understood?'

He shrugged, which could have been a gesture of defeat, or possibly merely one of acceptance. Either way, she was relieved when he turned slightly away from her and leaned back in his seat. Her relief was short-lived, however, for his movement caused the front of his jacket to part slightly. With fresh terror, Patricia saw what was protruding from his belt. It was the hilt of a knife, the blade protected by a leather sheath. The size of the hilt suggested that it was a large knife: a very large knife.

Patricia was immensely relieved when, in the distance, she was able to see the towers on York Minster from the train window. Although there had been no further approach from the man, and although she had avoided looking in his direction, she was aware of his gaze reflected in the train window, which had remained fixed on her for the rest of the journey.

Out of her eye corner, Patricia could tell both by the expression on his face and the way his focus of attention shifted, moving downwards as he examined every curve of her body, that the man was mentally undressing her. She felt her skin crawl at this loathsome inspection. She was desperate to leave the train; to put as much distance as possible between herself and the unwelcome attention he was lavishing on her.

The last few miles seemed to take forever, but even so, when the train eventually halted alongside the platform, Patricia remained in her seat, waiting for the man to move. When he failed to do this, she grasped the handle of her laptop case and stood up. She stepped past him, taking care to avoid contact with his knees, grateful for the space provided. She paused to lift her wheeled overnight bag from the overhead rack. As she stretched up, the temptation was obviously too much for him. His hand reached up between her legs, causing her skirt to ride up as he moved along her thigh towards his goal.

All the passengers were facing the other way as they crowded along the aisle, eager to get to their destination, or to a bar before they continued their journey to the football match. Patricia turned, swinging the laptop case. He flung his hands up, instinctively trying to protect his face; but as he did so she switched her target. There was a satisfying gasp of pain as the heavy case struck his groin, and as he bent double in discomfort, Patricia snatched her suitcase and fought her way past a group of protesting supporters as she exited the train at a half-run, halfstumble and marched down the platform, her pace masking the trembling in her lower limbs. As she surrendered her ticket at the barrier, she glanced back, but there was no sign of her assailant amid the sea of brightly coloured scarves and hats.

She reached the relatively safe haven of a nearby coffee bar, which was all but deserted. Presumably the supporters were aiming for places that sold something more powerful. She ordered a large latte and took the drink to a dimly lit corner from where she had a good view of people passing by. After a few minutes she began to hope that she had shaken off her admirer. She reached into her bag, removed her mobile and pressed a short-code. As the word 'Home' appeared on the screen she waited for Julian to answer.

Julian was disturbed by her account of events. 'Why don't you come home tonight? You're obviously upset, and you can always go to tomorrow's meeting from here. I've to be away early, I can make sure you're up in time.'

'I'd love to, Julian, but it isn't practical. The CEO wants to see me at 8.30, before everyone else arrives. To get there in time I'd have to leave home before seven o'clock.' Patricia hesitated. 'There isn't a train at that time in the morning. Certainly not one that will get me to Netherdale; let alone Bishopton.'

'Why don't you take your car?'

It was no good, she'd have to tell him. 'I can't; I forgot to tax it before I went away. The tax ran out three days ago.'

'In that case I suppose you'll have to carry on to Bishopton tonight. Please be careful, though, and be sure and call me from the hotel later on. Is it the Mitre you're staying at?'

'That's right.' She ended the call, drank the last of her coffee and glanced towards the wall clock. As she did so, she was conscious of movement in her peripheral vision. She turned quickly, but all she could see through the window were commuters drifting towards the platforms. She looked back at the clock and saw that it was time for her to move. She had to buy a ticket, and she was aware that the Netherdale train would depart from the most distant platform, which would mean hauling her case up and down steps and across the connecting footbridge.

She slipped the shoulder strap of the laptop case over her head and gripped the handle of her wheeled suitcase. As she threaded her way between the tables to the door, the man who had been watching her through the window shadowed her movement, making sure there were several passengers between him and his target. He was in no hurry. He had already bought a ticket in case she took the Netherdale train. Ivan was a great believer in forward planning. He watched from a safe distance as she queued at the ticket office. He rather hoped she'd decided to continue working and not go home. That would mean she would have to be disposed of, but Ivan thought he could have quite a bit of fun with her before the time came to kill her. The memory of her soft skin and the idea of what he would do to her was already exciting him.

CHAPTER EIGHTEEN

Nash spent an hour going through the paperwork surrounding the events at the holiday cottage, Stark Ghyll and the workshop. There were reports for the inquests, all meticulously drawn up by Tom Pratt. Not for the first time, Nash thought how lucky they were to have someone with such expert knowledge to work with them. His brain fastened on the word 'expert' as he considered the investigations that were still ongoing, the computer scam being uppermost. They needed specialist technical help – and needed it urgently, not only for the email scam but perhaps they could also look into the B.I.G. case. He remembered what Jackie Fleming had told him about the force's computer experts. They would not be free for months. By that time the email trail would have gone cold. Or even colder, to be more accurate.

Mironova and Pearce were in the outer office when Nash emerged. He waited for Mironova to come off the phone. 'I'm going through to Netherdale tomorrow,' he told them. 'I'm not prepared to wait for our own boffins. I'm going to plead with Jackie and the chief for us to hire an outside specialist. Viv, am I right in thinking you've done all you can in respect of the email scam?'

'Yes, Mike. I could try to go further, but I'm concerned I might trigger a virus which would affect either our computers or those of the victims.'

'I've also got to think about the Linda Wilson murder. I'm convinced it's connected to the Bishopton fraud, and we could do with some expert help there too.'

When Nash put his case forward, both the chief constable and Superintendent Fleming listened sympathetically, but Nash could tell by O'Donnell's face that he was going to be unsuccessful. However, before she could refuse the request, Fleming intervened. 'I've an idea how we could do this, ma'am, and possibly avoid any cost being incurred; or at worst, very little.'

'How do you suggest we do that?' O'Donnell asked.

'If we hire someone on a commission only basis, we could agree with the victims of the email scam that they would meet the cost of the expert from the funds recovered. A bit like those lawyers in America who take on the personal injury cases on a no-win, no-fee basis.'

'Or those companies that keep pestering me about PPI which I've never had, you mean?' the chief constable retorted. 'I'd go along with that if it can be arranged. Do you have anyone in mind?'

'Leave it with me. I have an idea, but don't want to make any promises, in case it doesn't come off. I feel sure if I can sort something, Mike will approve.'

On his way back to Helmsdale, Nash wondered about the slightly cryptic nature of Fleming's final remark and the mischievous smile that had accompanied it. He would have been even more intrigued if he'd known what transpired back in Netherdale HQ.

Fleming went back to her office and picked out a visiting card from her folder. She dialled the number and spoke. 'This is Superintendent Fleming. You remember our discussion a few weeks back? Well, I think I have something for you.'

Half an hour later, she returned to the chief constable's office. 'It's all arranged,' she told O'Donnell. 'The computer expert will start work tomorrow.'

Gloria put her pen down. 'Go on, tell me about it.'

Jackie explained, and eventually revealed the identity of the specialist she had hired.

The chief constable whistled. 'Now I understand. She's the young woman Mike met on that case connected with old London mobs. Don't you think that's a bit dangerous? She's highly attractive. Having her work alongside Mike is a bit like lighting a match in a fireworks factory.'

'Nash doesn't seem at all bothered about women these days.'

'An alcoholic can stay off the booze for more than a year, but I still wouldn't leave one alone in a brewery,' the chief said, with a grin.

'I still don't think he would succumb.'

'Twenty pounds says you're wrong.'

'I'd take that bet, but how will we know?'

'If the silly grin on his face doesn't tell us, Mironova's sarcastic comments will.'

'Right, you're on. Twenty pounds it is.'

Later that afternoon, Fleming phoned Nash and told him, 'The specialist will report to you tomorrow morning.'

'Who is it? Have they been given clearance and identity cards?'

'Don't worry about that, Mike. In view of the urgency I've skipped all the usual formalities. Identification won't be a problem either.' She put the phone down before Nash could ask for an explanation.

He had only been in his office next morning for a few minutes when the internal phone rang. 'Yes, Jack?'

'I've Dr Silver in reception for you, Mike,' Binns told him.

'Dr who?'

'No, not Dr Who, Dr Silver. The computer expert you were expecting.'

'I'll be right down. Hang on, when you said Dr Silver, is that Tina Silver?'

'You got it.'

Nash took the stairs two at a time and walked swiftly across to the reception area. 'Tina,' he greeted her, 'this is an extremely pleasant surprise.'

She took his outstretched hand and shook it. 'Hello, Mike. A surprise? Didn't Superintendent Fleming tell you I was coming?'

'She told me to expect someone. She didn't tell me the name of our expert. I think it was her idea of a joke.'

Tina let go of his hand and reached for her laptop case. Nash took it from her and ushered her towards the door. He held it open for her. His act of courtesy had no ulterior motive, although it did enable him to admire her legs as she preceded him up the stairs to the CID suite.

'Why don't you set up your computer in my office? I can work out here with Clara and Viv. That way you won't be distracted by our comings and goings when you're working. Whilst you're doing that, I'll make a drink. Tea or coffee?'

'Coffee will be fine.'

Nash was returning with the drinks when Mironova entered the outer office. 'Morning, Mike. Jack told me the expert is here, but he was a bit mysterious about it. He said I'd know them when I saw them. Who is it?'

'Open my office door and you'll find out. Here, you take this coffee. I'll go make another.'

Clara took the mugs from him and opened the door. Tina looked up, expecting to see Nash. 'Oh, hello, Clara.'

'Tina! So you're the specialist we were expecting?'

'That's right. Superintendent Fleming arranged it.'

When Nash returned a couple of minutes later, the girls stopped chatting and Tina informed him she was ready to start.

'In that case, we'd better wait for Viv. Then if you ask a technical question you might get a sensible answer. Without Viv to act as translator, you've no chance.'

Later that morning, when Nash took Tina another mug of coffee, she reported progress. 'I've made a start on the email scam. These are usually quite easy to trace or block, but this guy is a cut above the normal scammers. A few cuts above, to be fair, and I'm going to enjoy doing battle with him. I've not met many of his type before.'

'What do you mean by that?'

'The easiest way to illustrate it would be by comparison. You must have people on your books whose work you can recognize by their MO, burglars for instance?'

'There are a few,' Nash agreed.

'With computer fraud it's very much the same. The usual ones are those offering recipients lots of money. The best known of those would be the supposed relatives of dead Nigerian generals or politicians who have left a fortune that must be got out of the country.'

'I would have thought everyone knew about those by now – even I do. Surely nobody gets taken in by them anymore.'

'You'd be surprised. However, this one is way more sophisticated than that. The first email offering the saddles for sale was harmless, but the second one laid the trap. Whatever action the victim took, by simply clicking one of the response options, it activated a tracking cookie, but one with a specific objective. The next time the computer went online to view their bank account their login details were recorded and transmitted to the thieves without the victim being aware that anything untoward was happening. Once they were in possession of the codes, the thieves were able to impersonate the account holder and when they accessed their account, they could authorize payment to themselves.'

'I thought you needed one of those card reader gizmos before you could do that?'

'Unfortunately that's only true for certain banks. Sadly, a lot of them, even some of the bigger ones are by no means as security conscious as they should be. In most cases, all you have to do is enter the payee's account detail, the amount and then press go.'

'That sounds as if it was made simple for the thieves.'

'That's certainly so with the ones I've looked at so far, but I haven't looked at many of them yet. I'm having to work very carefully, which is why I reckon this guy is cleverer than a lot of them. I wouldn't be surprised if there's another level to this fraud that I haven't got to yet. One thing I do know, he's built in certain safeguards against people like me tracking him.'

'What sort of safeguards?'

'We call them bear traps. If someone tries to follow the trail of the money he's got some nasty surprises for them. The sort that will infect your computer and wipe your hard drive clean.'

'You keep saying "he" or "this guy", does that mean you've a clue as to his identity?'

'No, it's more a generic term. Although most of the hackers like this are loners, working in some solitary room away from prying eyes. Anyway, I must get on with the work. As I say, it's slow going.'

'I'll leave you to it.' Nash paused at the door. 'There is one thing. Let me know when you're about to start work on the Bishopton Investment files. There's some paperwork to look through to decide if any of it might be useful or not. It isn't here so I'll need to make arrangements.'

Patricia struggled across the footbridge between platforms, the wheeled case proving more of a hindrance than a help. Only when she had descended the steps at the far side did she look back. There was no one she recognized in sight. Her relief would have been short-lived if the angle of her vision had included the middle of the footbridge, where Ivan had stopped until he could see his target board the train. He waited, noting that she had opted for the rear compartment. That suited his purpose admirably. He strolled down the steps and entered the first of the two carriages.

He took a seat facing the rear of the train and immediately opened the newspaper he'd bought at the station kiosk. It was a broadsheet, ideal for masking the reader from all but the closest surveillance. Ivan turned the pages, eventually selecting one that contained meaningless lists of figures. His command of English was limited, but he could make out that these were stock market prices. He had no interest in such matters and had never owned a share in his life, yet he studied that page with all the diligence of the most avid investor.

It was only when the train began to move that Patricia relaxed. Her nightmare was over. The unwelcome admirer was a thing of the past, the distance between them increasing with every turn of the wheels. She would already be several miles away from the horrible creature.

Little more than thirty feet away from where she was seated, Ivan ceased his pretence of reading. He decided it was time to check the other compartment, to ensure the woman was still on board. He didn't for one moment believe she would have been clever enough to trick him and get off the train, but he had to make absolutely sure. He was being paid far too much to take chances.

He reached the division between compartments and stood far enough away to avoid activating the automatic doors. As he peered through the glass panel he could see there were only a few passengers in the other compartment. And there she was, her head bowed over the screen of her little computer. Ivan's excitement grew. 'Soon, my pretty lady. Very soon you will become mine. You will be Ivan's play toy.'

A passenger nearby stared at Ivan, wondering what the crazy foreigner was jabbering on about. All foreigners were mad, that went without saying, but those that mumbled away to themselves definitely needed locking up.

Ivan returned to his seat. He hadn't intended to speak aloud, hadn't realized he'd done it until he saw the man staring at him. It didn't matter. The likelihood of anyone on that train understanding Slovenian was extremely remote.

A dozen or so passengers got off the train when it reached Netherdale. Ahead of the rest of them, Ivan hurried to the barrier to surrender his ticket. He knew the woman would have to wait half an hour for her connection to Bishopton. But he didn't want her to see him. Not yet. Not until he was ready for her. After that, she could see all she wanted of him – for a short while.

Once he was outside the station, Ivan located the car that awaited him and drove to Bishopton, where he parked alongside the tiny single-platform station. Shortly before the Netherdale train was due, he walked across the car park and paused alongside the taxi rank, which contained only one vehicle. Noting the company logo, he dialled a number on his mobile. 'I am at Bishopton station. There is taxi. I need it moved. You can do this?'

'Yes, of course, give me the number.'

Ivan read out the number from the door panel of the taxi.

'Remember your instructions. Don't do anything; not until I've found out how much she knows.'

'What you want me to do?'

'Just keep her out of sight, and let me know when you have her computer. I want it switched on, then leave the rest to me.'

Ivan wondered again about the person he was working for. Apart from the one mobile phone number, he knew absolutely nothing about them. They had never met, and although he had been paid in advance for his services, the payment was made directly to his account. His employer was obviously keen on their identity being kept secret, and Ivan wondered why this should be. Still, it didn't matter, as long as the money was good. Ivan's business philosophy was simple. He was happy to do whatever was asked of him, as long as he got paid.

Within five minutes, the taxi moved off to collect the phantom passenger. All was now ready. He hoped there would be no other passengers on the train. However, with luck, even that should pose no problem.

Patricia alighted from the Sprinter and struggled to place her suitcase on the platform. Bishopton railway station was little more than a wayside halt. The single platform contained a no-longer-manned, dilapidated ticket office and covered waiting area, with three long benches that appeared to have been designed with the intention of causing maximum discomfort. The platform sat squarely between two sets of rails, and at one end, a broad set of steps led upwards, before they branched at a footbridge over the lines. Patricia groaned: not another bloody footbridge. There was no other way to exit the station. The only other passengers had already vanished. She hoped they hadn't commandeered the taxis. That was, of course, if there were any taxis to meet this train. The thought chilled her, but she felt sure even such a small junction would at least have a Freephone. She certainly didn't fancy walking into town dragging her suitcase along an unfamiliar route in the late evening. When she reached the top of the steps, she read a sign on the bridge. It told her that if she followed the arrow, she would find a public footpath leading to the town centre, a mile and a half distant. 'No, thank you,' Patricia muttered, and headed for the car park. Half a mile might have tempted her, had she been desperate. She wasn't that desperate – not yet.

On reaching the car park, one of her fears was realized immediately. There were no taxis waiting, no vehicles at all apart from a solitary car that was parked, probably belonging to a commuter who was catching a later train. In the gathering gloom, Patricia could just make out the skeleton stalk of a phone stand and the plastic waterproof bubble above it. She manoeuvred her suitcase over the low kerb and across the rough tarmac, trying to avoid potholes that were barely visible. By the time she summoned a taxi and waited for it to arrive and by the time it had ferried her to the Mitre Hotel, the restaurant would be sure to have closed. In such a small town during the middle of the week, the choices for a diner would be limited. Either chance an ethnic restaurant or hope that the hotel's room service could provide a snack that was approaching palatable. She set her suitcase into the upright position, and reached out for the handset.

CHAPTER NINETEEN

Late on the second morning that Tina had been working at Helmsdale, she reported progress. 'I've done about as much as I can. I'd better tell you where I've got to, which isn't very far. The problem is I've had to examine the software piece by piece. I'm trying to put this in layman's terms otherwise I'll have to spend half of the time explaining the technical details. This isn't the work of a standard hacker, but someone with an advanced knowledge of programs and how to write them. What they've done to protect themselves is to insert various devices, for want of a better word, which, if triggered, would activate a virus.'

She saw Nash's puzzled expression. 'Think of it as if you were a soldier walking across a minefield. If you took a slightly wrong turning, or walked ahead without looking down, you could hit a tripwire which would explode a bomb. If I were to miss one of their booby traps, it would wipe all the hard drives and erase any trace of the money trail.'

'Is there any way round the booby traps?'

Tina gave him a cold, piercing stare. Nash was secretly amused that she seemed offended by his lack of faith. 'Of course there is, if you know what you're doing and you don't spoil things by being impatient. The program writer probably thinks his system is foolproof, but it isn't; not against someone like me. All it means is that the process will take longer than I anticipated. The reason I'm telling you this is because I'm intrigued by the level of protection built into the scam. There's no way the designer could have foreseen that they would have been chased down by someone of my ability. Parts of the software suggest someone with a level of knowledge few people who set up these scams usually possess.'

'Belt and braces sort of thing?'

'More like two pairs of braces, a belt and a piece of string. In the meantime, you mentioned going to look through some papers to spot anything that might be relevant to the other case.'

'OK, I'll try and fix it up for this evening, if that suits you. I'll speak to Dean Wilson and I suggest we go there after work if that's OK with him.'

'That's fine. I have no plans.'

It was almost 6 p.m. when Nash and Tina pulled up outside Dean Wilson's flat. Dean opened the door and gestured for them to go ahead of him down the hall. When they reached the lounge, Nash made the introductions. Dean and Naomi had set out a stack of boxes on the dining table. 'There they are,' Dean said a trifle ruefully. 'I hope you can make more sense of them than I can.'

'I'll leave it to you, Dr Silver,' Nash said.

Tina gave him a glint of a smile at the formality.

Nash chatted to the young couple whilst Tina began her painstaking search of the papers crammed into the boxes. 'Have you seen your parents since you told them about Dean?' he asked Naomi. He thought it was still not up to him to reveal her true parentage.

'Not yet,' Naomi admitted. Her expression was one of fierce determination, much like the one Nash had seen when she'd spoken up in defence of Wilson. 'They can either like it or lump it,' she told him. 'Dean and I are going to be together no matter what they think his sister did or didn't do.'

Tina was now examining the third of the boxes. 'I think you can safely say that Dean's sister didn't have anything to do with the fraud at Bishopton,' she announced.

'Why do you say that?' Nash asked, getting his question in just ahead of Wilson.

'Because the papers I've set aside' – Tina gestured to a small pile on the table – 'show that she was checking Bishopton's customer accounts files. There are lots of figures circled in red and some comments scribbled alongside that make very interesting reading.'

'And your line of reasoning is that if she'd been the one committing the fraud, she wouldn't have needed to print this information off and check it. She would already know the details. Is that correct?'

'Yes, and that seems to indicate that she was not involved.'

'I'm going to phone your grandfather tomorrow and tell him that we no longer believe Linda Wilson was in any way connected to the fraud,' Nash told Naomi. 'Then your father will be certain to know. That may help to heal the rift.'

The young couple expressed their thanks, and shortly afterwards, Tina announced that she was finished. By then there was a quite sizeable stack of paperwork on the table. 'I should have brought my briefcase,' she said ruefully. 'I didn't expect there to be as much as this.'

'I'll get you a carrier bag,' Naomi offered.

Nash winked at Dean. 'Getting to be quite at home, isn't she?'

Dean smiled back. 'She is, and I love it.'

'I think you're a lucky man.'

Outside, Nash asked Tina if she'd care to go for a drink. They opted for the Fleece Hotel, where they took their drinks to the seat in the bay window of the lounge bar, overlooking the cobbled market square.

'Dean and Naomi seem a nice couple,' Tina said.

'Yes, they are, and they had a bit of a rocky start when Naomi found out that Dean was Linda's brother. Naomi's family were the biggest losers in the Bishopton fraud. That's why it's important that I drive the message of Linda's innocence home.'

'I'll remind you in the morning,' Tina promised.

'Anyway, enough about work. Things have been so busy I haven't had chance to ask you how your family are.'

'They're fine. Gran seems to have taken on a new lease of life since Dad recovered his health. He's doing really well. He's set up his own business as a market gardener and enjoying every minute of it.'

'How about you? What made you decide to go it alone?'

'Circumstances changed at the firm I worked for. We lost a large American contract when the people we were working for decided to source the business within the United States. That side of our operation was overstaffed, and when they had to make redundancies, the offer was far too tempting to refuse. So I took the money and set up on my own.'

'Are you still living in Leeds? It's a long way to drive home if you're going to be working here for a while.'

'No, I gave the flat up and moved back in with Aunt Margaret. She's really edgy about living on her own after … well, you know what happened as well as I do. I figured I owed her that much after she'd taken care of me all those years, and it helps keep my overheads down until I get properly established. The other advantage is that it isn't so far to travel when I go to Dad's or Gran's. I see my father every week or so, and make sure I visit Gran at least once a month.'

Tina reached forward and put her hand on Mike's. 'I owe you more than I can ever repay. That's why I'd have done this job for nothing. I was happy to take it on when Superintendent Fleming asked.'

'I was only doing my job at the time,' Nash protested.

'That's not how I see it. You gave me a family. The family I'd always longed for and never had. I used to be really envious of other girls at school or university when they talked about brothers and sisters, aunts, uncles and grandparents. That isn't all, though. Both Chief Constable O'Donnell and my grandmother told me the lengths you went to in order to keep my father safe. If you hadn't, we all feel certain he would have been killed. To me, that seems over and above the line of duty.'

All the time she was speaking, Tina was caressing the back of Nash's hand. A gesture of gratitude and no more, he thought.

'We can consider that debt paid if you can recover all those missing millions.' Nash spoke lightly, to cover the confusion he felt by the warmth of Tina's words and the thrilling contact of her hand on his. He was still wondering if he had misread the message in her eyes when they left the hotel and he bade her goodnight. Nor was he any nearer resolving his feelings when he reached home. A home that seemed a little colder and emptier than usual.

'Viv, I've got a job for you. In fact, both of you can do it. I want everyone who worked at Bishopton Investments interviewed. Ask them about this Mark Tankard character. At present, we know very little about him, apart from that description Diane Carlson gave us. Make that your priority.'

Once they had left, Nash brewed some coffee and took a mug through to Tina. 'Have you had another look at the stuff we got from Dean's place?'

'Yes, and it looks as if Linda Wilson was highly suspicious about what was happening at Bishopton Investments. From what I can gather, without checking the disk you got from Farrell, I think she'd printed off a set of account details for every one of Bishopton's customers. More than two-thirds of them' – she indicated a pile of papers on the corner of Nash's desk – 'had figures in red biro scribbled on them, but until I access the Bishopton system, I can't be sure what they refer to.'

'Still, it looks as if we're right in thinking that Linda wasn't involved in the fraud. I'll make that phone call to Christopher Macaulay.'

Once he'd spoken to Naomi's grandfather, he sat behind Clara's desk in the outer office going through the reports that she and Pearce had written up, concentrating on the interviews they had conducted with Dean Wilson, Diane Carlson, Peter and Christopher Macaulay and the CEO of Security Solutions, Jonathan Farrell. His reading produced little more than a vague feeling that there was something he was missing. He heard the phone in his office ring.

The normally easy-going chairman of Shires Financial Services had reached the group's head office in Bishopton much earlier than normal. It was no exaggeration to say that Sir Stuart Crawshaw was annoyed. He'd been careful to arrange his first meeting of the morning well in advance of the arrival of any members of his workforce. It wasn't that he suspected any of them of wrongdoing, but such was the nature of the work he had commissioned that forewarning them could have been counterproductive.

Nobody enjoys a visit from an external auditor, and with Shires Financial being a relatively small institution, they relied on the services of a freelance operator. This policy served two purposes: it was cost effective in that the group wasn't committed to a large annual salary plus benefits, and there was also no risk of the auditor and staff forming a cosy relationship.

Sir Stuart was concerned that there might be something amiss within the group. The bank, the building society, the insurance and estate agency divisions had all turned in healthy profits, as had the credit card operation, but he was uneasy nevertheless. He couldn't identify the cause of his worry, but his instinct had been proved reliable far too often for him to risk taking the chance of ignoring it.

When Patricia Wain didn't turn up, Crawshaw waited until an hour after her scheduled arrival time before phoning the hotel where he'd reserved a room for her. He was more than a little surprised to learn that she had failed to check in. And when her mobile went straight to voicemail, his surprise turned to unease.

His anger had dissipated in the face of concern when he was unable to get a response from her home phone number.

Crawshaw knew where Patricia's husband Julian worked, so when he contacted the man's employers he was able to obtain Julian's mobile number.

This time his call was answered immediately. Julian's concern was all for his wife, but Crawshaw had the additional worry that he had given Patricia access codes to the group software. If those codes fell into the wrong hands, there was no telling what damage could be caused.

Julian told Crawshaw that he'd spoken to Patricia the previous evening when she was in York, but that she'd failed to ring him from her hotel later as promised. 'I thought she'd simply forgotten, or fallen asleep. I know she was very tired.' As he was speaking, Julian remembered what Patricia had said about being followed. His alarm escalated. 'I'm going to contact the police.'

'Hello?' Jackie Fleming frowned, wondering if she'd misdialled. 'Clara, is that you?'

'No, it's Tina Silver speaking.'

'This is Detective Superintendent Fleming. Is Mike Nash there?'

'He's in the outer office. I'll get him. He's allowing me to work in here where I don't get disturbed.' At that moment the door opened. 'Hang on, he's here now.' Tina held the phone out. 'Superintendent Fleming for you.'

'Good morning, Jackie,' was all Nash said. For the next few minutes he listened as Fleming explained the reason for her call. After a while Nash started scribbling notes on the back of a large brown envelope that was lying on the desk. From her seat, Tina managed to decipher the words Nash had jotted down. They made little sense, and she wondered what the connection was. Mitre, Crawshaw, Wain and Shires. What did that all mean?

Tina glanced up from the envelope and saw Nash standing with the receiver in his hand, his mind obviously elsewhere. 'You haven't put the phone down,' she prompted him.

Nash took no notice. He seemed oblivious to her presence, to his surroundings, totally absorbed in whatever was going through his mind. Tina waited, aware how irritating it could be when one's train of thought is disturbed. It was one of the reasons she preferred to work in seclusion.

Nash turned and stared at her, or was he looking through her? At the same time he realized he was still clutching the handset and replaced it on its rest. 'A woman has been reported missing by her husband. She failed to check in at her hotel yesterday evening, where a room had been reserved for her. This morning she was supposed to attend a meeting in Bishopton, but didn't turn up. The man she was meeting alerted her husband, who called us.'

'She might have gone off with someone else. It does happen, I believe. I think it's called adultery.'

Nash smiled slightly, but shook his head. 'I don't think so, not in this instance. The meeting she was supposed to attend was with the chairman of Shires Financial Services, Sir Stuart Crawshaw. The woman is an internal auditor who was scheduled to start an audit of their branches and services today.'

He picked up the envelope and stared at the back for a second, before turning it over. For a moment he couldn't recall what the envelope was doing on his desk. Then he remembered. 'These are credit card statements. I removed them from a murder victim's house because I was curious about them. There might be some connection to the fraud. He had scrawled a load of figures on the statement but I didn't have chance to work out what their significance was, if any. In fact, I'm not sure I'd have been able to, but you might.'

He handed her the envelope. 'When you get time, try and make some sense of them, will you. I need to recall Mironova and Pearce. Looks like we've a manhunt on our hands. Or a womanhunt, to be strictly correct.'

Nash was about to return to the outer office when, out of curiosity, Tina pulled the credit card statements out of the envelope. She glanced at them, then looked up. 'Hang on, Mike. The statements are from Shires Credit. Isn't that part of the group you just mentioned? Where the missing woman was going?'

'That's correct. It started life as a building society, then converted to a bank and financial services group following deregulation.'

She examined the pencilled figures on the first sheet. 'It looks as if Ormondroyd was trying to calculate the amount they had charged him, to see if it tallied with the interest rate. Let's have a look.'

Nash watched as she turned to her laptop. She barely seemed to glance at the figures on the sheet, but within seconds, she said, 'There's a discrepancy. Only a small one, admittedly, but the amount Shires have charged for the number of days multiplied by the outstanding balance doesn't match the interest rate. The other thing that's wrong is the dating of the credit to the account.'

She held up the statement. 'Look there. That date in biro must be when he paid it. But look at the following month's statement when it hits the account. It says "Internet banking" alongside the date and amount, so we can safely assume he sent the money electronically. That should mean his account would be credited the same day, or the following day at the latest. However, the credit doesn't appear on the statement until three days later.'

'Might it have been made over a weekend?'

Tina took out a diary and flicked through the pages. 'No, according to the written date, the payment was made on a Monday, but the date it was credited to the account is a Thursday.'

'It could have been a glitch in the system.'

She held up the statements. 'Not if the rest of these come up with similar discrepancies. I know the amount doesn't seem much, but if you multiply it by the thousands of bank customers whose credit cards don't get paid off in full every month, suddenly the sums start to look significant.

Certainly an amount worth stealing. Especially if the scam has been going on for years without anyone noticing. The missing woman was about to conduct an audit. I bet part of her remit was to check the credit card operation. You may think that's a coincidence, but I don't.'

Nash nodded. 'My colleagues will tell you that I don't believe in coincidences. I take your point about the timing of her disappearance, but there's a flaw in your logic. How would the thieves know what she was going to do? Unless Crawshaw was in on the scam, or unbelievably indiscreet. When Jackie Fleming spoke to him, he told her that the meeting and her audit were kept top secret. Even his secretary wasn't aware of what was going on.'

'There is a way they could have learned about it. Ask Crawshaw if he supplied her with codes to access the company's software.'

'What good would that do?'

'If it had been me setting up a program to systematically extract money from a company's computers, I would have built in a fail-safe alarm that alerted me when anyone accessed that part of the software.'

'Like the bear traps you mentioned in the email scam?'

'That's exactly what I mean.'

'You also said that scammers like these usually stick to the same MO. Does that mean you think the same person is responsible for both frauds?'

'It seems highly probable. It would be far too coincidental for two people using the same methods to be operating in this area at the same time. And as you don't believe in coincidences, I think we can count that out.'

'I'd better get the others back here quickly. We must try and find this woman as fast as possible. I think I'll get Fleming over here too.'

As he was making the phone calls, Nash was troubled by a stray thought. It was something that had been said during his conversation with Tina, but for the moment he was unable to pin it down.

CHAPTER TWENTY

Jackie Fleming arrived as Nash was updating Mironova and Pearce. Tina Silver emerged from his office as the briefing ended. 'I've checked the rest of Ormondroyd's figures,' she told the team. 'He was being overcharged every month, and the credits were applied to the account late each time. No question about it, there is a deliberate fraud being carried out at Shires Credit. And if that's the case, I'd bet there are others taking place elsewhere within their systems.'

Fleming's alarm was mirrored in the faces of all the detectives. 'What other fraud could there be?'

'Oh, believe me, there are plenty of areas where they could be operating. We haven't started checking the accuracy of the overdrafts yet, or foreign currency transactions.' She looked at the confused expressions on their faces. 'OK, let's suppose you're on holiday in Spain. The easiest way to pay for something is with your card. Can you remember what the exchange rate was? By the time you get your statement you've been back home a few weeks. The rate shifts every day, so how do you know the rate they charged is correct?'

'You think Neil Ormondroyd may have discovered the fraud and somehow the thieves learned that he was on to them?'

'Quite possibly, if he tripped one of their security devices.'

'That could be why he was murdered,' Fleming said.

'I'd be very surprised if it wasn't,' Nash agreed.

'Which means,' Fleming continued, 'that the motive for Linda Wilson's murder might well have been the same. Either that or she was a convenient scapegoat. The MO was identical.'

Fleming heard Nash gasp, and turned to look at him. 'The same MO,' he muttered. 'That was it. That was what I was trying to remember.'

'Sorry, Mike, you've lost us.'

Nash didn't answer Jackie directly. He looked at Tina. 'When you described the email scam, you told us the initial email was only sent to provoke a response, correct?'

'More or less. They were setting the victims up for the second email, which was where they were trapped into a response that made it possible for the crime to take place.'

'And you also said that online fraudsters almost always stick to the same MO, right?'

'Pretty much. But I still can't see what you're driving at.'

Nash looked round, and it was obvious the others were equally puzzled. 'OK, here's what I think. What if the whole of the Bishopton Investment fraud was only like that initial email? In other words, what if it was designed to provoke a response?'

'I still don't follow you, Mike,' Jackie said.

Nash could tell by Tina's expression that she was beginning to understand. He switched his gaze to Pearce. 'Viv, do you remember our meeting with Jonathan Farrell? He bragged about the number of new clients he'd obtained as a result of the report he did on Bishopton Investments. What if the whole of the B.I.G. fraud was set up simply to achieve precisely that end result? Diane Carlson told us that she and Peter Macaulay had been asked for references on Farrell's company several times. After he compiled that report, Farrell got to supply software to Shires Group, Good

Buys Supermarkets, Dales Sports and a lot of other local companies. Most of them have a financial services division of one sort or another. Good Buys have their own store cards, and Dales Sports supply goods and holidays via an online catalogue with extended payment terms. If customers of all those companies are being overcharged, the returns would be far greater than the Bishopton fraud produced.'

'You think Farrell engineered all that? But how could he be certain that Peter Macaulay would insist that he was the person chosen to compile the report on B.I.G?' Clara objected.

'Peter Macaulay would have no choice in the matter if he was being blackmailed over his extramarital affair. I think we have to put Farrell at the top of our list of suspects.'

'It's a short list. He's our only suspect,' Viv pointed out.

'There is a way of confirming he's involved,' Tina intervened. 'If you can persuade Crawshaw to give me the codes for Shire Finance, I could trace the originating computer without springing any bear traps.'

'Sorry to appear thick,' Jackie complained, 'but could someone please explain these bear traps that you keep going on about.'

Tina told her, adding, 'Bear traps is the name they were given when we started installing them. The difference being, that we were using them as a defence mechanism against our systems being hacked.'

'Tracing the originating computer could take ages,' Clara pointed out. 'That poor woman could be dead already, and if it takes a few days to identify who might be holding her prisoner and where, her chances of survival will be practically nil.'

'Clara's right; finding her has to be our main priority, but we need a way of narrowing the search down.'

'How do you propose to do that, Mike?'

'I think I know,' Pearce interrupted. 'If Mike's theory is correct, and they stick to the same MO all the way through, my guess is that they will do what they did before and use one of the houses in Macaulay Property Holdings' portfolio. One that is currently unoccupied.'

'Good thinking, Viv. If we find vacant properties similar to the one they used when they killed Linda Wilson, that should give us the location. It has to be somewhere remote; somewhere they can be sure they won't be seen, and somewhere that's currently empty. There can't be many that fit all those criteria.'

'The problem is, how do we set about identifying the property without alerting the kidnappers?'

'We could try asking the letting agents.'

'That wouldn't work if Farrell has an associate working there. Someone with access to the keys, for instance.'

'I can think of a quicker, more effective way, and one that's totally safe.'

They looked at Tina. 'I can access the letting agents' website and see which houses are empty. I could even get a description which would tell us if they're suitable.'

'What about those bear-trap things?'

She gave Fleming a disdainful look. 'I was part of the team that more or less invented bear traps. I feel pretty confident I know enough to get round them.'

'OK,' Nash said. 'I vote we give it a shot. Meanwhile I think we should put an announcement in the local paper. Something along the lines of "Have you seen this woman?" and a few lines about her disappearance and how mystified we are.'

'Why do that, Mike?'

'Because the kidnappers will be expecting to read something like that.'

Fleming looked at Tina. 'How long will this take?'

'Twenty minutes; half an hour at most. I expect Farrell will have only done a cosmetic job on Wilson Macaulay's software. Sufficient to stop anyone else, but open enough for him to walk in and out at will, so to speak.'

As they waited for Tina to work her magic, they assessed the current state of the investigation.

'When we do go to raid a house, I want plenty of backup,' Fleming insisted. 'I'll ask Gloria if we can have a tactical unit from York. We've already got one body; I don't want any more.'

'I agree. You and I, plus Clara and armed uniforms. That frees up Viv, if that's OK with you. I've work for him to do in Netherdale.'

Fleming nodded. 'And don't forget you've got Lisa Andrews too. She came back off leave this morning.'

'This might take both of them, plus Tom Pratt as well. Here's what I want you to do, Viv. I need all you can find out on Farrell's background, plus see if Tom's had any success discovering anything about this woman, Hope Morgan, Peter Macaulay has been screwing. It seems she's not who she purports to be. So far, all we have is a neighbour's description, which could fit dozens of women.'

'Couldn't Dr Silver do that?' Fleming interrupted.

'I'd prefer her to concentrate on the fraud. We need some idea of how extensive it is.'

They didn't have to wait as long as Tina had predicted before she emerged from Nash's office. At the same time, the printer alongside Pearce's desk began to whir, then spewed out several sheets of paper. She marched across and plucked them from the document tray before handing them to Nash. 'There are three properties that seem to fit the requirements,' she told him. 'One at Bishop's Cross, one at Kirk Bolton and one at Drover's Halt. All the other empty houses are in the town centre. I discounted them.'

'I suggest we start at Bishop's Cross,' Nash told Fleming. 'That way we don't have to keep doubling back on ourselves.'

'Viv, when you get to Netherdale, ask Lisa to follow this Morgan woman. If we find out where she works, who she sees, it might give us some clue as to her identity. Her real identity, I mean. Also, when you and Tom are on the computer, cross-reference all the potential suspects in this case against the name Mark Tankard and see if that brings anything up.'

He turned to Tina. 'Farrell's company website lists their major clients. Can you have a look through the list and see which of them could be vulnerable to online fraud? There's one other thing; do you think it would be possible to find out where the money creamed off from the Shires credit cards goes to? You mentioned tracking an originating computer earlier. Does that include giving a location for it?'

'Not a physical location, but I could identify the owner or user, and if it's part of an intranet or LAN, I could pick out the individual unit.'

'I'm so glad you told me that. I'm not quite sure if it's good news or bad.'

'Put it this way, if we were talking about this building, I'd be able to tell which of the computer workstations it was at.'

'Right. Thank you! Will you make those tasks your priority? See if you can tie in a connection to Wilson Macaulay Industries. I feel sure someone working there is involved.'

She gave him a mock salute. 'Yes, Inspector Nash, sir.'

Patricia was cold. She was unable to see for the blindfold. She had a ferocious headache. Above all, she was terrified. When she recovered consciousness she was unaware of what had happened. Had she been in an accident of some kind? Or had she fainted? It was only when full awareness returned that the truth dawned. She had been knocked out. Then she had been stripped naked and tied up, her wrists and ankles secured to something cold and metallic. Confirmation of her location came via the softness of a mattress under her body: a bedstead. She had been kidnapped. And her position suggested the obvious reason for that.

Any doubt about this vanished when she heard her abductor's voice. She recognized it immediately, and the fear and loathing it had generated on the train returned, magnified a thousandfold.

'Pretty lady, I told how we should be together. Now you are here for me. Soon I will make the music to you as a man should. This you will learn to enjoy. Please to scream or cry if you wish it. Only I alone will be hearing this, and it makes encouragement for me. For now I must leave you, but soon I will return, and then, pretty lady, we will begin.'

Patricia struggled against the ropes that were restraining her, but in vain. Twice she opened her mouth to scream, but her tormentor's warning came to her in time. She must not do anything to further inflame his filthy, diseased mind. Her skin crawled at the thought that he had touched her, undressed her; examined her as she was lying naked and helpless. She bit her lip and swallowed to stem the urge to vomit and to avoid bursting into tears. For all she knew, a woman's tears might be another of his fetishes.

She was immensely relieved, if only temporarily, to hear his footsteps recede and the door bang closed before she heard the unmistakeable sound of stairs creaking. At least for the time being, she was alone, safe and unharmed. How much longer it would remain that way was something she dare not dwell on. She tried not to think of Julian and what he would be going through as soon as they found out she was missing. Nor did she want to dwell on what would happen to her, either at the hands of her vile captor, or worse still after he had grown weary of her.

A stray memory returned to her, of the bank in Kazakhstan; and of its manager. At that moment she would have given the world to have her hands untied and his machine pistol within reach.

CHAPTER TWENTY-ONE

The properties at Bishop's Cross and Kirk Bolton had yielded no result. As they pulled up a discreet distance from the house at Drover's Halt, Nash thought that this represented their best bet of finding the missing woman. The holiday home was over half a mile outside the hamlet, at the edge of a large belt of woodland. In a setting such as this, there was little chance of the activities of the kidnappers being seen – or heard. The location also worked in favour of the police, for they were able to park their vehicles where they would not be visible from the property. Nash walked to the edge of the trees. He could see the cottage and yet remain hidden from view behind a small brake of silver birch saplings that were in need of thinning out. From this vantage point, as he brought the house under surveillance with his binoculars, the first thing he saw was a car parked on the small open space beyond the cottage. He waved Mironova forward. 'Do an ANPR on this registration, will you.' He read the number out.

'I will if I can get the machine to work out here. I'm not sure if there's a strong enough signal, but I'll give it a try.'

Fleming had also joined Nash and was watching through another set of binoculars. As Clara was obtaining the information, Jackie noticed movement inside the building. 'There's someone walking about on the ground floor. Look at the two windows to the right of the front door. It looks as if they're pacing backwards and forwards. However, we can't be certain this isn't someone who rented the property after the computer was last updated.'

Mironova returned in time to hear Fleming's last remarks. 'I think you'll find this is the right house,' she told them. 'That car is registered to Helm Hire. I've been on the phone with them and they have it out on short-term rental,' Clara paused, 'to Mark Tankard.'

There was stunned silence for a few moments, before Fleming spoke. 'OK, so we've confirmed we're at the right place. The only problem now is how do we get inside without alarming them? For all we know there could be another of the gang with the victim, holding a knife or a gun to her head. We can't force entry without risking Mrs Wain's life. Nor can we walk up to the front door and knock.'

Nash was looking at Fleming as she spoke. She was dressed in a neat business suit comprising a tailored jacket and skirt, perfect for the idea he had come up with. 'Actually,' he told her, 'walking up to the door and knocking was exactly what I had in mind.'

He explained his plan to the others. Fleming thought it over for a few minutes. 'Before I agree, I want to consult our gunslingers.'

She summoned the leader of the armed officers. 'Do you think you can get a couple of your men alongside the front door without anyone inside the cottage seeing them? I don't want them to force entry, simply to be there as backup.'

'It would be tricky, but for that car being handily parked alongside,' he replied. 'That gives excellent cover for the distance between the end of the treeline and the corner of the house. Once there, my men can duck down below the windows until they're at the door.'

'OK, Mike, what do we need?'

Ivan was awaiting the phone call to give him the word to carry on. He was impatient, but knew better than to risk everything by letting his desire take control. He wandered to and fro across the lounge floor. He had switched the laptop on as instructed, to find that it was password protected. He'd sent a text to that effect, only to be told to leave it as it was. Now he awaited their orders. More than once, he was tempted to go ahead regardless. The thought of the woman upstairs, her naked body ready for his pleasure, made the pain of waiting almost unbearable, but still his fear held him back. He wasn't prepared to risk everything by letting his desire overtake common sense. Not over a woman, that was for sure.

His mobile rang and he leapt across the room to answer it. The message was short and to the point, no more than a short sentence. 'Switch off the laptop and go ahead.' It was all the encouragement he needed. A vision of the woman's naked body came into his mind. The computer could wait. He hurried upstairs and opened the bedroom door, his excitement mounting as he looked at the woman on the bed. His arousal was painful. He stepped forward, but at that moment he heard a knock at the front door. Ivan frowned: he wasn't expecting visitors. Surely they hadn't decided to attend in person? That wasn't the way they worked. He'd never met or seen them, only heard a voice on the phone. That didn't mean anything. For all he knew they might have wanted to ensure he carried their orders out properly. Better to be sure. He closed the bedroom door and walked slowly downstairs.

He unlocked the door and opened it. A man and woman were standing on the threshold. Both were wearing suits. The man was carrying a briefcase, whilst the woman was clutching a sheaf of papers in one hand. The man smiled at him.

'Good morning, brother. Are you prepared for the Kingdom of the Lord? Have you heard the word of God? May we take a few moments of your time and possibly interest you in a copy of *The Watchtower*?'

As the man spoke, his colleague thrust a sheet of paper towards Ivan. His reflex action to take the proffered document was his undoing. As he reached forward to accept it he felt something cold touch his wrist. At the same moment the man grasped Ivan's other hand and before he could defend himself, he was secured in handcuffs. Ivan looked down at his pinioned wrists in dismay. He heard the woman speak, but even then the sense of what she said didn't strike home.

'One suspect secure. Clear to enter the building.' As she was speaking, her male colleague dragged Ivan to one side to allow men wearing uniforms and flak jackets to charge past them. It was only when he saw them, and the automatic weapons they were carrying, that Ivan realized that it was all over.

Fleming and Mironova accompanied three of the ARU team as they searched the building. The women detectives found the victim and motioned to the ARU men to keep out of the room. They untied Patricia and helped her to dress. Fleming's assurance that her ordeal was over, that they were police officers and that she was safe had to be repeated several times before Patricia took it in. So too did Fleming's question as to whether she had been assaulted.

Patricia shook her head, wincing slightly at the pain this caused. 'I think he knocked me out. My head feels sore. He said he was going to … he told me what he was going to do….' Her sentence petered out as she burst into tears.

'It's all right, it's all over now. You're quite safe. There are armed officers outside the door to protect you, and the man who was holding you captive is in handcuffs. We need to get you to hospital and have that bump on the head examined. I'll see your husband knows that you're safe.'

Fleming looked at Mironova, who gave a slight nod. Once they were out of earshot of the victim, Clara asked, 'Do you want me to take her to the rape suite, just in case? We can't be sure he didn't do anything to her whilst she was unconscious.'

'I think that would be sensible. Purely as a precaution, although there don't seem to be any signs of a sexual assault.'

Downstairs, Nash had left two officers to guard the prisoner. 'Come with me,' he instructed a third man. 'I want to have a look around outside, and I'd rather have one of you with me.'

Unlike the cottage at Gorton, there was no garage attached to this building, but Nash saw a small shed towards the rear of the garden. He walked over to it, with the ARU man keeping constant watch alongside him. The shed door was open, but they found nothing more sinister inside than a collection of gardening implements. On closing the door, however, Nash saw the handle of another tool sticking out from behind the shed. He took a couple of paces to his right and saw it was a spade that had been left on top of a freshly-dug mound of earth. Beyond it was a deep hole, measuring approximately six feet by four. Nash stared down into the hole, knowing that this was the grave that had been prepared for Patricia Wain. His sense of relief changed suddenly to one of horrified disbelief. He turned to the ARU man. 'Fetch Superintendent Fleming. Tell her it's urgent.'

Fleming arrived and reported that Patricia seemed relatively unharmed. 'That wouldn't have been the case for much longer,' Nash replied, pointing to the open grave. 'I guess this was intended to be her last resting place. She had a lucky escape, I think. Unlike the current occupant.'

Fleming looked at him, then into the hole. Towards the far end she saw a small semicircle of grey-white substance. It was the size and shape of an eye socket. The grave had been used before.

'Good God!'

'Exactly. Unless I'm very much mistaken, I think we might have found the mysterious Mark Tankard.'

'I'd better summon Mexican Pete and a SOCO team. I'll ask for the one that worked at Gorton. They're getting to be experienced gravediggers.'

'If Clara takes Mrs Wain to hospital, will you see to the prisoner? The ARU men will take him, but I want Jack to make sure the arrest and everything that's happened here is kept under wraps. I'll stay here until Mexican Pete arrives. He'll feel lonely at a crime scene if I'm not about. Once I've turned the place over to him I'll join you back at the station.'

The leader of the ARU team joined them. Fleming gave him instructions, ending with an order to remain at the cottage as protection for Nash. 'OK, ma'am, but there's a laptop in the cottage. Mrs Wain says it belongs to her, but it's switched on. What do you want me to do with it?'

'Leave it as it is. It could be rigged,' Nash interrupted. 'I'll ask our expert's advice before we do anything.' He turned to Fleming when the ARU man moved away. 'There must be a reason that bloke switched it on.'

There was a strange irony in ringing his own direct number, knowing that Tina was seated at his desk. He explained the situation. 'What should I do with the laptop?'

'Bring it back with you, but leave it switched on and don't close the lid. Is the mains lead plugged in?'

'No, I don't think so.'

'Let's hope the battery doesn't fail before you return. If someone is in the middle of accessing the information on it, it's important that they don't get interrupted. That would be a giveaway that they've been rumbled.'

'The reason that Mrs Wain is unharmed is probably that they were waiting to see how much she knew. I suppose if they didn't get anything positive from the laptop, the hired muscle we've arrested might have been ordered to torture her. But what else might they have wanted to know?'

'Who she shared the knowledge with, for one thing.'

'Crawshaw, for example?'

'Yes, that sounds logical. Whilst you're on the phone, I've got news for you. I've taken a look through Shires' software using the codes the superintendent got for me. The fraud is more extensive than we thought. My next job is to attempt to follow the money trail. I hope to have some news for you by the time you get back.'

'The fact that Patricia Wain is safe and well is solely down to you, Tina. That's an immense achievement.'

Nash relayed the information to Fleming along with Tina's instructions.

'Tina Silver is proving very useful,' Jackie agreed as she carefully held the laptop. 'You seem to have developed a good rapport with our delectable computer expert,' she added.

Nash restricted his reply to a non-committal statement. 'I think she considers it to be just another job of work.'

Fleming smiled complacently. Nash was puzzled by her expression. But then he was not aware of the bet she'd made with the chief constable.

CHAPTER TWENTY-TWO

It was almost an hour later when the pathologist and the SOCO team arrived. 'If you keep unearthing corpses at this rate,' Ramirez told Nash, 'you're going to terminally damage the local tourist industry. People will be scared to book a holiday cottage for fear of what they might find in the vegetable patch.'

'I'm rather hoping this will prove to be the last one.'

Ramirez sniffed. 'I wish I had your confidence.'

The leader of the SOCO team approached, carrying an evidence bag. 'I'm sending this for forensic testing, but I thought you'd like to see it first. We recovered it from the lounge. It was in the inside pocket of the bloke's jacket.'

'You're sure it's his jacket?'

The officer held up a second bag containing a passport. 'Pretty sure.' He grinned.

Nash looked at the first bag's contents. The coil of thin nylon rope was clearly visible through the plastic. 'That looks like the missing murder weapon,' he agreed. 'It might be too much to hope that Linda Wilson's DNA or that of the person in the grave here will still be on it, but we could get a result from Ormondroyd's. And with luck, the rope should match the injuries to the victims.'

Having turned the crime scene over to the SOCO men, Nash returned to Helmsdale. Binns greeted him by handing him a sheet of paper. On it were the details of their prisoner. 'I got a hit from his fingerprints,' Binns told him. 'His name is Ivan Korosec. He's from Slovenia originally, but reading that lot he seems to have become an international celebrity. Several forces across Europe are keen for him to make a starring appearance in their courts.'

Nash scanned the document. 'They're going to have to wait a long time, Jack. Before he goes travelling again, he's going to have to answer charges here for the assault and abduction of Patricia Wain. And if results from the weapon we recovered prove positive, I think we'll be adding two, possibly three murder charges to the list. The victims being Linda Wilson, Neil Ormondroyd and one other, who we suspect to be Mark Tankard, or whatever the man's real name is.'

'I've stuck him in a cell for now. Do you want to interview him? At the moment he's playing the "no speakee English" card.'

'No, leave him to stew. That way he can't demand a solicitor, and it'll give us chance to get closer to the people who are paying him.'

'OK, Mike. I'll get him transferred to the cells at HQ for overnight. I think you're wanted upstairs.'

Nash entered the CID suite to find Fleming and Tina in conversation.

Fleming greeted Nash. 'Clara's just phoned from Netherdale General. Patricia Wain is none the worse for her ordeal apart from a possible touch of concussion. There was no sexual assault. They're keeping her in overnight, purely as a precaution. Her husband is with her and Clara has asked him to drive her to Netherdale tomorrow for Lisa to take her statement. In the meantime, Tina has news for you.'

'I followed the money trail without springing any bear traps. Thus far I've traced it to Wilson Macaulay Industries, and one particular unit on their intranet.'

'Whose computer is it?'

'The user name is Diane Carlson.'

Nash was surprised. 'Really? I have to admit I didn't have her down as a villain. Ambitious, yes, but not dishonest. Appearances can be deceptive.' Nash paused, shook his head and sighed, heavily. 'Of course: appearances!'

'What?' asked Jackie.

'It's all part of the scam, believing what you see. Jackie, do you look like your passport photo? Tina, do you?' Both women shrugged and agreed they had terrible photos.

'Exactly. Linda Wilson was reported to have been seen on the ferry and abroad, and what proof did they have? Her passport!'

'I get it,' said Jackie. 'Just because you have the passport doesn't mean it's you. Not if you look similar to the photo. And wasn't Diane Carlson supposed to be on holiday at the time Linda Wilson vanished?'

Nash grinned as he nodded in agreement.

Tina looked amused. 'Glad I was able to help.' She continued, 'Anyway, the good news, if you can call it that, is that when I checked out Farrell's website for Security Solutions, apart from those you mentioned, I couldn't see any other companies that might have been sold infected software.'

'Well, that's a relief. The question now is: where do we go from here?' Fleming asked Nash.

'I think the first thing we need is to know what progress Viv's made with identifying this woman Peter Macaulay's been seeing, and also if he's discovered anything about the mysterious Mark Tankard.'

Nash was about to pick the phone up, when it rang. 'Speak of the Devil,' he said, 'I was just going to ring you. I take it you have news?' He listened for a few minutes before saying, 'That's ridiculous. Sorry, Viv, but you dropped a bit of a clanger there. Never mind, we'll talk about it later. Any news on Tankard?'

Nash put the phone down and Fleming saw him shaking his head. 'What's ridiculous?' she asked.

'Viv slipped up when he checked the entry on the electoral roll for the house where the woman lives. He and Tom spent hours searching for Hope Morgan, a woman who doesn't exist. He forgot that on the electoral roll, the surname comes before the Christian name. He should have been searching for information on Morgan Hope, who most definitely does exist. Now that he's looked for the right details, he's discovered that she works as a secretary at Wilson Macaulay Industries, which would explain where she met Peter Macaulay.'

'Anything about Mark Tankard?'

'No, he remains a mystery at present. Viv's got Tom working on that, whilst he concentrates on Morgan Hope's past.'

He was still speaking when the phone rang again. He listened for a moment, and the women saw his expression change. 'Thanks, Viv. That is extremely interesting.'

He replaced the receiver and looked at Tina. 'Are you prepared for a sleepless night?'

She smiled faintly. 'That depends what you have in mind, Mike.' Then added, 'If needs be, of course I am. Why, what have you found out?'

He told them, and after he finished, Fleming asked, 'What do you want me to do?'

'If Tina can get me the information I need, I want you to sort out some arrest warrants, and also to arrange a meeting for me.'

Nash turned to Tina. 'Would you be in a position to give me chapter and verse before morning on exactly how the frauds were conducted?'

'No problem, I'll get working on it now.'

Nash watched her disappear into his office and glanced towards Fleming, who was staring at him, an odd expression on her face. 'Something wrong?'

'No, I was waiting for you to give me details for these warrants.'

'I need to speak to Mexican Pete first, and then I might have to ask Tina to do a special job for me. However, whilst you're not doing anything else, would you try and arrange for the directors of the companies we've identified as Farrell's clients to meet at Wilson Macaulay Industries tomorrow? You'll need to get Peter Macaulay's approval first. By then, all being well, I think we'll be in a position to wrap the whole thing up.'

'Mike, what exactly are you up to?'

He explained, and as he spoke, Fleming's expression changed from surprise to incredulity and then acceptance. 'How on earth did they get away with it? And why did nobody spot anything untoward?'

Nash shrugged. 'If you're told something, you tend to believe it unless there's something to make you suspicious. It was simple, and that's probably why nobody raised any awkward questions. However, just to be certain, let's talk to Mexican Pete.'

He dialled the mortuary. 'Professor, how are you progressing?'

'I've recovered the remains from the garden, if that's what you're driving at, but it will take a while to give you any answers.'

'There is one piece of information that might be useful in the meantime.'

He explained, and Ramirez said, 'Wait a minute, I'll find out.' Nash listened as the pathologist rummaged through paperwork. A moment later he gave his answer.

'Thank you,' Nash said and put the phone down. He stared at Fleming for a moment, but she realized he wasn't looking at her.

'What is it?'

'I think we've become ghost hunters. We're chasing phantoms rather than real people. I think I do need Tina to do a spot of computer hacking after all.'

'Whose computer is she going to break into? Or shouldn't I know?'

Nash told her. Fleming should have got used to the surprises Nash was capable of springing, but this one made her gasp. It was only after he gave his explanation that she agreed, with great reluctance, to turn a blind eye to what was about to happen.

CHAPTER TWENTY-THREE

Jackie Fleming and Mironova arrived at Wilson Macaulay Industries' head office next morning, well before the scheduled time for their meeting. They were ushered into the boardroom, where Peter Macaulay and his father were waiting, along with Diane Carlson. 'What's this all about?' Christopher demanded.

'I prefer to leave explanations until after everyone is here. It will save having to go over everything twice.'

Fleming had barely finished speaking when her mobile rang. She answered it, but her part of the conversation gave little clue as to who she was speaking to, or the subject matter of the call. 'How did it go?' she asked, and after hearing the reply, 'Any problems?'

Mironova saw her smile, and deduced that the news was positive. 'OK, get here as soon as you can.' Fleming glanced across at Mironova and nodded, but there was little for the others to gauge whether the call related to them or not.

Sir Stuart Crawshaw was the first of the visitors to arrive. He was followed into the boardroom by the young, dynamic managing director of Dales Sports. Having greeted the other executives, he turned to the detectives. 'Superintendent

Fleming? What's the reason for this meeting? Your message yesterday was rather short on information.'

Jackie repeated her earlier comment. Fortunately, they did not have long to wait before the CEO of Good Buys Supermarkets arrived. 'I believe we can start now.' Fleming looked at Peter Macaulay. 'I think it would be advisable to have someone to take notes of what's discussed here. Do you have someone available to do that? Your secretary, perhaps?'

Macaulay looked slightly uncomfortable. 'She's covering for our receptionist, and I don't have anyone else available at the moment,' he explained.

'That's not a problem. I'm sure Detective Sergeant Mironova won't mind doing that for the duration of the meeting.'

Clara left the boardroom, and a minute or two later Morgan Hope entered, carrying a shorthand notebook and pencil. She took her seat at the far end of the oblong table, nearest the door. As soon as the secretary was ready, Fleming addressed the meeting. 'With the assistance of a computer expert loaned to us specifically for this inquiry, we have been investigating the systematic theft which has resulted in large-scale fraud committed against the customers of all your companies. Along with that inquiry, we have been pursuing murder inquiries in connection with the killing of three people, and the abduction of a fourth, who we believe would have been another victim had we not intervened in time. To cover up their involvement in the fraud, the criminal gang set up scapegoats. When they were threatened with discovery, they murdered a local solicitor, Neil Ormondroyd, who had found evidence that confirmed one of the crimes. They then abducted an independent specialist, Patricia Wain, who was about to conduct an internal audit at Shires Financial Services which would have given the fraud away. They also wanted to discover how much she had gleaned from her initial examination of the Shire Finance software, but fortunately we were able to rescue her before they attempted to extract that information.'

She looked at each of the executives in turn. 'Our computer expert has uncovered elements of the fraud that involve all your companies. She has not only identified the source of the problems, but has followed the money trail from the point where the excess was creamed off your accounts, to the originating computer where the stolen funds ended up. That computer is right here in this building.' Jackie paused and smiled slightly. 'It isn't coincidence that I asked for the meeting to be held here today.'

She turned to look at Diane Carlson. 'By accessing and examining the Wilson Macaulay Industries' intranet, our expert was able to establish categorically that the computer in question was yours.'

Diane Carlson looked horrified.

As she finished speaking, the boardroom door opened. 'Right on cue,' Fleming remarked. She held her hand up to stem the barrage of questions being thrown at her. 'My colleague, Detective Inspector Nash,' she introduced the newcomer. 'He will explain more about how the crime was committed, and identify the fraudsters.'

'I'm sorry for my late arrival,' Nash began, 'but I was otherwise engaged. However, I am pleased to be able to tell you that we now have two members of the gang under arrest. To put it in simple terms, the fraud involved the corruption of software supplied to all your companies. In the case of Wilson Macaulay Industries and Dales Sports, the effect was less lucrative, as it was only committed against those of your customers who took advantage of the extended credit offered via your Internet sales operations. By far the larger share of the criminals' proceeds came from the clients of Good Buys Supermarkets, and especially Shires Financial Services. The fraudsters extracted additional interest from any of the store card or credit card customers who did not settle their full balance every month. They did this in more ways than one. They massaged the interest rate so that the amount on the statement sent to clients was in excess of that due, and they delayed crediting the accounts with the payments received by as much as three days in some cases. Thus earning interest on capital that had already been paid off. In addition, if anyone used their credit card abroad, the exchange rate applied for conversion to sterling bore no resemblance to the actual rate in operation on the date in question.'

Nash turned to address Crawshaw. 'Not content with that, they applied the same methods to all your overdraft, mortgage and loan customers. Anyone who owed money was vulnerable. The methods they used are far beyond my ability to explain in a technical sense, so I prefer to leave that until our expert arrives, which should be quite soon. In the meantime, please reserve your questions until she is here.'

There were no questions, merely a stunned silence. After a moment, Morgan Hope stood up and asked if she could be excused to organize refreshments. 'Of course,' Nash smiled, 'take as long as you need.'

As they awaited her return, the mobile in Nash's pocket bleeped, signalling an incoming text message. He glanced at the screen and smiled, before showing the gist of it to Fleming. Morgan re-entered the room pushing a small trolley from which she handed out mugs of coffee before she resumed her seat. She took up her pencil and looked towards Nash expectantly, but the detective didn't speak.

After a couple of minutes, the door opened again. 'Allow me to introduce our computer expert. This is Dr Tina Silver, who is on secondment to us for the duration of this case. Dr Silver is a leading expert in cybercrime and counterterrorism, and we are extremely fortunate in having use of her outstanding skills with regard to computer software.'

Nash invited Tina to explain more about the technical aspects of the fraud. She began, her voice clear and confident. 'The whole thing began with the collapse of Bishopton Investment Group. That was designed to act as a Trojan horse by creating panic in the boardrooms of local companies, which in turn led them to take preventative measures. Unfortunately, in so doing, they allowed the very people they were trying to keep out to access their systems.'

She glanced at Nash, a clear invitation for him to contribute. 'The other reason for the Bishopton Investments fraud was to create ready-made scapegoats in the shape of the two people who disappeared at the time Bishopton collapsed: Linda Wilson, and the man known as Mark Tankard. According to local rumour, they were living the high life in some tropical paradise on the proceeds of their crime. The truth of the matter is very different.'

Tina continued, 'The software you all commissioned from Security Solutions contained a hidden program. It was this that allowed them to steal from your customers on a systematic basis. Although the individual amounts involved are minute, the cumulative effect over the last three years of robbing thousands of people, month in, month out, runs into millions. The scheme was highly sophisticated, and every aspect was carefully managed so that the paper statements you sent out via computer to your customers did not match the amount shown on your system. Nor did the amount received via direct debit or even by cheque. As soon as the account number appeared on your system, the excess was diverted and the amounts made to tally.'

Nash watched the group, who all appeared poleaxed by the revelations. He wondered what their reaction would be to the far greater shocks that still awaited them. 'The scheme is one of the most sophisticated I have ever encountered,' Tina told them. 'And the measures taken to avoid detection and discourage attempts to penetrate the areas within your system where the fraud was committed were all but impossible to bypass. That is except by someone with the very highest level of computer expertise.'

She turned to look at Diane. 'Ms Carlson, I believe? I was able to follow the trail of the diverted funds. It led me to a partition in the hard drive of your computer. From there, the money was transmitted on a regular basis to an offshore account. That account was not in the Cayman Islands, or anywhere near there,' she added. 'That was simply another myth created to throw people off the trail should they get that far with their enquiries.'

'You don't believe I was involved, surely? I don't know enough about computers,' Diane protested indignantly as the others round the table stared at her.

Crawshaw leaned forward and looked at Nash. 'If you're right and the software from Security Solutions was the cause, are you suggesting Jonathan Farrell was behind this? Did he sell us software simply to enable him to steal money from our customers?'

'Yes, and no,' Nash told him. 'As far as I'm aware, Jonathan Farrell has never committed a criminal act in his life. If that appears to be a contradiction, let me explain. The man you know as Jonathan Farrell is actually Mark Tankard. The only mistake the real Jonathan Farrell made was to be too trusting. He trusted his wife and he trusted his best friend. They both betrayed him, as they've continued to betray and use people for many years.'

'Can you prove all this?' the CEO of Good Buys demanded.

'And have you arrested this man Farrell, or Tankard, or whatever his real name is?' Crawshaw added.

'The answer to both those questions is, yes. Farrell was arrested over an hour ago. That was why I was late arriving. Interestingly, a short while ago, a text was sent to his mobile that read "Operation Armageddon activated." That was to inform him that a virus had been triggered.' Nash nodded to Tina. 'Dr Silver will explain.'

'The effect of the virus was to remove the whole of the credit balances from the accounts of all the companies within your organizations. The liquid assets of Dales Sports, Good Buys Supermarkets, Wilson Macaulay Industries and Shires Financial Services were all transferred to the offshore account of the fraudsters, leaving your companies in meltdown. Within days you will be facing the same fate as Bishopton Investments. Having transferred the funds, the virus then erased the full contents of your systems, leaving it impossible for anyone to trace the money or the perpetrators.' Tina stopped as the outraged voices of the directors threatened to drown her out. She watched the horrified faces staring at her for a moment before they quietened and she relented, then added, 'Or rather that's what "Operation Armageddon" would have done, had I not protected your software from it.'

The look of relief on her listeners was apparent, but with one exception. 'Do you know who sent that text?' Christopher Macaulay asked.

'We believe it was sent by the only member of the gang not yet under arrest,' Nash told them. 'Let me explain. Jonathan Farrell was an orphan, whose parents had left him quite well off. He was also a brilliant musician. He went to university to study music, where he became friendly with another student, Mark Tankard, who was studying computer science. At some point, Jonathan Farrell met and later married another student, who was also on the computer science course with Tankard. She was exceptionally talented, but from a much poorer background. So much so that she was forced to supplement her meagre grant by working as a prostitute.

'That ceased after her marriage, so probably the sole reason for the wedding was money, certainly not affection. Whether she and Mark Tankard had become lovers before then or later, I don't know. What is certain is that it was their alliance that led to the scheme that would give them both a life of luxury. However, to throw investigators off the scent, they needed scapegoats. The first of these was with Bishopton Investments. Tankard was working on contract to the company and when he and Linda Wilson vanished and allegedly ran off with their ill-gotten gains, Mark Tankard's identity died at the same time. In actual fact, he had merely assumed the persona of Jonathan Farrell and set up a company which sold security software.'

'I don't understand.' Peter Macaulay spoke for the first time. 'If the man we all knew as Farrell is this Tankard character, what happened to the real Jonathan Farrell?'

'He suffered the same fate as Linda Wilson. Murdered by their hired thug, a Slovenian hitman nicknamed Ivan the Terrible, and buried at one of Macaulay Property Holdings' holiday cottages. The murder took place well before Bishopton Investments went belly up.'

Nash stopped to allow Tina to take up the story. 'Having examined the student records, I can vouch for the fact that although Tankard was competent enough to design some of the software and install it, the real talent lay with Farrell's wife. The pair had disposed of her husband and Linda Wilson, so she now used her influence within Macaulay Industries to force them to recommend the software to all of you. As you'd all lost money in the Bishopton Investments collapse you were only too glad to avoid something similar happening to your companies.'

'You mean Diane Carlson did all this?' Crawshaw was seated next to her and moved his chair further away as he spoke.

'No, we believe Ms Carlson to be simply another convenient scapegoat.' Nash smiled at her to reassure her. 'No, the person responsible was Peter Macaulay's mistress and she either bribed him or blackmailed him into taking up the Security Solutions package and promoting it to others.'

Peter Macaulay looked aghast at the revelation of his affair and the accusing glares of the other executives round the table.

Nash continued, 'I'm referring to Jonathan Farrell's widow, who works as Peter Macaulay's personal secretary and now uses her maiden name, Morgan Hope.'

Morgan was already on her feet before Nash revealed her name, and attempted to dash from the room. She flung the door open, but found her way blocked by DS Mironova and DC Andrews. She was led away, as Nash continued his explanation. 'When she excused herself from the meeting a little while ago, she went next door to Diane's office and activated the virus using Diane's computer. However, Dr Silver had already blocked it, so that didn't work.'

213

'We also have a direct witness to the activities of their hired assassin, Ivan the Terrible,' Fleming told them. 'Patricia Wain, whose planned internal audit at Shires together with the murder of Neil Ormondroyd led to the uncovering of the whole plot.'

'How did you find out that Tankard had switched identity with Farrell?' Crawshaw asked.

'To begin with we were convinced it was the missing Mark Tankard in the grave we'd found, except there was one thing niggling me. Diane Carlson said that Tankard was no more than medium height. Having seen the skeleton in the grave, that didn't seem to fit. Either her memory of the man was wrong, or that wasn't the right corpse. I got our pathologist to check, and he confirmed the body was that of a man over six feet tall. We obtained details on both men from the university, and sure enough, Farrell was six inches taller than Tankard.'

'You may be happy enough that the crimes have been solved,' the CEO of Good Buys grumbled, 'but that doesn't help us.'

'You're quite right,' Crawshaw agreed. He looked at Nash. 'Do you have any idea of the sums involved? We will have to reimburse customers for the amount they've been overcharged. We'll have to stand those losses, but without some indication of how much is involved, we won't be able to make adequate or accurate provisions on our balance sheets.'

'Our job begins and ends with apprehending criminals for the offences they've committed,' Nash told them. 'We have to deploy other agencies and specialist departments to recover the proceeds of those crimes. I think at this point Superintendent Fleming and I should check that the arrested woman has been processed correctly. In the meantime, it may well be that Dr Silver can give you a more accurate picture of the current situation than we can.'

CHAPTER TWENTY-FOUR

'What the heck was all that about?' Jackie asked when they were outside the boardroom. 'You know very well that Clara and Lisa are more than capable of following the right procedures for detention of suspects.'

'I know, but there are times when it is better for us to appear to be ignorant of what is going on. If we were inside that room, we would be unable to deny knowledge of what is being discussed if the matter becomes an issue at a later date. Tina explained that she has been able to access information which will set our friends in that room at ease. However, in a technical sense, part of what she has done is, shall we say, open to misinterpretation. She thought it would be better for us not to hear this part of the proceedings. So I suggest we pay a tactical visit to the coffee machine in the reception area. Tina assured me that what she had to say wouldn't take long. Then we can wrap things up here and start questioning our suspects.'

Nash grinned. 'The guys in there have had some huge shocks already, but they're nothing compared to the ones Tina has in store for them.'

As Nash and Fleming were walking downstairs, the executives in the boardroom listened to Tina's explanation of what had happened. 'The reason Inspector Nash and Superintendent Fleming left is because I suggested it. I understand from them that the repatriation of stolen funds is a very tricky situation to resolve, and is not always successful. Normally, it can only happen with the cooperation of the bank involved and often the government of the country where the funds have been lodged. On more than one occasion, the authorities have taken the opportunity to seize the money and hold onto it. Even if that weren't to happen, the funds could only be repatriated following lengthy and expensive legal proceedings conducted in a legal system that is alien to our own and quite often extremely corrupt. The very reason that perpetrators choose those places to lodge their money is because of the difficulty involved in retrieving the funds later. Given the less than satisfactory nature of that procedure, it has become more common practice to bypass such processes and act unilaterally, wherever possible.'

She paused, aware that what she was about to tell them was, to put it mildly, contentious. 'With that in mind, once I was in possession of the requisite codes I was able to access the overseas accounts where the criminals had lodged the money and remove it. I have transferred that money to the United Kingdom. I have to tell you that the sum involved runs into eight figures.'

Tina smiled as one of the listeners whistled with surprise. 'That's nothing compared to what they might have got away with had they succeeded in emptying your accounts completely. Had that happened, they would have been able to buy a small country to hide away in.'

'Where is the money now?'

'For the sake of expediency I have lodged it in an account belonging to Wilson Macaulay Industries. However, before any of their directors rush out to order a new Rolls Royce, I would add that I have ring-fenced that sum with a login name and password known only to me.'

There was obvious relief amongst her audience, but Crawshaw still had an important point to raise. 'It's going to be a nightmare trying to sort out refunds. How will we know which customers have been overcharged and by how much? The mis-selling of PPI was bad enough to resolve. This will be ten times worse.'

'That would have been a problem,' Tina agreed, 'had it not been for the meticulous lengths that Tankard and Hope went to when they set up the scam. I've only had a brief look at their software, but I can confirm that every individual transaction is coded and logged to identify dates, amounts and the customer reference numbers within your systems. They needed that to ensure they demanded the right sum, and it has actually worked in our favour. Organizing the refunds to your customers won't be as difficult a task as you might have imagined. Although it will incur considerable cost in man-hours, that will be nothing compared to the losses you might have been facing, and the potential damage to your companies, both in cash terms and the loss of reputation. Overall, I'd say you've escaped quite lightly.

'There is one more point,' Tina continued. 'After the distribution of the refunds, there will be a residue, which should represent, at least in part, the money taken from Bishopton Investments. I don't for one minute think the full amount of what they stole will still be there, but what there is should go to the creditors of Bishopton and the people defrauded by them. I have to tell you there is one more crime the fraudsters planned to commit. Possibly the most callous of all, apart from the murders.'

She handed those nearest her two sets of envelopes. 'Please pass these to the person whose name is on them, but don't open them yet. In addition to removing money from your companies' accounts, they'd also accessed the personnel files of all your employees. A program was set up to drain their accounts of every penny they possessed, with no exceptions, from the office cleaner or supermarket shelf stacker right up to the board of directors. To test the effectiveness of their software I hacked into it and downloaded your personal details. I printed them off and the results are in those envelopes.'

The only sound for the next few moments was that of paper tearing, followed by gasps of surprise and dismay, accompanied by some less than businesslike language. Tina knew she had already convinced them, but had one more unpleasant surprise left.

'I also found another program which would have acted in the same way on the accounts of all your suppliers, customers and shareholders. The only mistake I made was in saying they could have bought a small country. I think, to be accurate, they could have bought quite a large one.'

The reaction of all the executives was one of relief. Half an hour later, Fleming and Mironova escorted the grateful businessmen from the building. Nash went back into the boardroom to collect Tina. As they reached his car, Nash asked why she was looking so cheerful.

'I've been asked to supervise the distribution of the funds retrieved from the scammers,' she told him. 'And each of the clients wants me to write them a proper security program. I'd say that will keep me in work for the next three years, and it's all thanks to you, Mike. It seems that once again I'm hugely in your debt.'

Nash took hold of Tina's hand. 'I'm glad about that, because I have a question to ask you. A very important question.'

Tina looked at him in surprise. Nash seemed to struggle with the words, but eventually managed to convey what he wanted.

Tina stared at him for a long time, her surprise evident. Eventually, she put her arms around him. 'Yes, Mike. Of course I will.'

It had been a long and tiring day, but in the end, highly satisfying. When Nash returned to the station, Binns greeted him with a smile. 'Don't go near the interview rooms without earplugs,' the sergeant told him cheerfully. 'All three of them are singing like canaries, and the sound of each one accusing the others is deafening. Viv's got Ivan, Clara's got Hope, and the superintendent's dealing with Tankard. You're redundant, I'd say.'

Next morning, Nash received a phone call that surprised him. It was from Christopher Macaulay. 'I thought you'd like to know that we had guests for dinner last night. Naomi and her young man. The atmosphere was a bit frosty to begin with, but I think Dean has now forgiven us for our suspicions about Linda. Naomi told us all you did for them, and with what your team and Dr Silver have achieved, I think you can expect a lot more phone calls from grateful executives in the area. I had chance for a long chat with Naomi and Dean. They're planning to get married as soon as Naomi graduates. I don't know what will happen with my son's marriage, and I regret to say both my children have been a disappointment to me. Other than my son agreeing to raise his sister's child, that is, and for the moment I believe we are right in keeping that information strictly confidential.'

'I assure you, Mr Macaulay, that information has been treated as you requested and has not been documented in any of my reports. It was not necessary, so no one else is aware of that fact.'

'Thank you, Inspector. However, your assessment of my granddaughter was absolutely correct. She's going to start working for the company as a management trainee when she has her degree and my hope is that eventually she will take over as managing director.'

The church was almost full when the chief constable and her husband arrived. They managed to find two empty seats on the pew alongside Superintendent Fleming and took their places. After a few moments of mutual admiration of outfits, both women looked towards the front of the church. O'Donnell focused her gaze on the spot where the groom was standing alongside his best man, awaiting the imminent arrival of the bride. 'Mike looks a bit nervous,' Gloria whispered to Jackie.

'Hardly surprising: it's a big day for him.' Fleming was about to add more, but her attention was caught by the arrival of Tina Silver. She nudged the chief constable and they watched in delight as she walked up the aisle with her chosen attendant. Young Daniel Nash was beaming with pride. 'Just like his father,' Gloria muttered, 'never happier than with a lovely girl on his arm.'

The organ was already playing the familiar theme and as the bride took her place alongside the groom, the vicar began to intone the familiar words, 'Dearly beloved, we are gathered together here in the sight of God, and in the face of this congregation, to join together this man....'

After the ceremony, the guests watched the photographer take a seemingly endless succession of photographs, before they dispersed to the reception. As the bride and groom greeted each arrival, Nash smiled happily at them. 'Congratulations, Naomi, or should I say, Mrs Wilson?'

'Thank you, Mike, and thanks for standing in as best man at such short notice. Typical of the army to send Dean's CO overseas just before the big day.'

Nash felt a dig in his ribs and found Clara alongside. 'I must say I was surprised by your choice of companion today.' She glanced at Tina, who was chatting to the groom while Daniel was eyeing-up the buffet. 'I do hope you're behaving yourself,' Clara added severely.

Nash looked shocked. 'Clara, you should know better than to ask. Don't I always behave myself?'

It was several moments before Clara recovered sufficiently to explain the reason for her sudden outburst of laughter to her fiancé.

Sometime later, the chief constable and Superintendent Fleming stood to one side watching proceedings. Gloria smiled as she observed Nash and Tina dancing; saw the way he was holding her and the look that passed between them. She nudged her deputy. 'Jackie, you owe me twenty quid. Hand it over.'

THE END

The D.I. Mike Nash Series

FREE KINDLE BOOKS

Made in the USA
Las Vegas, NV
16 January 2021